Under My Wings
Everything Prospers

By Curtis Harnack

UNDER MY WINGS EVERYTHING PROSPERS

WE HAVE ALL GONE AWAY

PERSIAN LIONS, PERSIAN LAMBS

LOVE AND BE SILENT

THE WORK OF AN ANCIENT HAND

CURTIS HARNACK

Under My Wings Everything Prospers

1977
DOUBLEDAY & COMPANY, INC., GARDEN CITY, NEW YORK

ISBN: 0-385-12501-1
Library of Congress Catalog Card Number 76–42334
COPYRIGHT © 1966, 1969, 1976, 1977 BY CURTIS HARNACK
ALL RIGHTS RESERVED
PRINTED IN THE UNITED STATES OF AMERICA
FIRST EDITION

*Portions of this book have appeared
in Tri-Quarterly, Diplomat, The North
American Review, and The Southern Review.*

For Horace Gregory

Contents

Under My Wings
Everything Prospers

Voice of the Town

Theodore Rueff took on his life as if it held no mystery he couldn't solve. He tithed his income and served as elder in the Protestant church, sang the gaunt, sad hymns from his usual spot on the aisle in the fifth pew—even God seemed taken care of. But behind this amiable show of certitude we saw the looming figure of his youngest son, Danny, who by age fifteen was seven feet two inches tall.

As he began to sprout, Clara Rueff joshed with her friends about what a big boy she had produced. They squinted behind their smiles and let her think what she wanted. Theodore was put to the trouble of buying special shoes and clothes in the city, but all he talked about was what a swell basketball player Danny would become. Years later Danny's surprising marriage to La-Vonne seemed to fulfill his father's hopes of a normal life for his son—hopes which we of the town knew Danny could never possibly realize. All the time Danny and LaVonne lived and worked together, we saw their alliance with our own eyes but groped for an important truth lurking somewhere in their privacy. Who would tell of it? Theodore never cracked. He was Kaleburg's leading banker, keeper of the public confidence, and no one ever knew what torments of doubt or unease afflicted him. Finally he was to go to the grave clean and fast with a heart attack, before any audible whimpers could begin, or any revelations. Because of men like Ted Rueff the general faith is held—or deeply doubted. One wonders why anybody'd like to see himself in such a dubious role, and why we always expect someone to play it.

The Rueffs' was the third house in from the highway as you entered town, green clapboard with steeply pitched eaves and one hundred running feet of porch, all of it screened. There, on card-party evenings, Ted Rueff was the smiling host clearly visible through the windows to passers-by in automobiles, as if he were on display. At the party everyone talked a great deal—but mostly about the tricks just taken and who should have trumped but hadn't. The four Rueff children, according to custom, were kept out of the way. But Danny the giant, dazzled by the company, would climb like Jack-and-the-beanstalk up into those rooms of people from the basement playroom. "What were you doing in the cellar, big fellow?" a guest might call. "Lifting the house?"

"Hey, how's the weather up there?" (This from one of Clara's twinkly friends.)

He never answered. Even his face was peculiarly unresponsive; his round jowls simply hung there like a peeled eggplant. "Danny, you get your sleep," Clara said, in her soft-sigh way. "Go on now —you're the youngest," an excuse she used to hide the fact that sometimes he got so tired he fell asleep standing up or sitting in a chair and had to be caught before he hit the floor and broke his flesh open. He couldn't bear the cold in winter like the others; he fainted from the heat if he went out in August without his blue baseball cap. Germs found a haven in his huge interior, and nothing could stop their proliferation—as if inside, not all the caverns had yet been accounted for.

Clara was like the hen that sat on a duck egg along with her own and she refused to see a difference among her offspring. She was very bosomy, such an enormous pillow that it seemed ample not only for the Rueff family to cushion its fears upon but also for anyone who might need this reassurance. In winter she draped herself in a fox-collared coat, soft as a dog's shank. Her creamy pearls—a double strand, for years the only real pearls in town— stood for the things which were not of flesh, and she believed in them.

While he was young, Danny moved along from grade to grade, but at the start of high school the principal had a closed-door talk with Ted Rueff. Soon Danny showed up as clerk in his father's bank. "Hey there, big boy," customers called, "got your hands on the money yet?"

Cheerful as always and now even somewhat handsome in a blown-up way, he'd grin and wave his baseball-mitt hand. But he never said much. "He understands real good," said the teller. "He's taking it all in," said the cashier. "He'll be a banker yet," said Ted Rueff, thinking he was among friends, but it soon got around town.

Danny performed simple clerical errands such as going into the vault with a customer's safe-deposit key. He swept the floor and kept the cooler filled with water. Try as he might, he couldn't learn to work with figures. He found it hard to concentrate, sitting at a desk, his spine curved like a wishbone. Ted had new furniture built, but Danny still couldn't remember the multiplication table. "What do they teach in that school!" Theodore shouted one day, and a farmer at the grilled window overheard and passed it along. "What do they *teach*? What do they *teach*?" was savored in taverns and stores all week. To think, Ted Rueff hadn't been taught the difference between a soft-head and a normal person!

Danny was dismissed on orders from "someone higher up" and for a time not even the family seemed to pay much attention to him. The two older boys were busy suiting-up for basketball after school; they dribbled down the glistening floor with the cocky good feeling of being loose in the joints. Girl friends tumbled to them quickly. They had no time to look after Danny, and even his sister ran out on the old tender responsibility. She became a cheerleader.

"Luckily, Danny's found something he likes to do," Clara announced, smiling, imperturbable. "He just *loves* cars!" Although Danny couldn't pass the written driver's test, he knew how to operate them. He'd take the wheel whenever it was offered and barrel through the curves of the nearest winding road. Each hairpin turn and two-wheeled squealing corner seemed to thrill him into a skin-close consciousness otherwise unattainable. A couple of no-goods around town got a kick out of letting Danny loose on the highway. As he laughed aloud at the nearness of death, for a few vital seconds he did not feel buried alive in his body. The result was, however, he rolled a car over and was in the hospital half a year.

"He's not the same," Clara said, when Danny got out. "He's been affected," she told her card-playing cronies, shaking her head, and they let her talk. At last she'd been given a respectable excuse.

"He's got to learn a simple trade," said Ted, urging a farmer who was heavily in debt to the bank to take Danny on as a harvest worker. But it didn't work out. "The lummox," said the farmer, "he's always on the ground under the bundle-wagons, sucking on a lemonade jug."

In no time Danny was drifting around the pool halls and one saw him drunk in the middle of the afternoon. Sometimes Theodore Rueff in his neatly pressed blue suit, gold-flecked tie, shiny shoes, and snap-brim hat walked right down the sidewalk past his sprawled, half-unconscious son, who was loafing on the bench in front of the bank. They wouldn't look at each other or speak.

When the Korean War broke out, the two Rueff brothers, who were graduating from college, arrived home in their uniforms and made their last romantic impact upon the town: the one in Air Force blue with silver buttons, the other in ROTC Army officer's twill. One on each side of Clara, with Ted Rueff following behind, they walked down the church aisle under the eyes of God and the town. In the excitement they forgot to include Danny, who awoke from a late sleep to find the house empty, the church bells ringing for the world but not for him. He wept, and he was still weeping when the Rueffs gaily tromped back into the house.

"Danny—Danny! Don't be such a big baby!" called Clara, one arm still around Army, the other looped to Air Force.

"Hey there—" both brothers cried out and leapt to Danny's side to pick up the easy old romp of their childhood.

"Don't punch him," called Clara, "you know how easy he bruises."

"Leave me alone! Just leave me alone!" Face still shiny with tears, he loomed up and entered the stairwell, mounting the steps carefully to his room, a giant on business. The family was stunned, almost offended by the discovery that Danny felt he had a right to his own emotions—which might not be theirs. He would not come down to dinner, nor could he be persuaded to tag along as the Rueffs bid farewell to their patriotic sons, later that afternoon. "If they don't come back," Clara said finally, taking leave of him, the horn honking, "just *think* how bad you'll feel then!"

He looked at her angrily, stirring his huge limbs, and for the first time she felt afraid of him—and fled the house. She didn't tell her husband what had made Danny so furious, only that "he looked about to hit me!"

"If it gets any worse," said Army, "you know what you'll have to do."

"But we always said, your Dad and I (Ted sitting right beside her in the backseat), "why have him put away when he's so harmless?"

"Some of the women in town are starting to worry," said Air Force, who'd spent most of his leave getting reacquainted with high school loves. Both boys had already confided to their father that Danny was actually no threat on that score, since he was impotent. They were certain of it. Some years back, in an attempt to explain sex to him, they'd sat on a pasture gate and watched a pony stud in action. Much to their surprise, Danny wasn't the least interested. Now the rumors of his threat to the local girls was just the dirty country gossip one might expect, given his outsize proportions in that department, too. Every time he was caught taking a leak there were guffaws and comments. But neither Rueff boy could bear to inform their father of the indecent nature of this talk—yet they felt some little warning should be voiced.

The following week Danny insisted he be allowed to enlist in the Navy. Theodore Rueff went through it all: helped Danny pack his bag, watched him bid farewell to his Mom, and drove him to the Navy recruiting office above the city post office. He and Danny walked up the steps as if they truly expected to get somewhere. "My son here wants—" Ted began, apologetically, while the petty chief on duty, red-faced from seawinds, widened his eyes, pushed back his chair. "My son—"

"I come to enlist in the Navy," said Danny, his deep, half-muffled voice seeping out of the tower of himself. "I'm of age." A blush suffused his neck and lower cheeks, as if the blood of his life were coming forth, once he proclaimed himself a man.

The five-foot-three petty chief grinned and leaped to his feet. With a side wink to Rueff he reached up and thumped Danny on the back. "More fellas like you and we'd win this war in no time!"

"Where do I go?" Danny twirled his little satchel nervously, while Rueff blinked, looked embarrassed, and turned to gaze out the window.

"Trouble is—you're so big you'd put the fleet to shame."

"I'm too big?"

"No, *they're* too small!" He marched Danny into the examination room, laughing to leeward all the way. It was a slack day, and the medical officer was waiting. "Look what I've brought you!"

They took great pains to describe the narrow, stacked seamen's bunks on a typical U. S. Navy vessel. They showed him skivvies and bell-bottoms so that he could see that none of them fit him. When the interview was over they shook hands with Danny, called him a fine American, urged him to stop in and see them whenever he liked.

"Well, son?" said Theodore. "Ready to go home now?"

Danny nodded agreeably but with a new independence. At last he'd gone beyond his father—and the family's network in Kaleburg. He'd been seriously discussing his life with representatives of the United States Government. All the way home he couldn't keep the grin from his face.

Then, through a pool-hall friend, Danny got a job with a pinball machine company, Idle Hour Games. They helped him pass his driver's license exam and loaned him a car. His chief duty was to collect revenue from pinball machines and punchboards. Although they were illegal, most bars had several kinds of punch-boards for the customers' amusement. You could buy a punch for a dime or a quarter, the whole card bringing the company ten times the cash value of the prize for the lucky-punch winner.

Danny took a room in a small hotel in the city, where he could receive messages that came while he was on the road. He collected coins from the pinball machines and learned to fix broken ones. Without his father close at his side, he managed to keep his accounts straight. After three months he was courier for half a dozen shady operations, including a numbers pool, ball-game pools, and a system whereby servicemen met girls. He was known and hailed as he made his rounds. Men would clap him on the shoulder and pump his soft hand, and Danny would bray with pleasure, showing his long-toothed, horsy grin.

But suddenly Theodore Rueff received a call to bail Danny out of jail. He and the Idle Hour Games people had been arrested and charged with racketeering and procurement for the purposes of prostitution. An understanding judge commuted Danny's sentence, sending him home in the custody of his parents, who were henceforth to keep an eye on him.

"We've been all alone here, Danny," Clara whimpered. "This big house and all the children gone but you." However, she couldn't make him her baby any more. Before a week was out he fled. They didn't know where he'd gone and were afraid to ask the authorities to hunt him up, since surely then he'd have to be "put away." Both Rueffs became highly guarded on the subject: and while the addresses of the two boys in uniform and the girl in Los Angeles studying fashion were printed in the church bulletin, Danny was left out.

Soon everyone read of Danny's marriage—to LaVonne Zimmer —before a justice of the peace in a town forty miles away, one of those many villages where Danny had become known as a traveling man. Clara said it was wonderful "to have somebody taking care of Danny." The Rueffs helped settle the newlyweds in a Kaleburg house available for twenty-five dollars a month, provided Danny and LaVonne "look in" on the eighty-year-old lady who lived alone next door, their landlady. Wedding presents arrived, but Clara gave no tea to introduce her daughter-in-law, and suggestions of a bridal shower were quashed for no reason, unless it was that Clara and Ted didn't want to pretend they expected grandchildren from this alliance.

The old rumors about Danny's sexual abnormality began to surface—*he* wasn't interested in girls, everybody knew. So, what was going on? LaVonne was tall and squarely built, as strong as Danny was weak. Her dark brown hair, the color of flaxseed, was done up in a coil over each ear and flat spit-curls just above her forehead were held in place by hairpins that seemed to staple her crown. She had deeply recessed, small blue eyes and run-together eyebrows. Her mouth was a neat, thin line, and except for her nose, which projected a modest distance, she seemed almost bereft of the usual features that distinguish one of us from another. Everyone thought she was up to no good and had probably married the village idiot in order to cash in eventually on the Rueff money. Clara made a point of telling her friends that LaVonne had nursed her father through a long illness, that she was a good, shy, devoted soul—hard to get to know, but in every way worthy of her son.

LaVonne didn't entertain in her home nor did she accept any of the invitations to join women's clubs. "He's being looked after," said Clara joyously, "that's what counts." The life of the elder Rueffs separated easily and decisively from that of their son and his wife. Soon nobody thought to remark that it was odd Danny and LaVonne were never seen in the big green house on Main Street. It was increasingly hard to remember he was a Rueff at all.

When the old drunk who ran the dray service got run over and killed by his own cart, Danny and LaVonne took over his business. They acquired a sorrel gelding used to plowing and corn-planting and shod him for service on town streets. LaVonne showed the horse where to graze on the strips of pasture along the railroad embankment, and in the evenings he cleaned up the spilled oats and corn around the spouts of the Farmer's Elevator. The wagon was an ancient, heavy box on four thick wheels; panels slid into place making a rectangle four feet deep—or the wagon could be stripped down like a railroad flatcar. Originally there'd been a pair of horses for the outfit, but something had happened to one of them. Since the old man couldn't afford a new horse, he'd adjusted the rig; the load could be pulled from the whiffletrees, by a single brute in harness.

You may wonder what need there is for a dray service in a town as small as Kaleburg, since most citizens have cars and could make periodic trips to the dump with tin cans, glass, and junk that won't go into the backyard compost pile. But some people hate to run the risk of having their tires cut by broken glass or nails. They detest the sight of rats among the refuse, should they go out there in daylight—or the bright little rat-headlights gleaming all over the place at night. They called Danny's Dray. Customers also phoned to have salvaged bricks hauled to the site of a foundation for a new house; or to carry lumber in a hurry, when the normal delivery couldn't be made. Even the stores employed Danny and LaVonne to transport heavy merchandise. The price for service wasn't high, and thanks to LaVonne the job was always done neatly and in good time, without much fuss.

In going about their business, Danny and LaVonne wore over-alls and heavy work shoes, the leather so thick it didn't much matter what dropped on their toes. The only way to tell it was a man and a woman on the cart, not two men, was that LaVonne wore a babushka, except in summer, when she was forced by the intense sun to wear a farmer's straw hat. Unlike junk carriers the world over, they never seemed interested in their burdens or considered their freight in any light except that it was something to be disposed of. No little trinket was ever filched and kept in secret at home. When something of possible value was included in the load, LaVonne would speak about it to the person employing her. "That hairbrush?" the woman might reply, "*Ach*, its bristles are mostly broken. No, it ain't good for nothing but curryin' your horsie." And then LaVonne would use it for that, as long as it lasted. She seemed to understand the dangers that might develop if she ever wised up to the business she was in. She was, in short, incorruptible; but the town believed nothing of the sort. *They* thought she ignored salvageable items because she was waiting for the Rueff fortune itself, when the old folks died off.

Meanwhile, Danny's Dray made money, though they never seemed to spend any. Now and then they'd go to a movie, settle themselves in the front row where Danny had always sat, share a nickel bag of popcorn, and watch the cowboys galloping across the screen. They put a dime or two in the collection plate when they attended church, which was infrequently. They didn't drink liquor or even beer because LaVonne said (what everybody knew), it didn't agree with Danny. Their car was a beat-up 1939 Chevrolet. Every morning LaVonne was first at the bakery for day-old bread. She kept a sizable garden and canned all summer. She knew what farmers could be approached about picking the tart plums in a forgotten lane, to be made into preserves. The grocery supplies LaVonne bought were of the austere, pioneer sort: flour, sugar, salt. Even the meat supply was arranged for privately, during the country butchering time in February. The town speculated that perhaps Danny preferred the safety of his mattress or the sugar bowl for his hoard, rather than his father's bank.

Years later the true tale leaked out, in the surprising, appropriate way these revelations occur. In the prosecution of one of Danny's pinball-machine buddies, who'd been released after serving his term only to return to his rackets, the district attorney discovered that Danny Rueff had been paying hush-money sometimes amounting to two hundred a month. The convict had terrorized him into believing he could be re-arrested at any moment, and even LaVonne was convinced. Nowadays some blame Theodore and Clara for not inquiring into the reason why Danny and LaVonne's back-breaking drudgery showed so little profit. But misery is often obscured because of the pride everyone takes in hard labor, the virtue it entails—the fact that "work never hurt anybody."

But it broke Danny—or rather the strain did. He was such a big, calm, plodding creature no one thought he might be a mass of anguish inside. One day he got into the Chevy and drove to the state insane asylum twenty-five miles away "to turn in." LaVonne was summoned for interview, and the authorities talked to Clara and Ted, each of them separately. Danny planned to remain safe inside the walls, LaVonne reported; "He's real happy there." She spoke without bitterness or even resignation. "Now I got to carry on with the Dray alone, I guess."

The town would have speculated at length about Danny's surprising action had not Clara succumbed to a stroke the same week. Her right side was paralyzed from top to bottom. She could only speak disjointedly with half a tongue, smile with half a mouth, and think with half a brain. It happened because of her grief over Danny's collapse—that's what people said. LaVonne immediately began to nurse her. In the morning she'd go over to the house on Main and fix Theodore's breakfast before he walked to the bank, then lift Clara from her bed, carry her to the bathroom, wash her and dress her and put her in the wheelchair. After a ramp was built over the front steps, Clara's trips in the mobile chair could be down the block or even to the stores, LaVonne always in attendance. The dray service dwindled, but she still maintained the business. She continued to live in the little house next to the very old lady (now in her nineties) and checked each morning to see if the woman was alive.

Clara was expected to regain use of her arm and leg; there seemed to be improvement for several months. But Clara enjoyed being taken care of by LaVonne and wasn't much interested in using the doctor's spring-contraption to exercise her hand, biceps, and calf. She had no reason in particular to want to get up and walk again. "I've got it pretty easy, wheeling along," she'd say with a laugh. "I don't know's you folks have it so good." She would never be quite right in the head again, that was the trouble. There were no devices to fix that lesion. The doctor told Theodore that the end would most likely come suddenly, one of these years, with another series of strokes. Hard to tell just when.

During this time the three other Rueff children didn't come back. They had youngsters of their own, of course, which was fair excuse, but it seemed odd that in those four years none of them was able to make the trip home. Mostly it was thought the reason was guilt over Danny—and shame that he was where he was, when the Rueffs could certainly afford a private sanitarium. But who would start doing something? Theodore washed his hands of it—he had enough to think about with Clara; his face in profile was pewter gray and stern, the look of George Washington on twenty-five-cent pieces. The letters between the Rueff children flew back and forth, from New York to California and Washington, guardedly speculating on what should be done about the home situation. But the last word was always, "Thank God for LaVonne!"

When Theodore died of a heart attack, all of them came back. What a strange procession they made: the children in their well-tailored dark clothes walking behind the coffin, along with dotty Clara, who was weeping, snuffling, and carrying on aloud; and sober, lean-faced LaVonne, pushing the wheelchair down the church aisle, looking no more grim than usual—in fact, she was "just the same's ever!" She was about as tough as a mortal could be, in the best sense of the word, for no matter what was dished out, she took it without a whimper.

She was not entirely of iron, however. A few weeks after Theodore's burial, when she moved into the house on Main Street in order to be closer at hand in ministering to Clara, she put her horse in the barn out back, which had been used as a garage. The city fathers said there was an ordinance against it. She received an official letter from the mayor, warning her that she'd be fined if she didn't remove the animal. But she *had* to have him close by, not in the shed giving onto a pasture (outside the city limits) where she'd formerly kept him. She was wildly attached to the beast who'd been her companion all these years. She wouldn't give in—no, she'd pay the fine.

But the penalty, it was explained, would be levied again next month and each succeeding month until she did something about complying with the city ordinance. Ladies who came to visit Clara got a full, emotional report from the invalid, slightly off-key, a peculiar wheezing screech, as if a half-melted phonograph record were being played on a faulty machine. "She got Theodore's pistol out—oh yes, she found that! And she cleaned it up real good, and dug up some bullets, too. Just you wait—anybody comes trying to move her horse—you'll see some shooting, you will. Our property, ain't it? They can't do this to us. And after all we've done for this town!"

That kind of talk, bruited about the village, was just the sort of thing the high school hoodlums liked to take up. They deviled LaVonne as she walked the streets or drove her dray cart in the alleys. They cackled and hooted and even threw firecrackers, daring her to shoot the pistol. She never gave them the satisfaction of paying any attention.

A special dispensation for the horse was finally granted "in respect to the memory of Theodore Rueff." Everybody knew LaVonne had won because of her strange, fierce love for that animal. In farm country you seldom hear of anyone getting affectionate over a cow or a pig or a workhorse because that sort of thing upsets the system. These beasts are in bondage to man; it's not the other way around. If only LaVonne had had the sense not to put that straw hat of Danny's on the creature, cutting out holes for his ears. If only the horse hadn't had such big blue eyes which did indeed resemble Danny's; if the animal had been given some name like Nick or Dobbin. But he had no name, and so the high school kids began calling him Danny. Then you began to see other connections: the fact that he was a gelding; his lumbering gait and size; his sad, half-witted look. The effort LaVonne made protecting the horse got her into closer alliance, really a companionship. Cart, horse, and woman roamed the alleys even when there was nothing to be hauled, the cart empty.

Some village gossip must have written to the Rueff daughter in California, describing the situation and saying that Clara was being neglected because of LaVonne's infatuation with the horse. A practical nurse was suddenly engaged to come and live in the house. LaVonne was no longer to attend the invalid. The stranger, sent by a city agency, was a hearty, gray-haired, meat-and-potatoes sort. She was righteously indignant over the filthy condition of the house, which apparently hadn't been cleaned for a couple of years. Moths had infested the clothes, mice and rats had the run of the basement and attic, and even poor dear Clara Rueff herself was so dirty on the back of the neck that she had to be scrubbed hard with a rough washcloth and strong laundry soap. Purveyor of all this juicy news, the practical nurse was welcomed into every household on the block.

She told more than she should have. Or rather, she kept repeating everything Clara said, and these ravings were increasingly unreliable and not to be listened to. For one thing, apparently LaVonne had been in the habit of caressing the old woman in those regions where one would imagine only the young feel intense pleasure. Clara liked to be handled gently, dreamily, and for a good long time, until she went off to sleep. LaVonne, questioned about this by the practical nurse, who was shocked by such manipulations, was reported to have answered: "She'd smile and feel so good, I never had to give her no sleeping pills. That's more than *you've* done for her!"

The remark, coupled with Clara's own peculiar notion about

LaVonne, began to spread. The nurse quoted Clara as having said: "LaVonne's got whiskers like a man. A girl ain't supposed to have a chin like that. No, I don't think she's a girl at all." Actually, LaVonne had always carefully shaved the stubble she'd been afflicted with on her upper lip and chin. As these growths flourished in later years, she'd tried to cover them up with talcum powder. But one time Clara's hand had happened to reach out, in a moment that might have been ecstasy, in the evening when the light was dimming in the bedroom, and LaVonne was soothing the old lady for the night. She touched LaVonne's face—her eyes widening—suddenly she thought she understood the mystery of this creature who'd come so accidentally into the Rueff household and now was such an indispensable part of it. "Always in overalls, she is. Works like a man. No wonder my poor Danny sent himself away!"

So when Clara died, and after the funeral and the dutiful visits from the far-off children, when the practical nurse lost her job and had to return to the city, in the settlement of the estate the clapboard house on Main went to LaVonne, plus a small income from farm property—largely because the Rueff children realized that she'd forever make those twice-a-month visits to the state hospital, keeping an eye on Danny. She lived alone and never went out in the streets or alleys with the cart anymore. The horse was too old, and nobody phoned to have LaVonne do a job. They knew her circumstances had changed. By now LaVonne's hair was streaked with gray, and she wore it severely back in a bun and looked like some prairie sod-house woman of the nineteenth century. You might guess that she'd be left alone to live out her years in peace, with whatever private hells she experienced, and wherever she found her heavens. But you don't know our town, if you think that.

The kids kept talking about the rumor that LaVonne was really a man dressed up in woman's clothing. One night in late spring a bunch of the graduating seniors, out drinking and celebrating, sneaked through the backyard and walked right into the Rueff kitchen—because nobody, not even widows and old maids, locks their doors. Maybe she knew why they'd come and what they meant to do to her. She did not shriek or run for the telephone. They tried to corner her in the front parlor, but she escaped up the stairs. Yelling like animals, they were hot after her. They thought she was merely fleeing—and she was in part—but she was also trying to remember where she'd put Theodore's Colt .45. Finally they pinned her down on a musty bed in a back room and ripped every shred of clothing from her body. She fought so wildly that the young athlete astride her got aroused—a local football hero I shan't name, for he later joined the Marines and died in Vietnam. With his teammates co-operating, as they used to do on the playing fields, he made the full discovery of her womanhood, something no man had ever done before—not even her husband Danny. They saw the deep stain on the bedspread and knew her secret, a different one from what they'd come to find. She writhed free of their grasp in the moment her assailants saw the blood. The pistol lay on the washstand next to the only window with a clear view of the barn door. She grabbed the gun and, naked in the starlight, flung herself through the window, shattering the glass as she flew.

Aghast and suddenly sober, they raced downstairs and out the front door, got into their cars and spurted away. They didn't even have the decency to go round back to see what might be done to help her. They just wanted to get away and not be caught. A neighbor heard the crash but couldn't figure out for a long time what had caused it. Then he saw the pale, nude figure on the lawn, slowly moving through the grass, long hair down her back. He'd have gone over at once if he hadn't also noticed that she was entirely naked, her breasts flat and loose. There seemed to be some dark stuff like paint here and there on her body. He figured that whatever she was up to, she wanted to do it alone. She squirmed across the long backyard lawn, hung awhile on the picket gate till she worked the latch open, then slumped down again to wiggle through the hollyhocks. It took nearly twenty minutes for her to get to the barn—the horse whinnying and trampling the earth as she came. She reached him at last and somehow managed to pull herself upright in the stall—so that she could explain to the horse and to herself what she was about to do—in a voice none of us ever heard give utterance to anything that mattered.

You can be sure she spoke. She got very close to his wall-eye, we know from the wound, and pulled the trigger. Then she shot herself, left hand clutching the mane, a fistful of sorrel hair. Her head lay near his furry ear, as if she'd just stopped speaking. Those who came up after the pistol fired and saw the naked woman sprawled across the horse's body said, later, that Lady Godiva herself had not been more beautiful. Isn't it just like them to say something like that? Her leg had been broken, the doctor reported—*her* leg, not the horse's.

My Son, Stuart

After finishing work brought home from the office, I felt like a swim but knew Tina was bare-ass, soaking up the last rays beside Stuart. My lecherous son and his willing girl friend. How is it possible these days for a parent in situations like this to be natural, offhand? I'd teased Stuart about their nude scene, asking what happened when motorboats passed close, and he said his two hands on Tina did the cover-up. Now from the deck on our cottage I could see Tina stretched out, still awfully pale for this time of year, rather ordinary breasts, dark triangle where her legs began —quite good legs, too.

"Watching the sights?" asked Mary wryly.

"Not all that much to see."

"You're looking though."

"I know. I've seen better."

"She's not interested in measurements—or comparisons—or any of that male oppressor stuff, so don't start it."

"Don't start what?" I put my arm around her bottom.

"Aren't you about ready for a drink?"

"Well . . . suddenly . . . you know? I've a *different* idea."

"Now?"

"While they're safely out of the house."

"Can't say I feel flattered—considering what you've been ogling. Is it *ohg*-ling or *ahg*-ling? I've never known."

She talked resistance but we moved into the bedroom. By the time Tina and Stuart climbed the bank, after the sun had set, we were dressed again and sitting on the deck, with our cocktails. "Aren't you going for your swim, Dad?"

"Yeah, I might. How about it, Mary?"

"I'm feelin' too good. Why spoil it?"

Tina glanced at her with dark, sexual knowledge, then at me—the precocious kid always making connections.

"Oh, come *on!*" I pulled Mary out of her deck chair. Just as well we were away from the house while Stuart and Tina had their hot shower together ("To save water, Dad").

"But my bathing suit's still wet from this afternoon."

"Forget the suit." I pulled her toward the lake.

"What's that girl *doing* to you?"

On the dock I stripped and dove in, rising to the surface just in time to see Mary, breasts flying, in mid-air above me before water enveloped her. "Beautiful!"

The chill lake doused whatever erotic afterplay still hovered. We scrambled out quickly, rubbed ourselves with rough beach towels, and leaned against the pilings to take in the Adirondack sunset. "Wish we had those drinks down *here*," Mary said. "Wouldn't that make it perfect?"

I yelled up to Stuart but there was no reply. After a while I mounted the steps to the deck and walked into the living room. They'd neglected to hook the latch on their bedroom door and it'd swung half open. He had her pinned against the wall, her legs curled around his thighs, and he was humping hard to the finish. I felt a flash of embarrassment mixed with anger over the imposition on our privacy—but I tiptoed into the kitchen, courteous as a pimp, fetched the ice cubes, and slipped out the back door.

I decided not to tell Mary anything, since such news was no news to her—or me either. We lay there silently sipping drinks, but as so often happens after love-making, she was exceptionally attuned to me. "What's the matter?"

"I'm wondering how long . . . before we get back to normal around here. The way it was before Tina."

"Well, Stuart's grown! Though I wonder if we *shouldn't* have had another child, no matter what the doctor said. Or adopted."

"What's he going to do for girls in the Middle East?"

"Is *that* what you're thinking!" she laughed.

Yes, truly I was.

Later, Stuart hosted the barbecue and served us all, ebullient, fairly singing with joy, and I thought, well, if Tina does this to him she can't be all bad. But with me he solemnly discussed solar-heated dwellings and wondered why low-income housing projects utilized none of the scientific discoveries in this area, about which *she* knew everything. In short, we had one of our usual conversations. Soon as they left for a drive-in movie we headed for bed, not sleepy at all, ready as honeymooners.

Afterward, I lay awake and thought about Stuart, whom we'd always regarded as an old-fashioned, Henry Aldrich sort of boy. "Stuart's so *normal*," our friends used to say, most of them on the rack over a dropout offspring. Loving and easy with us as if this psychologizing century hadn't been invented. I worried that Stuart was half-living *our* lives with us and would be unprepared to spend his later years in his own particular, contemporary way. Nobody could be so out of kilter with his generation and not suffer eventually. Stuart must've realized this too, or he wouldn't have taken up with Tina, who didn't in the least resemble the local upstate New York girls we'd seen him date. Her complexion was sallow from bad health-food-store eating or too much marijuana smoking, and her messy hair was sheepdog. A bristling aggressiveness played around her like static, an anger which fascinated Stuart, as if she were the nutpick needed to pry him open.

Tina undercut his cheerful confidence and mocked his thus far unshakable smugness, until in frustration he'd lay hands on her. But what did his muscles prove? That he was so strong he could push her under the water any time he wanted to? Well, she knew *that!* How did he justify this lakeside cottage, when little slum children in Harlem had nothing but an occasionally opened fire hydrant? He'd safely bypassed Vietnam while dark-skinned American counterparts nearly his age had done the fighting and dying. She ridiculed him for using underarm deodorant—and shaving, when he had a perfectly good beard eager to come forward and represent him—for still buying sports clothes of a fatal preppy sort which had gone out years ago.

After a week of Tina, Mary wondered what in heaven's name Stuart saw in her. "Something he needs," I said, and we both knew I wasn't referring to sex, though an awful lot of it was going on, perhaps because she was trying to teach him that his tool was no weapon with which *she'd* be manipulated.

"We're not exactly the kind of bourgeois pigs Tina's out after," Mary said. "I mean, you a city planner . . . and me a school-teacher. *That's* not as bad as some parents she could find around."

"But bad enough. Low-income housing projects are only land grabs, serving real estate interests."

Stuart knew what Tina was doing to us, but he grinned blank-eyed, expecting his Peace Corps travel orders any day. The only time I heard the girl laugh was when Nixon's name was mentioned on TV. (I kept quiet about having once voted for him.) We didn't know what Tina was on vacation *from,* since she hadn't been in college with Stuart. I suspected she was getting over some lover in New York who'd ditched her, which might account for her bitterness. She met Stuart at a United Nations rally for population control. Little references suggested she was four years his senior: first hearing the Beatles in high school (Stuart was only about ten); going to Washington to protest the Kent State killings (Stuart was in high school). Tina caught me trying to put her history together and stared at me in a hostile way that seemed far too adult for poor Stuart to cope with. "I wish they'd go live with *her* folks for a while, if she's got any," I said to Mary.

"Oh, she has! Stuart told me. Pretty impeccable parents—both university professors."

"Of *what,* though?"

"Psychology."

"It figures!" We both laughed and felt better, then ran down to the dock and climbed aboard the old Chris-Craft. We revved out into the sunset just as always, riding the waves at a delicious angle, as if in some smart roadster rumble seat of our youths. In the early 1940s, when I'd longed to own a smart car, I'd barely enough money for a breakfast bun—which is why our brick house in the nearby town and this shore-front camp shimmer somewhat unreally. I can never quite believe in my possessions. Nothing Tina could comprehend!

Twice a summer we throw a bash for everybody around the shore, and a few friends drive over from town. Our first Saturday party went much like the others except that Tina, in an Algerian jibbah of undyed, handwoven cotton, padded barefoot among the tartan-trousered gents and clunky-jeweled, bare-necked ladies like a genie we'd let out of a lake-bottle floated us from the other side of the world. She'd washed her hair, and it fell from a severely centered part down both sides of her poker face, all the way to the unpressed or unpressable North African garment. Tina passed nuts and chips, holding out the salvers mysteriously and weaving through the mob, saying nothing, never a smile, just staring out of that hair with dark, intent, almost Arabic eyes. Some of the gin-lit men fancied themselves love buccaneers and tried to elbow her into a corner, but she cooled them off plenty fast. Stuart bartended as if he were hired help: polite, smiling, but extraneous to the whole affair. After a couple rounds of martinis, even Tina's disapproval couldn't be felt by anybody. Then she and Stuart disappeared in his Vega, no doubt to talk us all over.

When the last car had gone, only a radiant violet light hovered on the water; the wilderness night reclaimed our camp. Mary moved softly in the dark, picking up glasses, emptying ashtrays. "Good party," she said, as always.

"Was it?"

"Everybody had a fine time, didn't they?"

"It was barbaric and you know it!"

"Well of course, these things are."

"Why do we do it then? Just because the neighbors do?"

"Now you're sounding like Tina," she said dryly, moving into the kitchen.

Not *one* of those glad-handers with their leather-skinned, heavy-smoking wives would I ever really care to see again. Not a single idea had I exchanged with anybody. Not one new fact of interest, or celebration—just a miserable drunken huddle. The pines were breathing, sweetening the soft lake air, purifying me. I lay sprawled in the dark, blissfully open to the balm of a forest evening.

"Come, your steak's ready."

"What's the *matter* with me, anyhow?"

"Alcohol's a depressant. You've had too much and now you're coming down."

"Yeah, too much . . ." There's a melancholy of middle age caused solely by the witless repetitions one has gotten into the habit of.

"Hair of the dog," Mary said, pouring me another drink as I ate. I didn't stop her.

The following days, whenever Stuart and I were alone on grocery-shopping expeditions, washing the car, or sailing, we avoided the enormous fact of Tina as carefully as matters of sight are excised from one's conversations with blind men. Whereas our old companionship had been so unself-conscious it was almost as if we were the same person, now I was separated from him. His flashing smile and glib cracks kept us from doing anything to remedy this distance we both felt. Was he insensitive emotionally— too boyish, still, for somebody his age? Tina seemed an old lady in comparison. Perhaps he figured he needed maturing, and useful instruction from her. Surely this was our last summer as father and son in even a semblance of the old way. Maybe in tribute to *that* sentiment Stuart pretended to be the cheerful, competent boy of yesterday, the kind of kid he thought his Dad wanted him to be just now, for what parent has a right to know the true life of an offspring? Did *my* parents really know anything about me?

But why bring Tina into the remnant months of his childhood, unless he wanted to show us something about his new adult self which he thought we absolutely *had* to know? With the special responsibility an only child feels toward its parents, perhaps thoughtful Stuart was weaning us away from him—and bringing home Tina was a deliberate act, out of love for us. Or maybe he just wanted a sexual companion to bide the time until the Peace Corps snapped up his life and like many young people worked the situation to suit himself, without much thought for anyone else. He'd spent every summer here, employed by the marina or counseling at one of the camps. This year he was on a loose string and couldn't make any job plans—so Tina might've seemed a perfect solution to keep from getting bored. I realized, after a month of it: Mary and I would no longer brood over whether Stuart fitted into his time, part of his generation. We were as baffled by him as any parents I'd heard of. We'd joined the modern age.

Finally the telegram arrived: Stuart must immediately demonstrate proficiency in spoken Arabic at a testing in New York, then he'd be off to the Middle East for two years. All of us (even Tina) welcomed the news, merely to have our expectations fulfilled. I accompanied him to the airport thirty miles away, leaving the women behind. He planned to return in two days for the final pack-up and departure, at which time he'd take Tina to New York with him. Now he grabbed the driver's wheel for a final American highway kick, on his last good pavement for a while.

Got your Koran with you? No more pork or ham, infidel. And the females will be veiled to their eyes, my boy. Say good-by to all these trees and Northern Tissue.

We quipped along, laughing with our teeth and mouths, but I felt a tearing away in my rib cage. Stuart, what's to become of you?

At the mesh gate as the flight was called, he suddenly turned and embraced me. "Dad!"—and quickly headed into the runway wind. I waved and smiled, flushed with relief, for all along *he'd* felt as I had. He'd be all right. Nothing much could go wrong.

The drive home in the heavy, hot afternoon was no fun, the route clogged with desperate city vacationers returning south to the cities. Our cottage was twenty degrees cooler than the roads, but when I opened a beer and settled down to rest, Tina started in on me. "Did you ever figure up how much of your income tax payment goes for armaments?" I told her to shut up for a bit. She sulked in her dim room with a book, then strode down to the shore for a solitary swim at sundown. Mary's polite, determined conversation got us through supper.

"Tomorrow, I hope you're not planning to leave Tina with *me*," Mary said later, in bed.

"I'm expected in. By noon."

"She's awfully neurotic."

"Ignore her. Go down to the dock. Let her fix her own lunch, shift for herself. My God, she knows the place by now, I should think."

"Actually, I'm a little afraid of her."

"She won't *hurt* you! Come *on!*"

"I just wish my relief at the prospect of seeing her go—and my sadness over Stuart's leaving—didn't get everything so mixed up— I feel like crying!"

"It's *that* time of the month, you mean," I said softly, for she never tipped to what was wrong.

"It *is,* but my feelings are still valid. Don't take *that* away from me." She sounded quite hurt and angry.

"Tina's poison—crawls under bedroom doors."

Mary rolled over and yanked a pillow on top of her head. I lay there in the still, close air, unable to sleep. I rose stealthily and slipped out to the deck for more air, but mosquitoes zeroed in on my naked flesh, driving me back inside. "What's the matter?" she asked groggily, when I lay back.

"Nothing, nothing." I filled my mind with that spoken answer until finally I was gone.

Next morning I couldn't bear the thought of driving into town, so I called my secretary and took the day off. "*Wednesday'll* be a good day to start my week at the office."

Mary thought I did it for her. She lazed around, feeling edgy, downing aspirin, while I kept Tina's attention by working on the Chris-Craft motor, which I'd been meaning to get at for a month. Tina squatted on the dock watching, genuinely surprised I knew how to clean carbon off spark plugs. I fixed us all sandwiches and iced tea for lunch, which we ate in cool places of the house, alone.

Upon finishing the job, in early afternoon, I decided to test the engine on a run of the lake. Tina accepted my invitation to ride along, but chided me for owning such a stinkpot, when we had such a fine alternative—the sailboat. Fortunately, the motor noise ruled out conversation. I looked with respect at the powerful thunderheads building in the west. Little squally gusts made the lake choppy, the trip interesting.

Then, without a cough in warning, the pistons simply stopped. Tina thought I must be teasing her the way Stuart so often did. We went through a lot of no-really-I'm-serious before she moved her ass enough for me to get at the dead motor. The rubber cap on the distributor seemed loose, perhaps water had gotten in. I removed my T-shirt and wiped out the hood very carefully.

"Got a paddle?" she asked. "We could row to that island."

No paddles or oars, no success with the engine, either. Maybe it *was* the generator all along, as Stuart insisted. I hadn't paid much attention to him because he's usually wrong about motors. We were drifting farther and farther from home and a storm was whipping up rapidly. I became sweat-soaked from my small exertions, plus anxiety. Even Tina showed the wholesome effects of the elements and perspired heavily. So few boats on the lake, too. Possibly a bad-weather report on the radio had driven them all to safe harbors.

"What about lightning? Could we be killed out here?"

"Sure! Or tipped over by a little twister. This lake is famous for waterspouts. I'm awfully glad you can swim." And that she'd come prepared, in a bathing suit.

"But I can't . . . not really."

"What do you do down there on the dock?"

"Sunbathe. As *you* know very well. And then wade in."

We were wading in, all right. I didn't look at her. I kept grinding away at the starter, hoping one of the sparks would catch. Pretty soon the wind changed and it began to blow hard. A heavy sheet of water advanced down the mountain toward us, relentless as the final devouring of the world. She stared at me with the first look of fright I'd seen in her. Maybe this breakdown out here was worth it, just to see Tina humbled—if not by Stuart in rut then by this brutal Adirondack thunderstorm.

When the rain hit we crouched, drenched in an instant, the water surprisingly lukewarm. I threw back my head and laughed right up at it, lifting my arms and rising to my feet, teetering, yelling my fool head off—the only way to go back at Nature. My antics alarmed Tina and she grabbed my arm for support, or reassurance. We bobbed around on the waves and shipped quite a lot of water. I hauled out the life jackets from under the seat, just in case, and insisted she put one on. We hung in there until it was over, fifteen minutes later.

"*Now* what?" she asked, querulous.

"Can't you be quiet for a while? Or heroic—like Tallulah in *Lifeboat?*"

"What's that?"

"Never mind." To my astonishment, the motor started right up, the first try.

"I knew it! You planned this all—to scare me. Just like Stuart! Really, what's the point? Why should *you*, a grown man, go to such trouble?"

"Tina, if you say two more words I'm going to throw you overboard."

"Stop at that island—will you? Right over there."

"No! Why should we?"

"I've got to step ashore."

"*Why?*"

"To crouch in the bushes—okay?"

"Okay."

Mooring was no problem because the state owned the island as a picnic spot; there was a large NO CAMPERS sign because it'd be such a beautiful place to spend the night. Picnic tables, cook-out pits, and plenty of bushes for whatever. Plus a very neat little rock jetty. Tina leaped out and made us fast with the rope. My soaked shorts were clammy and my joints ached a little, but I felt refreshed by the adventure out there. How good now to stretch! I paced up and down, wondering if I should've kept the motor running. Wasn't thinking about Tina—hadn't noticed where she'd gone—but suddenly when I turned around she stood a few feet away, with nothing on at all.

"What do you think this place *is*, Tina—Buff Beach? The mosquitoes will have—"

"You've been spying on me every day—so here I am, close up."

"Fine. You're a very liberated young lady. And I'm a conventional, middle-aged man." I picked up the moor-line. "Shall we start on back? But haven't you left . . . something . . . somewhere?"

"Why can't you look at me? Are you afraid of yourself?"

"I'm looking."

"You aren't, either. You're hiding behind the next thing you're going to say. Whatever that'll be."

"I've already said it. Put on your bathing suit and let's get going."

"I'm not ready. We just got here. My suit's drying out."

I thought of the forest ranger's station half a mile upshore; he often passed by, checking the state grounds. Just our luck to have him witness this absurd scene. But I knew what she'd answer to *that* kind of cowardly remark. I couldn't in fact think of anything to say *she* wouldn't find evasive. I didn't have long to search, for she stepped close and took my hand and made it do things I had no intention of doing. Mary and I'd gone to a triple-X-rated movie once, just to see what the fuss was about, and emerged feeling ashen, ripped off as well, remembering the five-dollar apiece admission. Here was one of those wanton, celluloid creatures, alive and prancing about. I'd always thought a seduced man pretty ridiculous, but I'd never had a naked woman stalk me on a desert island—only in fantasy! She had my shorts off in no time and began doing crazy things with me. We ended up on top of a picnic table, surely in full view of any passing forest ranger. It happened so wild and fast I could scarcely catch my former self.

"Now what the *hell* is this all about!" I said, when I could speak at all.

"Don't you *dare* say you haven't been after it from the very beginning. You God-damned hypocrite, Mr. Middle America himself! Look at you!"

I pulled on my trunks hurriedly because she was looking.

"You don't know—anything, Tina." She was so wrong I couldn't even find words for her. I'd never been unfaithful to Mary in the twenty-three years we'd been married, and before that I'd only slept with three women—the first a sort of town whore, the other two I'd loved and thought of marrying. I value my unpromiscuity, but what could Tina know of such sentiments? The virginity she'd lost was not that hymen-breaking of long ago. I may have missed a few sensual detours through lack of variety, but what I've enjoyed has been bonafide sexual intimacy. Tina knew the harem girl's arts, in a sleek, professional way, but poor Stuart! That he thought he needed this sort of sex—when all he must've wanted was somebody to love him as dearly as his parents had, in childhood.

"Come on, we're heading back. I'm putting you on the evening flight to New York."

"Oh, what guilt is swirling, swirling. Lie—and say you didn't enjoy it. Go ahead, I'm listening."

"The novelty . . . must've given it a certain edge for you. Incest isn't exactly the right word. I don't know what *is*."

"I don't either—what difference does it make?"

I'd struck something. "It made a difference to you, Tina, didn't it? Or you wouldn't have gotten me out here the day after he'd gone."

"Poor Papa!" She tried to be mischievous and light, kid me out of it, but she understood I recognized her contempt for Stuart in this act.

"Where's your bathing suit—come *on*, Tina." I thanked the motor for starting up, because I surely didn't want to talk any more. She'd done enough damage without persuading me into a disgust for us all. As I unknotted the rope, she leaped aboard respectably garbed, basking in her triumph. Both Stuart and I'd been trying to figure out ways to overcome Tina, and here she'd put us in our places in a rather age-old way, by splitting us. She possessed a headful of power now, and Tina was a girl who'd know how to use it. I had to get off by myself to figure things out a little.

"I understand why you want me to leave today—but how're you going to explain it to your wife?"

"That's my business, thank you."

"I'm not allowed to have a 'story'? No explanation? You're not very good at this, are you? Don't you think she'll think it funny—since I didn't plan to go away—when we left a couple of hours ago?"

"I said I'd rather not discuss it, Tina. You suddenly have to go, that's all. That's enough."

Mary *was* bewildered but sensed my outrage and extreme distress and didn't question me. She'd seen us through the binoculars foundering out there. For a second I wondered if the lenses were powerful enough to pick us up—on the island—then remembered we'd circled around to the other side of it.

While Tina packed, I pulled on slacks and a shirt; we'd barely enough time to make the plane. "We've got to leave *now*," I told Mary when she entered the bedroom, hoping to speak to me.

"But Stuart said—"

"Forget Stuart!" If only I could.

On the way to the airport, Tina kept trying to add a coda. "I don't know if I've really got you figured out. I mean, is it the prude in you that can't accept what happened? Or your basic hostility toward women, which you *know* you have—or should know. Once you've been with a woman, you despise her for letting you have what you wanted all along. In fact, such an attitude isn't really far from the homosexual's—"

"*Can* it, will you?"

"I thought you were so proud of your—'openness to life'—I think that was your phrase. Always willing to examine any—"

"I said shut up!"

She did, for three minutes. "I don't have any money for the plane."

"I'll put you on my BankAmericard."

"Wouldn't that be compromising?"

"Sure."

I signed for her ticket just as her flight was called. She moved off toward the plane, then turned: a quizzical, peculiar expression, as if she could only be honest once a separation made it clear she wouldn't be involved. Across thirty feet of cement we gazed open-eyed for the first, and of course the last time. I saw a vulnerable, bewildered girl who'd no idea why she did the things she did, except that some people can only find squirming life by picking up rocks. How hard they work at it!

The minute she arrived in New York (Stuart was staying in her flat), she'd tell him: not that I raped her on the island, nothing dishonest like that, merely that I'd lusted and succeeded, which was more or less the truth. She'd flay his innocence just to blur his blue eyes, bring a little rank odor to that lithe, pure body—knock him in the belly so he'd never get up the same as he went down. She must do this in order to make her tremendous point. He'd not understood her—before—but now he would. Of course, he'd be too furious to have anything more to do with her, but she'd feel she'd done what was needed. In the future there might be hope for him to have some kind of "real" connection with a woman, but he wouldn't realize *that* now, or ever send her belated thanks. Never even think of her, except in rancor.

Whatever joyous illusions Stuart possessed about his father and his childhood (or was I being maudlin?) would be shattered. He'd never be tempted to cling to his boyhood happiness; everything over. Nor would he be easy or natural with me ever again, not in his whole life. I felt so bereft I slammed the car door and wept on the steering wheel. Airport grief is so common, people getting into their cars nearby glanced calmly at my red eyes and wet face, thinking only how much I must love that girl I'd said good-by to.

So I'd lost a son—I accepted it, but what about my wife? If I didn't tell Mary what happened on the island (as most men in my place wouldn't) a new kind of doubleness would enter our marriage. She might not realize it for some time, but I'd be keeping this tremendous secret from her and always worrying about when the truth might spill out of Stuart: the reason he refused to write and never came home to visit. Yes, his two years in the Middle East would be a cushion—and the delayed suspense might continue for a decade. ("Why's Stuart so odd with you? Why didn't he invite us to his wedding? Why doesn't he ever phone?") I'd always be out there, beyond the ring of our marriage, looking at poor Mary. So, I decided she'd have to be told immediately and somehow made to understand just how it had happened.

At first she couldn't seem to hear me. "You *what*? With *Tina*?" When it registered, her face grew pale and she sat down abruptly. "You bastard!"

"Now wait—" I explained how haphazardly nutty the incident had been, how lacking in real meaning.

"Oh, for Christ's sake, shut up!" She escaped to the bedroom, slamming the door, and bolted the latch so I couldn't enter.

Early next morning she packed a suitcase and phoned a taxi to take her to the bus station. She was off to visit a recently divorced cousin, with whom she'd gone to Keuka College, and who now lived in Boston. "You'll get word from me—after a while," she said flatly.

If we pulled through this mess, perhaps on the other side we'd be wiser. I made the mistake of saying something like that out loud, and she gasped as if I'd slapped her.

Later, I checked in at the office because I had to hang onto a real world somewhere, but I spent most of the day thinking how I'd respond to Stuart's rage that night. He *had* to come back to pick up his carefully planned Middle East gear: khakis, binoculars, L. L. Bean canteen, and Clarks desert boots, all in a bundle and ready for weeks. Having had no contrary word from him by phone, I drove to the airport to meet his plane. He waved from the disembarkment steps like a campaigner, hair flying, full of grins. Obviously, he'd heard nothing. It turned out he hadn't even seen Tina. "She's not *here*? Where'd she go to?"

"Back to New York."

"I couldn't get into her apartment! The super wouldn't let me in because my name wasn't down in the book, or something. Even though I had the damned keys!"

"What'd you do?"

"Checked in at the Y. And today they hand me a plane ticket. The government's sending me straight out. Here—to JFK and Pan Am flight number one. I won't get back to Manhattan at all."

"She'll miss you—then."

"Funny . . . she took off like that. And here I had a terrific line —for when we say good-by. I'll have to write it from Cairo. Though it won't sound the same."

"No . . . it won't." And *my* misjudgment of future events had gotten me into needless trouble. Why hadn't I waited, before telling Mary? In wars or marriage, *never* volunteer. As we approached our camp, I informed him his mother had gone to Boston to see a sick cousin who suddenly needed family.

"It's serious then," Stuart tried to look sober because of the suggestion of death, but he wasn't really concerned, still so far from it himself.

"Mary thought so."

We ate supper at a steak joint on the lake road and drank a lot of beer. Stuart was so high over the prospect of foreign adventure, I kept forgetting my new life circumstances. Oddly, he omitted mention of Tina as if the girl hadn't been tightly in our lives, as if she'd never happened to us. Looking at Stuart, I saw my old self, for we do closely resemble each other. Near him, I could almost believe I still inhabited my old days. I felt strong, good-humored, confident I could take on anything—no calamity could make a serious dent.

Up to yesterday I'd been just like Stuart, really. Though I'd not known it till this minute. No wonder back in June when he emerged from college into the world I'd feared he wasn't maturing or changing as he should! I'd felt my own innocence melting in his eyes. Somewhere up ahead in years for him, along a way he couldn't even imagine now, something would happen to make him—like the rest of us. Diminished from what we once were. Never to recover. I wished to God it'd be a long, long time from now.

"You're a good boy, Stuart!" I burst out.

His face was so alive it almost sparkled, but a slightly quizzical expression entered his eyes as he looked at me in my awful desperation. "I'm not a boy any more, Dad. I'm a man."

"Are you really?" He could stay sober longer than me—I was a bit high from all the beer.

"I'm old enough—for *every*thing." That cocksure smile.

"Are you really?"

"You damn right!"

"Then let's hear how you take this: Tina made a play for me the second you left."

"No kidding!" He laughed, genuinely amused—or mocking me.

"Where the fuck did you pick up that wench?" Anything to wipe off that grin.

"She balled you—really?" Still smiling. "She made a bet she *would*."

"You realize what you've *done*, Stuart?"

"I didn't know you were so vulnerable. I really didn't."

"You've broken up our marriage!"

"Mom found out? What happened?"

"I *told* her."

"Oh, Dad!"

"I'm an honest person."

"My God, you really fucked up, didn't you?"

"Is *this* what we've come to? You track in filth—into your own house—and laugh about it?"

"Dad—you didn't have to screw her did you?"

"Don't *talk* to me like that! I'm your father!"

"Okay, okay." He wasn't smiling now. "Don't take it so hard. Mom'll come back, you'll see. She'll get over it. Easier'n you will."

"But what've we got left now?"

"The rest of your lives—I should think."

"Little *you* know, Stuart, about *any*thing!"

"I realize you're awfully upset. But can't we—I mean, this is my last night in the States." He raised his hand to the passing waiter. "Cognac, please. Dad—you'll have another? And I'll take the check." To me with a wink: "I'm on a per diem. *This'll* be on the government."

He knew how to end it—me, him, and his childhood. I had to hand it to him. Only I *still* wonder why these kids think it's necessary to murder the old before they can move on into their years. Soon we were talking about baseball and who'd win the pennant. When he paid the bill he swaggered out, toothpick cocked, ahead of me, holding the door not in deference or respect for my age, but kindly, because he felt sorry for me.

"She called me a hypocrite, son."

"You can understand Mom, though . . . she must've been in a state of shock."

"*Tina* did."

"Tina called you a hypocrite?"

"She did. Is *that* what you think, too?"

"Let's not make a heavy scene of this, Dad. It's my last night. Mind if I drive? I'm really gonna miss it." He took the wheel and with the windows down, the wind was too loud for talk. When we got to the cottage he said: "I suppose you want some kind of apology from me—is that it?"

"I'm not asking *any*thing. Forget it."

"Okay—I will." He slammed the door.

We need them more than they need us, that's the trouble, and here was another youth who knew it. "What kind of a civilization are *you* going to represent—out there in the Peace Corps? What kind of ideals?"

"*You* probably should go in my place. The Peace Corps was founded on talk like that. But if you want to pick a fight, Dad, let's have the right subject."

"I don't want to fight."

"Think I'll go for a swim—care to join me?"

"Yeah." For peace between us. Also to clear the head.

On the dock in twilight we stripped, as we'd done hundreds of times. I looked at his marble nakedness as if my *Doppelgänger* stood there under the stars, his shoulders wide as mine but firmer, his genitals a replica of my own. I knew every cell of him; he seemed the only thing left of *me*. He'd taken my body from me, and I was helpless. The worst of it was, I sensed no pity in him, though he seemed stirred by the intimacy brought on, in this crisis, almost cheered to have found me here next to him, naked inside and out. "Race you to the float, Dad." He clapped my back in a gesture of peace. "What d'ya say?"

Like a bomber peeling off, he dove in. Me after him, the lake cool, marvelous, and the rhythm of the crawl put me at ease, for I could always do this well. It gave me the feeling I could do *any*thing, even get Mary to come back home from wherever she'd gone.

Stuart splashed ahead, his kick-kick like a dance on water, white waves on the black surface. This moonless night, the sky and lake bottom shifted places, rolled; the stars sparkled in the water like phosphorus. We were amphibious creatures making our innate way forward, driven by biological urges too powerful to controvert. It was almost joyous thus to expend ourselves, *he* swimming on as if he'd never fall back.

"I won!" he called, bonging the metal top of the buoy over the shoals.

"Okay! Okay! No contest!" It surely never was.

We rolled over and swam the backstroke home, reaching and gliding, hand over head. Side by side the way it *should* be—and never is.

The Empty Rooms

The American troops had already landed in Sicily when I, a seventeen-year-old high school graduate, enrolled in a small Iowa college composed of three hundred and seventy-nine women but only nineteen male students. The men's dormitories had been shut down entirely for the duration, and we were to live in an off-campus house which had been an auxiliary women's residence. Pine Tree Cottage, with its pink and blue interior, chenille bath rugs, fringed drapes and swathes of white curtains was redolent of recent females. There were wooden clothes racks in the bathroom for drying undergarments, and bathtubs rather than shower stalls. A faint odor of perfume seemed to emanate from the woodwork, and the bedroom carpets were smudged with face powder.

"There must be some mistake," said my roommate, Stan, who arrived with baggage, blankets, tennis rackets and golf clubs on the afternoon train from Chicago. He was red-haired, blue-eyed, the sort pictured in October Sunday supplements, if not in a blue football uniform on a chalk-lined turf, then wearing the proper suede stadium coat and sitting next to a blonde who waved a three-cornered banner of Old State.

We shook hands and looked closely at one another, solemnly aware that this was one of those fine, fateful moments. In August we'd exchanged introductory letters: mine was awkward and brief, Stan's rich in biographical detail and filled with personal convictions of what he expected from his college year, even though it was wartime.

"What *is* this place? The men's dorm? How awful!" He flopped down on the bed I'd left for him and put his head in his hands. "We'll have to redo the whole house, not only this room."

"Wait'll you see the upperclassmen," I said.

"What's the matter with them?"

"You'll see. The freshmen will probably do, though. I can hardly wait for dinner. We eat with the girls, you know. They've assigned us two tables right in the middle of 'em all."

"I'd better unpack right away." He swung the heaviest suitcase onto the bed, unlatched it, and began taking out an array of handsome sports coats, slacks, and sweaters. "I hope these wrinkles hang out."

"We get our mail in their mailroom—and we're supposed to use their laundry, if we want."

"Anything else?"

"We're the luckiest bastards I guess ever lived."

But Stan wasn't so sure. When we trooped down the stairs to cross the street, the men of this campus were such a peculiar collection he could not hold back a snort of disgust. The spindly seventeen-year-old freshmen were uncomfortable in their ill-fitting suits, and they clearly felt inadequate to dine with three hundred and seventy-nine women. At the head of our band were four medically discharged veterans, back from the wars, with haunted eyes and an attitude of distance from the rest of us; two of them were paraplegics getting used to prosthetic legs, and all of them seemed to be veterans with women as well as battles. Of the 4-Fs (who were quick to explain just what was wrong with them), two had heart trouble, another a punctured lung, one was partially crippled from infantile paralysis, another had a cleft palate, two wore thick-lensed glasses, and one was hard of hearing.

Our entrance into the dining room was greeted with ogling, giggles and a kind of excited murmuring that seemed to become more and more voluble. Stan swore to do something to show the girls "we meant to hold up our end of things." He'd come eager for the fabled experience, the kind of thing sung about in "The Whiffenpoof Song" and "By the Waters of Cayuga," which the girls that first evening rendered for us, over coffee and cigarettes. We squirmed, listening to these masculine ballads sung in soprano. It was as disconcerting as watching women dance together (which was customary in my home-town ballroom) because the men had gone to war.

He spent the evening rounding up a chorus to serenade the women after-hours. Under his insistence, and with the jesting co-operation of the house president and the veterans, a brief rehearsal was held in the parlor. The girls whistled and cheered as we came singing across the lawns. They were clustered in their dormitory windows as thick as angels in a pre-Raphaelite painting. No matter how off-key, or how we dragged through "Let Me Call You Sweetheart," the coeds applauded and shrieked—even, in the anonymity of the night, called, "Give us a kiss, honey," and "Come on up, boys!"—which got most of us pretty excited, though Stan seemed to think they were either making fun of our performance or else didn't understand the ritual at all.

On the upper end of the campus the eight men's residence halls were empty, the playing fields unused, the football stadium deserted and the tennis courts green with weeds. During physical-training period in the great, drafty gymnasium we played basketball on only one of the four courts. Though we did not have enough able-bodied players to make two teams, we shouted as robustly as we could, our echoing calls dying among the rows of bleachers, scaring the sparrows in the rafters overhead. Afterward in the showers, how thin, few, and white we seemed in that vast tiled room furnished with an array of nozzles which could have soaked a whole football squad.

At night I never liked to walk up past the men's dormitories when I went out with a girl toward the town park and golf course, a blanket tucked under my arm. The shifting reflection of the street lamps, shining through wind-blown elms, made shadows on the windowpanes like the ghosts of the absent men—who envied my luck, who wished they could be doing what I was about to do, even though during peacetime they'd never been able to sample as freely the variety of girls at my disposal.

In my room at midnight I would nod over French vocabulary and be unable to comprehend chemistry. I was solidly scheduled for eight o'clock classes, and if I didn't sleep through them I usually failed the inevitable drop quizzes. I seldom got enough sleep, since I couldn't bear to waste time that way, and by Christmas I was so thin that my family, when they saw me, was alarmed over my health. How could I ever explain that I had strung myself upon the harp of youth and was all melody and song? Though the war bulletins were filled with disasters, I was delirious over life's sweetness.

And so was Stan, but in a very different way. He saw us both as figures in the foreground of a varsity dream. I did not even know his references, which ranged from those students Hamlet and Laertes to Amory Blaine, poems of Housman, and songs from *The Student Prince*. We dutifully wore our freshman beanie caps in reverence for the tradition. We did not walk on campus grass. We prepped for the upperclassmen in the time-honored way by shining their shoes and going for food at midnight. And if we got black marks for failing in our tasks—which happened every week —and were swatted at Monday night house-meetings, we received our blows with a certain satisfaction. It was good for these tattered bits-and-ends of humanity, our upperclassmen, to play their part, and it was necessary for us to do so, even though we ran the student council, the newspaper, the drama club, and were the real Joe Colleges of our time.

Saturday, the rah-rah day of the week, was the most difficult to get through. There was nothing for Stan and me to do except visit the local tavern. After downing quarts of beer we'd stumble up toward the women's quadrangle, singing songs to make everybody aware that some college men were still around. By nightfall, when our dates were expecting us, we had usually sobered up. Occasionally, formal dances were held in the dining hall (cleared of tables but smelling slightly of pork chops). All nineteen men, black ties or not, were forced to show up with a date, and every coed who could manage it invited from home a serviceman on leave and put him up at the hotel or in Pine Tree Cottage with us. One way or another we were enough of a crowd to fill the dance floor and make the evening balloon out into nostalgic rosiness. Almost before the "Good Night, Ladies" from the three-man combo, the experience of the evening was a glow of memory which had become "our fabled college life."

Sunday morning, Stan and I would be up and dressed in time for eleven-thirty chapel, where we participated in the services, first as ushers or readers of the Bible, and finally as preachers, because the war made it difficult to get guest speakers. Slightly hung over, but in our best dark suits, we found the occasion emotionally charged and trembled at the sound of Bach on the powerful organ. My religious feelings welled up easily, along the same channels as my outpouring of sentiment over college itself, as a result of the wonderful time I was having. In the black gowns of the non-denominational chapel, speaking glibly of God's will and ways, we no doubt fancied ourselves capable of being masters of ceremony anywhere, in heaven itself. The wonder was that the more cynical professors in the congregation didn't snicker out loud at our performance. They must, I think, have been glad to see us on hand, for it helped to take away from the barrenness of the choir loft, where only the high, sweet voices of girls sang.

After the recessional, while the congregation slowly filed out, I studied the commemorative brass plaques on the rear walls of the chapel. The most magnificent were for the Union soldiers. At the outbreak of the Civil War all but four of the college men had enlisted and gone off. From the Spanish-American War there were only ten dead heroes, but World War I names filled plaque after plaque and the list stretched into the hall. There wasn't room for another war, and yet I knew that the alumni already killed far outnumbered all of these, and their names would be posted somewhere here when the war was over. I tried not to think about it. And yet, there was no way of avoiding it, for I was still connected to the outside world through the usual family alliances. My two brothers, in uniform, wrote me in that firm-chinned, quiet tone I recognized to be fear. In the newspapers I secretly studied the campaigns on the western and eastern fronts, and I listened to newscasts when Stan wasn't around. The war was not a subject we discussed.

As the months wore on, we fell in with older coeds, the upperclasswomen who admired our concern in carrying on varsity traditions. The freshmen girls with their perfervid talk and Gibran's *The Prophet* tucked under an arm seemed awfully young; and perhaps most important, the older girls were granted later hours. By spring Stan and I were mostly going out with the eight women who had no lock-up time at all: the house presidents of the dormitories.

One of these was Sue Blakely, whose boy friend was killed in Italy in January. The day the news came, a telegram from his parents, we were sitting in the drawing room after dinner. The girls led Sue away to her room, heads bowed in the time-honored, awful way. I tried to hold back my cheap feelings of sympathy, for I knew it would be easy to elevate Sue Blakely and her mourning into a new, thrilling item for my collection of collegiate emotions. I restrained myself from going to her side and sitting with her at meals, or in any way showing what I actually felt: a hot, stomach-twisting sensation of love, every time I saw her. I painfully kept my distance until the day I noticed she no longer wore her diamond engagement ring. Then I began playing bridge with her after chemistry lab in the afternoon, and at dusk we'd have a quiet cigarette together in the arched passageway outside the dining hall—saying little to one another, just looking up at the afterglow of the sunset. I spent hours with her, listening to records or walking along the clipped paths of the arboretum, the sky reflected in the still, glassy waters. We found peace in each other's company, or so I imagined, from her almost nunlike calm. The white skin of her face seemed pellucid; her long blond hair was held back by a simple heavy barrette of silver which the dead man had once given her. What vast despair her silence indicated I now from a distance wonder, but at the time I read it quite differently, little realizing that my own ease had come about because here was the one girl in the entire school with whom I didn't have to be the varsity man, who in fact would have been offended had I tried.

One Saturday night in May, after a picnic Sue and three of her friends had prepared, we wandered back from the golf course through the dark loggia of the men's dormitories. Someone suggested breaking into the dorms and exploring. All the girls had attended open houses here before the war, and they seemed to be taunting Stan and me with the fact that we only knew the inside of Pine Tree Cottage.

Immediately, I scouted about to make sure the night watchman was not in the shadows. Stan jumped into the soggy casement and slipped off the storm window, then tried to lift the sash. The lock snapped out of the rotten wood and the window was easily raised. Stan leaped in first, the rest of us following quickly, and we found ourselves in the dining room. The high-backed oak chairs at the trestle tables resembled bent-over men, as if a whole silent company were devouring an invisible meal.

We began to grope forward with suppressed, housebreaker gaiety. The girls found the swinging doors which led to the staircase, and they reminisced about Sunday night exchange dinners they'd once enjoyed here. They seemed to forge ahead of Stan and me, dismissing our juvenile company. We caught up with them in the utter blackness of the hall as they giggled and lurched against the wall. "Where's the railing?" asked Sue.

"No, that's *me!*" said another.

Now they were at our mercy again. I grabbed whichever one was nearest and ran my hands over her body, all in the blindman's buff of the moment, as we stumbled together on the stairs. They broke away from us and explored the smoker on the first floor. Even in the gray half-light it seemed to be the very den Stan always said true varsity men inhabited. There were a sofa and chair in front of a massive, wood-carved fireplace, and above the mantel was a painted shield of the house—magnificently Old English. The dark leather furniture was grouped together in alcoves, where, on open-house nights, one could get down to business with a girl. The women now inspected every cranny. They studied the framed photographs of intramural athletic teams, though it was too dark to identify anyone and we dared not light a match.

Upstairs on the second floor we opened a door, and I could make out the ghostly shapes of the wooden toilet cabinets and shower stalls. A towel still hung by its name tag on a peg, and I wondered if upon closer inspection I'd have found a used tube of toothpaste on the washstand or dried shaving soap on the mirror.

In a three-room corner suite on the top floor, the girls sat down on the striped mattress of a single bed. Light came quite strongly through the dormer windows, and I saw the desks under the casements, the chairs in front of them, the gooseneck lamps bent low over plain, uncluttered surfaces. The doors to the two other rooms stood ajar, open to the companionship of the neighbor, or as if in a moment we were to see the occupants themselves, coming forward.

"You'd think they'd have *cleaned* the rooms, at least," said one of the girls.

"I suppose nobody thought of it."

"The janitors went, too—to the defense plants."

I realized what they were talking about: the room had been left in its after-packing state of chaos, just as it had been that June day following commencement. The unwanted stuff was still lying about: a broken-string tennis racket, a torn shirt, a few old yellowed magazines and newspapers, a couple of ragged textbooks. I didn't need light to tell me that the pennants on the wall were in the primary colors of one's college years. Although none of us opened the closet door, no doubt some toeless socks and a few soiled ties were in there among the fallen coathangers.

I saw Sue bend over, her long hair spilling forward in that wonderful way it always did. She put her face into her cupped hands, and I knew she was crying. Each of the girls looked in a separate direction, their eyes not meeting—and perhaps no longer seeing—as they turned their attention inward. They were as oblivious to the presence of Stan and me as if we were merely the boisterous companions of their idle hours; the playful inhabitants of their house, passing the time while they, the Penelopes, threaded out their days and waited.

That was in late May. Stan and I stayed in college to finish final examinations, but only with reluctance; then we drove to the state capital recruiting office and joined the Navy. Both of us still had several weeks to go before reaching eighteen—time to cavort about and enjoy the sanctuary of youth—but we'd had enough of it and were ready for war. I received my boot training at Great Lakes, but Stan for some reason was sent to Farragut in Idaho. Later he was assigned to a destroyer bound for Okinawa and on the way was killed when a kamikaze fighter plunged into the ship.

After two years, when I came back to the campus, ex-servicemen were packed into the dormitories and doubling up in temporary quarters all over town. It was hard to find privacy for a good night kiss, provided you were lucky enough to get a date at all. The men had returned in such numbers that whenever I thought of Stan, I wondered what empty rooms his spirit might inhabit. It seemed there were only occupied, overfull rooms, for us who'd survived and were living our unused college years as extravagantly as we could.

We never return to empty rooms, even those of us who manage to keep alive. Leave a room empty, and time will fill it.

Madness

On the Kemp side of Nora's family a taint of madness ran like a cleft of mold in aging cheese, though she herself felt free of it. Like inverted primogeniture it passed through the women only. "Keep reading those books, you'll end up crazy as your Aunt Clara," her father used to say when he caught her emerging from an alcove on a rainy day, eyes red from *Elsie Dinsmore* or the fairy tales of Oscar Wilde. He operated an implement shop for Iowa dirt-farmers, never had time for books, except the black ledgers in which he kept accounts. Saturday nights, the farmers with their wives and children, in wagons, buggies, and Model T Fords, filled the streets of the town. They seemed to Nora ordinary as most other creatures of the earth, mundane in their pursuits, and her father was like them; he was normal.

Therefore, the madness in the Kemp family annoyed him. He

railed against the expense of keeping his sister-in-law, Clara, in a private sanitarium, even though Nora's mother paid the bills out of her own inheritance. One time the inmate had been allowed home on a visit, but Nora's curiosity soon turned to terror. "Ah, my little niece, my *only* niece, come here to your Aunt Clara!" She slapped her knees, laughed, eyes rolling. Nora refused to let the strange woman touch her, ran quickly outdoors to play. The visit ended badly, with Clara fighting her return to the sanitarium, weeping hysterically, and Nora's father had to lift her and carry her to the back seat of the car, like a prisoner. "Keep the windows rolled up, Nora," he muttered, as they started off. "She might try to jump out."

Nora's mother paid dearly for that unwise home visit, and although Clara never returned, whenever there was a parental fight, her father brought out *this* ultimate weapon. "Your whole family's crazy! Insane! Why should I listen to *you*?"

Nora learned to use the idea of madness when she sought better treatment. By acting a little queer (coming home from school wearing only a sweater in the middle of winter; refusing to eat favorite foods like ice cream and cake) she'd receive days of careful attention. At age twelve when she started getting her periods painfully and was possessed by wild thoughts, she wondered if the traditional insanity weren't coming out in her, too. The Kemp family tree interested her mightily. Who was the cousin locked up most of her life in the state asylum? And what about Grandmother Kemp, who swallowed too much medicine, did herself in. "She was old and sick—it was an accident," her mother maintained, with little conviction.

When Nora was summoned home from college by her mother's illness, she guessed the nature of the trouble at once, though nobody else did. Her father by this time had gotten so separate in his days and indifferent to his wife at night (except as that female he shared a house with) he was baffled by her tantrum of seclusion. She refused to step off the front porch, go down the sidewalk, wouldn't attend church—because the whole town was talking about the awful thing she'd done; and yet she couldn't tell her husband what the act was or why news of it was so well known. The doctor decided she'd suffered a breakdown and recommended shock treatments in Omaha.

"Shock? Is she that bad?" Nora asked.

Someone her mother's age, he explained, might be receiving the wrong brain messages through minuscule hardening of the arteries. "We'll have to wake up her system."

"How awful."

"A bit of juice now could work wonders."

"Like a criminal—in the electric chair!"

" 'Fraid you don't understand, young lady."

Nora hated the patronizing way he talked to lay people about medical problems, for she'd gotten all A's in biology and knew a few facts about the body, too.

Her mother embraced the notion of "treatments," however; seized upon the idea as if she'd been waiting all along for somebody to suggest just that. Of course, it *was* crazy of her to accede so readily, Nora thought. But the doctor and her father were delighted to use the woman's irrationality for such therapeutical good ends. She went off smiling.

The spurts of electricity had little effect at first; she stayed in the hospital for a while, resting, until ready for the next round. Nora had to return to college or she'd lose a whole semester's work. Like a conspirator, her father urged her to leave, insisting the situation was well in hand.

A month later her mother died of a heart attack induced by the voltage. "Now and then these things happen," said the doctor lamely.

"What can a fella do?" echoed her father.

"I should've stayed home!"

"No, no . . . we have to keep on living."

"That's so easy to say, Dad."

"What else is there?"

Her father felt bad in the usual, self-incriminating ways, for he'd a dim idea he'd treated his wife rottenly but couldn't figure out where the wrong turning had come. Nora guessed he was also lamenting his wasted life, consumed in a close round of business routine and small-town civic obligations, none of which suddenly seemed important at all. In addition, with farmers losing their land and banks closing, he felt poor, cheated of his life's energies. Nora sympathized but couldn't reach out to console him because the ground had widened and split open between them—and they'd never been very close.

Now, her intimate problems couldn't be revealed, certainly not to one's father. She'd spent the last two weekends with a graduating engineer, a rather frightening and not enjoyable time. She'd bled a lot and soiled the mattress, about which the hotel was extremely unpleasant. Tom was scared he'd be reported to the university authorities, perhaps denied his diploma. He turned resentful, though the whole experiment had been *his* idea in the first place. The second time was to be their "honeymoon," and Tom even provided her with a dimestore ring, so there'd be no hardlooks at the registry in *this* hotel. In bed she pretended the proper spasms of joy at what seemed the crucial moments, and later he asked her to marry him, so she figured she'd done pretty well.

Tom—her husband? She looked him over with awe, feeling distant, suddenly, because he was so near. He'd a fine lanky body, a handsome profile, good facial bones, but a certain ruthless quality bothered her. "Tom's *all* boy," he said his mother used to remark.

"And *this* scar?" Nora asked, pointing to a white slash on his thigh.

"Football . . . this appendicitis . . . a dog bite here . . . a knife, this one. My worst fight."

The snarl of hair on the back of his hands and wrists, the blue, ropy veins in his powerful arms suggested flesh very different from hers. Was it best for opposites to couple this way? He'd take over her life as he took over her body, hard and insistent; she'd have to give way, seek fulfillment in submission—or pretend to, convincingly. Should she try? (Didn't everyone?) "I think I'm going to love you, Tom Summers." More in hope than belief, and she agreed to turn over the dimestore ring for a diamond. They planned a June wedding following commencement, though perhaps it was unseemly soon, after her mother's death.

"Daughters shouldn't mourn too long," her father said. "You've got to get on with your life."

In May they made love on a blanket under the full moon. Tom couldn't get enough of it, made jokes about "the bean-bag," a little heart-shaped pillow he carried across campus as they headed for the privacy of the arboretum. Tom, an engineer, figured out the proper angles and placed the bag under her bottom, just so.

She saw the moon rise between her knees as she lay back, felt it coming up into her. She was pregnant after the first month, the wedding barely in good time. Because the news meant a worsening of their financial predicament, it didn't bring them closer together, as she'd expected. Would he land a job, even though these days nobody was hiring engineers? Now there was no chance *she* might find work. Perhaps she'd never really feel intimate with Tom (children shatter the bond between parents, she knew— make it different), as her mother had remained distant from her father—even officially, in a separate bedroom. She'd only to decide if *that* might be the way she preferred her marriage to go. After all, there was the Kemp nuttiness, which caused her to look at other people as if they belonged to the normal human race, while she was doomed to remain just a little outside, watching. Nobody knowing the difference.

That winter after the birth of David, when she was still in the Des Moines hospital, her father wrote he was marrying a local widow who was "comfortably off." The two of them scooted out to California, away from the snow. The family house was sold in April, and Nora doubted if she'd ever see the home town again, since no relatives remained. But an eerie turn of destiny brought her back. Her husband, a municipal utilities specialist, was offered the job of supervising the installation of a new power plant in the town; at the same time the waterworks, long privately owned, was to be converted to a public system. Tom was asked to remain as city engineer—not much salary but a "safe" position, these uncertain times. He'd just enough experience with Des Moines utilities to long for a chance to be his own boss.

And so Priscilla, their second, was born the following year, when they were settled into their lives, having made peace with their overblown, early expectations. They didn't want any more children—scarcely discussed the matter—as if they were the unspoken embodiment of Depression years statistics on the national birth rate. In bed as elsewhere, they'd struck a compromise. A little apologetically, Tom still came to her for it at least once a week, and though she tried to be a good sport, she didn't bother with the show of former years. No little yelps or shudders —she just lay there until he was finished. Really it hardly mattered to her one way or the other; there was no question, a husband had these rights. The sexual failing was hers, she admitted to him. He shouldn't let it interfere with his natural pleasure; and yet she knew that his inability to arouse her was the only nagging flaw in his life circumstances. Too bad. She realized his professional limits when she saw his satisfaction in that small-punkins job, knew all too clearly how their life here would roll the years away.

She began to live for the children. At least *they'd* be getting somewhere, and the focus or direction didn't matter, only that promise lay ahead. Nothing yet had happened to cut them back; she'd see nothing did. The old home town *was* a good place for them to grow up, even though she knew it'd never contain them.

Nora urged Tom to purchase the Kemp homestead on the edge of town when it came on the market. She had the fun of fixing up her childhood room for Priscilla's use. All the ghosts seemed to smile a welcome, and when she climbed out of bed in the middle of the night she could navigate to the bathroom as if born blind.

Tom became president of the school board and head of Rotary, began believing in the image others had of him, got pretty porky with her. He'd tuck his toes under the footboard of the bed each morning as he performed a series of sit-ups to keep his belly lean. Sometimes he seemed to have sexy periods precisely because his interest in that department was flagging. He'd try to hop into bed with her before she'd a chance to slip the diaphragm in place. Then he'd kid her about it, asking why in hell she was so particular—until she finally had to spell it out: with two healthy children, they'd better count their blessings, not press their luck, risk a baby. "You know my family history as well as I do, Tom."

Nora realized it was a phony reason but preferred not to pursue the matter for fear of ending up too close to Tom for daily comfort. The children, even, shored-up their parents' set ways of dealing with each other. There were good family times together, Ma and Pa in the front seat on rides down forgotten dusty roads on hot evenings; fishing trips to Minnesota; and movies on Bank Night. The children were kept in ignorance of what went on behind the closed bedroom door; nobody in town knew details like that, fortunately! Tom's coarseness—or insensitivity—was perhaps, Nora figured, the difference between women and men when it came to sex. He viewed stag movies at the Elks and returned home horny; she loathed him for it, but what could she say? He took after her, used her like a whore, fantasies in his head, eyes closed; she submitted to this madness as best she could.

On Pearl Harbor Day, huddled around the radio after church, listening to the news, Tom said: "You know, I'm still draft age. If this thing gets serious, they might take me!"

Such speculation bloomed into "I wish they *would* take me!" The Army was too slow in getting around to the older men, but Tom interested the Navy in his engineering skills—and he passed the physical.

"My God, Tom, why do you have to tear everything up this way?"

"*I'm* not to blame. It's Hitler—and Hirohito!" He thought it good for David and Priscilla to have a different idea of their father, even though he'd be missing from their daily lives for a while. They'd understand what a man was—not just a breadwinner who goes off to work each morning. "Probably over in a few months. I've only enlisted for the duration." Their alarm gratified him; he felt loved by his family as never before.

Nora knew he'd meet prostitutes, the war merely justifying his quest. "A man's got *needs*," he was fond of saying, cupping his genitals as he came toward her. How uncomplicated, depressingly primeval, a man's needs seemed to be compared to hers.

She never in the world imagined he'd be killed—Tom wasn't the type. Nevertheless, the awful telegram arrived, and the blue star in the front window was eventually replaced with one stitched in gold. No recovery of the body—he was blown out of existence, simply ended, "needs" and all.

Through the ordeal of small-town showcase bereavement, Nora kept her arms like angel's wings around the children—scarcely able to believe the news, nor could they. With only a memorial service, no body for evidence in front of the altar, death was unconvincing. Nora pretended to be in mourning when in the presence of others because the children might be harmed by her lack of tears. But in the confines of her quiet, solitary bedroom, she let a slipping sense of relief come over her and give her peace. Never had the sheets seemed so wide and clean—like celestial raiment, what angels wore up there. (Not that she believed in heaven—Tom was nowhere, the end was the end, that's all.) He'd left her a solid packet of insurance, an interest in the implement business, and the house was entirely hers through the death clause in the mortgage. She'd never have to lift a finger or get a job, if she didn't want to. So like him!

"With the children in school, what do you *do* with yourself all day, Nora?" friends asked, jackal-eyed.

She enjoyed being alone. Something wrong with that?

Of course.

"Got the whole house to keep clean, clothes to wash and iron—meals to fix. What do you *mean*, what do I 'do'?" and a round laugh to make it seem okay.

Everybody was watching her, especially her own children, anxious side-glances, wondering if she'd be able to hold up the roof for them, keep all this going. Priscilla calmed down first. She played her own sweet game best of all, quickly caught on to the town's implicit rules and put herself to the test, confident of her success. She fell right in with schoolgirls her age and was a favorite among them. She'd fool with Nora's lipstick and eyeshadow, dab perfume behind her ears—simply couldn't wait to be the flirtatious tease no little boy of the neighborhood guessed was here already. Not a sign of the Kemp streak in Priscilla, not yet at least. "She's so normal!" with a laugh of pleasure to a neighbor, who wouldn't catch the note of exasperation.

David had the tough lot of trying to be a man before he was ready. It nearly made Nora weep to hear him slam the front door when he returned home from school and shout "What's for supper?" in exact imitation of his father. For a little kid to have absorbed so much of his father's mannerisms amazed her, and underscored her conviction in like-father, like-son, with its echo: like-mother, like-daughter. But she hated having David carry it so far as to promise he'd never marry because no one could be as beautiful as his Mom, or cook like her. The more she retreated from being too strong a female in his life, the more he sought her out, pulling her from hiding upstairs, covering her with kisses. "Oh, David! Don't pay attention to *me*. Go play ball with the others. I can manage the chores okay."

He wouldn't hear of it. None of his friends at age twelve could be head of household, and he enjoyed swaggering about as if he owned the place. He could fix leaky faucets, drive the car, handle a saw, hook on storm windows, repair things that broke down. Since mechanical inclinations were symptomatic of manliness, she'd nothing to worry about. He was "all boy" and could have a harem of women about him, without suffering any kind of diminishment, or sissifying.

With only two years separating the children, they formed an unusually strong bond, full of torturous infighting, but also mutual support, as if, welded together, they made up for the missing parent. Their visible growth gave purpose to the household: she was feeding their lives (and indeed her pies at church bazaars were always bought first). She attended PTA, raised money for band uniforms, did a lot of chauffeuring. The seasons tumbled them along. Just through Christmas and here's Valentine's Day! Where'd the time *go?*

She'd a vague sense of being diddled out of her life but wasn't sure where the thought came from, since nurturing one's children was obviously *the* experience for a woman; managing a house alone made her gallant role that much more certain. Townspeople were almost patronizing, the way they recognized the lineaments of her life, knew positively what her duty was: she'd lost her husband in the war, fighting for his country, his home, but her thriving children would keep her on an even keel, force her to think hopefully of the future.

She felt so lonely! None of her housewife neighbors said anything but tiresome, surface chit-chat—their idea of conversation. Back home they had husbands who shared a bed with them, talked now and then in the night when anything might slip out— things that mattered. These women still believed in it all, this whole silly life they lived, but Nora didn't. She felt imprisoned in a pageant and didn't know how to get out of it.

David and Priscilla suspected her plight but made the choice children always do and looked sharper to their own developing interests. They'd far to go and didn't want to be hung up on the snags of their mother's life. Her growing obesity pleased them, as if she were a blimp from which now they could easily push off. But just in case they fell back, she'd be a doughy, heavy cushion to fall into.

While the madcap pace of the high school years prevailed, Nora had little time for gnawing reconsiderations. She met no eligible men, and no effort was made by anyone to introduce her to new male companions. They were all somebody's husband by this time; or not interested. Summer months were her happiest times, with work in the garden and trips to the sandpit, where she'd bake in the hot sun until absolutely exhausted. But a couple of times out there on the beach she was approached by men, some of whom knew she was a widow and others who'd just ask any woman for it. She got rid of the lechers before the children noticed, but memory of these crude overtures filled her head at night, in bed, and what she thought she'd kept tight control of burst out, stronger than it'd ever been while Tom lived. Memory of sex with him seemed ghoulish, morbid. She couldn't remember the exact features of his face but knew precisely how he'd looked down there. She felt wild, on the edge, miserable, and sometimes little screams, more like gasps would come out, startling her. Once she arose at 2 A.M. and ran downstairs, jumped on her bicycle and wheeled through the hushed, empty streets, round and round the merry-go-blocks. The saddle felt good under her. She crept up the dark stairwell afterward like a naughty teen-ager, hoping her children wouldn't waken.

David suddenly began avoiding her. His room became such a sacred bastion she wasn't allowed even to clean it. He spent hours behind the locked door, getting acquainted with his new pimply-faced, bass-voiced self. Masculinity settled over him like deep musk from a tall wood. He was rangy, good at basketball, and passionate about sports-car models. They could only speak now in false, standard, American mother-son ways. David would never let her kiss and hug him, and soon she didn't try. She'd have to be content imagining her son's life—conjure up his present, a success in the classroom and gymnasium, and glow with pleasure over his future.

"Stop looking at me that way!" he'd reproach her, when he caught her staring at him.

"Oh, was I?" Her mother-love had X-ray strength, could pass through doors, enter minds. God, what power! Yet, nothing to be done with it.

Priscilla dated the prime high school athletes but wouldn't let them get very far, as she told Nora even before motherly caution could be voiced; she was waiting for the right boy to come along

—later, in college, perhaps. The usual nursing or teaching careers didn't interest her, for she'd far rather help her husband in his profession, whatever it turned out to be. A doctor's wife, say.

"Smart girl!" Nora smiled but was secretly in awe of this smooth, determined youngster. Something heartless about her. No acne or menstrual cramps softened her, no excuse came along for them to fall upon each other's shoulders. Nora felt denied the chance of half reliving her youth through Priscilla (only this time with understanding); no mother should be cheated of the pleasure of making the child's life easier than hers had been. If these cycles didn't prevail, what hope was there for the future? It was a curse to have such a queenly adolescent, this pretty paragon. At times Nora succumbed to uncontrollable dislike or envy, a mad impulse to lash out and crush Priscilla's smugness. Those moments, she remembered the family history—as if her taut face glimpsed in the mirror were already hanging in the hall of ancestors downstairs by the front door.

David left home first, as he always knew he would. The Kemp madness had nothing to do with him, just as it'd nothing to do with his father. The men here endured, turned in with their thoughts, turned out to the world with their bodies; never hung around very long. The moment David set his face sternly and placed the college brochure in front of her, the crimson emblem like a drop of blood on the creamy paper, she knew he'd fixed upon a plan of departure that would wound her. "RIP? What's that?"

Priscilla, who knew what David was up to, said quickly, laughing, "No, Mother, *RPI*. Rensselaer Polytech Institute. You know, the famous engineering school."

"Isn't Ames good enough anymore?"

No, it was too nearby to seem distinctive; too many around town had gone there. The eastern college would put him in line for top industrial jobs "anywhere in the country." He was going.

She hoped to get used to the idea and never once counted the days on her desk calendar until the time he'd be off. Clothes weren't discussed between them, only cash and how much he'd need. Like a husband who'd decided he must break the marriage, David was severe with her; no irrelevant questions permitted. On the actual day of his departure by train for Chicago and points east, she felt a wrenching like the moment she'd given birth to him, an awful ripping away. On the station platform she threw herself at him, weeping, caressing his back—her stony, embarrassed, beanpole boy. He didn't flinch, allowed her to have the emotional scene all by herself; it'd be the last he'd have to endure. But in spite of his resolve, he was moved, she knew, for they'd shared a life together and a piece of time like that counted for *something*, had to be recognized. With surprise and a melting relief, she noticed his eyes were teary. And yet he so thoroughly hated demonstrations of affection, his love turned to hate at almost the same moment. If allowed, she'd ladle out the love in such gobs he'd feel like a smothered parfait. "See ya' at Christmas," he said, turning and jumping aboard.

The first vacation, David returned to measure his progress, see how far he'd come from his Iowa boyhood, but the following summer he counseled in a Maine camp and Nora didn't glimpse him for a whole year. "Why should I come home?" he said bluntly over the phone (she was grateful even for a call!). "School's starting Monday. Have to be there."

Priscilla chose a fancy girls' college near Cleveland that nobody'd ever heard of. Nora supposed she'd found a booklet full of glamorous pictures and the right sort of sales pitch, for all kinds of admissions folders lay around the high school guidance office. Once the girl's mind was made up, that was that, but Nora failed to understand how such an important decision became fixed, irreversible, and blamed the school for letting youngsters have their own heads too often.

Perhaps worry over Priscilla was a sentimental indulgence not squared with the facts. Some parents couldn't get free of overly dependent children, couldn't shove them out of the nest. Nora would far rather have an offspring like Priscilla than a helpless, meandering girl who couldn't get headed toward anything.

"You'll be all right—alone here, Ma?" Priscilla asked, upon leaving, as if *she* were the guardian. Such concern might lead to future closeness, for the strong must make the first gesture of conciliation toward the weak, the child must make a move to forgive the parent, or they can never be friends in later life.

"Sure, I'll be fine! It's my old home after all. Little empty, but I've the dog to keep me company. And lots of fine memories."

"That'll be enough?"

What glorious concern! "And friends, of course."

"Yeah, the bridge club." Priscilla showed no trace of her usual disdain for the Where-You-Go-I-Go Club.

"Keepin' up this place, I'll be so busy I won't have *time* to think."

"Good." That, as everyone knows, is best of all. Priscilla gathered together her matching set of luggage, called the porter, and kissed Nora good-by.

The first night alone in the creaking house she scarcely slept, but after she had mowed the lawn all next day, exhaustion put her out at sundown. The rose garden and shrubs needed attention; she poured such energy into the flowers, people stopped to comment. "Nora, how do you *do* it?"

"Like to feel the earth, touch my roots, you might say."

"Ain't you somethin'!"

"Our family's been here a long time, and the ground knows our fingers."

"Ha!" A rather queer look.

Maybe with *that* remark she'd gone too far.

All that autumn she prepared for the children's Christmas visit, laying the groundwork carefully with David, so he'd be sure to come. Not too many letters but all of them assuming she'd see him before long. "And Priscilla's eager to talk to you, too."

When David arrived, looking filled out, somewhat older, no boys his age seemed left, and those available were strangers to him. The girls were bespoken. Mostly, he sat around the house, but if he fetched mail from the post office or bought beer, he hoped he wouldn't run into anybody he once knew. Reacquaintance seemed painful, pointless. There was nothing in this town for him any more. He was only home because of *her*, and he'd surely never come again, because his mother wasn't worth a fifteen-hundred-mile trip.

"No use gettin' sentimental," he said when he left after New Year's, waving his hand as if to a half-stranger. "S'long."

With a part-time mechanic's job in Rensselaer and a full scholarship at the Institute, David was on his own, never wrote for money. She'd plenty to give but knew the bondage such transactions entail. "Keep it for your old age," he wrote, returning her hundred-dollar check.

Events in David's life were dry statistics gleaned from letters—high grades, Dean's List, job offers—pegs for her to hang her life on, because after all she was his mother, he the only son. She felt wounded, noble in her silent grief, occasionally angry over his ingratitude and indifference.

"Yes, David graduated *cum laude* . . . works for General Electric now . . . uh huh, married the prettiest girl you ever saw. She's from right there . . . Schenectady . . . he sees a lot of her family."

Although Nora hadn't received an invitation to the wedding ("No big deal, just a wedding, period"), and wasn't asked to visit them in their new home, she received snapshots by the dozen and vapid letters from her daughter-in-law, then photos of the baby, Little Tom. Phone calls on holidays were stiff—didn't work. David ceased writing altogether. If Nora could only believe reckless passion and baby-on-the-way had produced the marriage, she'd have felt easier, knowing David's settling was deliberate, inevitable. Queer, the way he closed all the gaps in his life just as quickly as possible, everything shut tight. Nothing the years could do but age him.

The bank managed her financial affairs so well that even though Priscilla's college bills ran high, Nora had enough to spend a bit on herself, her own pleasures. But what would they be? She didn't look well in *any* clothes, being too stout; no yearnings for travel or taste for luxurious automobiles. If she took a trip somewhere she'd get too far off her routine, might succumb to a bunko artist, a con man, somebody guessing her loneliness and love-susceptibility. The best way to keep the hatches battened was to stay home.

Nora headed the library board, served in Mission Society, said yes to every request for public service, played bridge—they had her coming and going every day of the week. Sometimes she forgot to rip off a month on the calendar until weeks after the first day. Evenings, she dozed in front of the television but always came to when "The Star Spangled Banner" played, the screen white-gray. "Got to Stand up—the National Anthem!" she said to the dog, who'd also been snoozing. In the morning, just after waking, during that fulgent time before the trappings of one's life are fitted into place, she tried to suspend thought, hold despair in abeyance, quickly perked a pot of coffee, flipped on "The Breakfast Club," loud with laughter, tinkly music, and the sort of busyness that prompts one to step aboard the day.

Despite these ordinary activities, Nora didn't quite have a soul-settling belief in her own existence. She expected the bland sameness to end before long, even sought out signs of decay—in her hearing, memory, sight; this devilish quest, she figured, might be the old Kemp trouble asserting itself now in her declining years.

There were these signs: a tendency to talk overly much to the dog as if he were a human being; an occasional mumbling aloud to herself; more than normal fears about living alone on the edge of town. When she ordered three phones installed, for bedroom, kitchen, and basement, it was because she could dial the police quickly should a marauder break in. Her sleep was far from steady, and whenever she woke in the night it seemed the enormous breath of the wind had aroused her. The steady, unnerving winds of the plains came to play upon her nerves like the unending sound of the same note. Nothing, after all, could be done about the wind.

Nora tried to laugh herself back to normalcy, but her cackling seemed further evidence of disorder. The stiff smiles she wore on the streets were symptomatic of just the opposite of gaiety. At last she *had* to talk, between hands at bridge, much to everyone's annoyance, for aside from weakening their concentration on the game, they were afraid Nora might say something which would get them more involved in her troubles than they wished to be. Last night's dream about the vegetable salesman who didn't know his watermelons were bleeding was quickly disposed of by her partner's comment: "If you'd drink a glass of warm milk before going to bed, you wouldn't dream so much."

"That's what they say."

"'Course, you might have to get up and go to the bathroom in the middle of the night. Ha!"

"If it's not one thing it's another, I guess."

Terrifying, to watch them resolutely avoid recognition of what they were doing to themselves. Every *one* of them saw the chinks, light of some awful awareness streaming through, but refused to

admit it. They preferred to talk endlessly about their grandchildren. Several believed devoutly in God and the afterlife. A few
dumber ones were pretty well enmeshed in the trivia of existence
and hadn't the wit to wonder. But even these women sensed
something dangerous in Nora that might cause them all trouble.
Health preoccupied them, for the Major Enemy usually came dis-
guised as illness, if not accident. They exchanged useful lore about
cures, and when somebody in town died, there was quiet, unspoken self-congratulation since *they* continued to live. Nora knew
she was viewing her cronies harshly, but her compassion ebbed as
the years did, and whereas once she could find good in almost everyone or at least an explanation of crotchets and perversions,
now the whole lot seemed deservedly cast aside by their remote
husbands, distant children, and indifferent American society.

Nora resigned from the library board, protesting their decision
to accept federal funds for a new building. "We'll lose control of
the library—don't you see? Next, the government will tell us what
books to buy." She stopped attending the Mission Society because
she felt Christianity was devastating the innocent heathen of the
primitive world. Withdrew from all activities except the bridge
club. Nobody fought to win her back or tried to seek her out in
her seclusion. Thank God! She was as tired of them as *they* surely
were of her.

No scale in the house worked, but she knew she was getting
heavier, for she couldn't fit into any of her dresses, felt too enormous to be seen in public. She ordered groceries by phone and
had the boy pick up her mail at the post office, transacted business, paid all bills through the mails. Because the phone made instant conversations possible, it was months before she realized
she'd actually seen no one but service people at the back door.
"Being hermits suits us!" she said to the dog, and he nodded.
They talked a lot these days.

David and his wife urged Nora to fly East for a visit, but she
knew she'd drop an airplane with the cargo of herself on board.
Those two were almost middle-aged, parents of growing children,
and perhaps felt a fresh alliance in the offing, now that they were
candidates to join *her* generation, high up on the shelf. The awful
effort involved in travel canceled out the possible pleasure she'd
have, crunching into immortality at last, glimpsing kin of the new

generation. David had made the overture, however. "The latch-string's out," said his wife, and she could go there sometime.

Priscilla's good manners led her to scribble "Come visit!" at the bottom of her infrequent, newsy notes, but Nora didn't take the invitation seriously. Fairfield County, Connecticut, sounded pretty fancy. She didn't have to gaze at rolling hills, stone walls, and landscaped estates to be convinced Priscilla had achieved the mark set for herself years ago.

Nevertheless, one day up ahead Nora feared she'd get into such a fix somebody would have to help her out of it. No provision as to who'd come or what kind of aid there'd be, aside from Blue Cross and a pile of cash in her savings account. Very likely the precipitating incident would be a fall, for she was abominably clumsy, or a simple cold that developed into a strangulation net of pneumonia; or a sinister, quietly working carcinoma somewhere in the mountainous regions of her flesh.

"I'm pretty good on my pins yet," she remarked to the dog. Her legs in stretch-bandage casings were bearing up quite well, considering the weight they had to carry. Therefore, she was surprised when a varicose vein hemorrhaged and she was rushed to the hospital in an ambulance. The staff doctor scolded her for having neglected the malady so long; now they'd have to roll up her veins like string on a kite, "all of which'd be a lot easier if you didn't weigh half a ton," smiling as he said it, but no-nonsense serious, too. He suggested a spinal, but Nora loathed the sound of it and feared an incompetent nurse might slip with the needle and paralyze her. The old gas mask was best, for she'd rather not know anything until she came swimming out of the anesthesia.

Later, she realized intimations of disaster were sparking at her right and left. The aides washed and sterilized her body, hung about her person as if she'd no longer any say. She felt dreadfully exposed, vulnerable—danger so real prickles rose on her nape. In such moments the worst could happen from almost any direction of the void. They wheeled her to the elevator and she ascended to the operating room. All the while she was going under ("wave your finger if you can still hear me"), she twitched her hand violently to show she was still fighting.

During the operation or shortly afterward, she suffered a stroke which partially paralyzed her right side. Neither the surgeon nor the nurses knew what had happened until Nora complained, after coming down from the recovery room, that her right arm kept trying to slip away, was hiding behind her. With her left hand she attempted to recapture her runaway right member. The nurse frowned, puzzled by Nora's weak struggle, not comprehending the garbled words. She pinched toes, upper arm, cheek. "Can you feel me? *Can you?*"

There was a strange space between her thoughts. She could only get over that emptiness with words thrust ahead like planks over a chasm. "I . . . know . . . the . . . words . . . but I . . . can't say them."

The surgeon arrived, examined her quickly, a glance of pity, parental seriousness. Nora felt dropped off at the end—of somewhere. Would she never rise from bed again, never walk? Along with the billowing fright was a weird, pleasurable completeness—the closing of a door that'd remained open too long. Her affliction had come! The unreal waiting was over. Nora tried to smile at the nurse, after the doctor'd gone. "Is . . . is . . . my daughter? . . . can't think . . . of her name . . . is she—?"

"Been notified, dearie. Probably on her way." Tucked the blanket under the mattress, a good nanny. "She'll take care of you, don't you worry."

So this is my fate! Now, how about it? Her relief having things clarified was so great she began to chuckle. Mirth spilled out in the form of a gasp, a rattling in her throat; she shed a lopsided smile. The nurse, nearly out of the room, heard Nora's unseemly noise. She wheeled around, a scolding expression in her sterilized blue eyes, stepped quickly to the bed. Nora lay deep in the pillow, helplessly laughing. In the nurse's eyes suspicion changed to cynical understanding. Nora felt herself slipping away from the ordinary world at a very fast pace. Quickly removed from where she wasn't sure she'd ever belonged anyhow. Common existence was a platform already in the distance as her fast-moving bed-vehicle sped off. *I'm gone, she thinks, gone out of my head!* It was too funny for words.

The Kemp madness—just this! Nora's laughter didn't stop, though she soon was weeping with almost no intermediate transition between emotions. The nurse left her to her bedlam diversions, whatever they might be.

News of Nora spread to aides on the floor, to the personnel on the next shift; soon the entire hospital knew, then the town. But the fuzz in her head came merely from physical causes, Nora realized—nothing congenital, nothing for anybody to feel *that* way about. She'd suffered a stroke, that's all. Didn't they *know?* It could happen to anyone.

"We'll get you out of here in no time," Priscilla said.

She thinks *her* reputation is at stake, too, madness in the family tarring everyone alike.

From the bed, Nora watched her daughter pace the hospital room, stare down at the parking lot, light from the windows hard on her Wrigley-girl features. Thinking what?

"Oh, Priscilla . . . oh . . . my dear!" Now *she'd* become the parent, forced to cope. There was still no softness about her; she relaxed with great sweeps of a cigarette, back and forth to her determined mouth. Nembutal at night to put her out, she said. Spine slightly curved, the Connecticut debutante slouch perhaps; clothes tweedy, tailored, very expensive, right down to neat little lizard shoes with gold buckles.

After ten days the paralysis weakened. Nora could almost make a fist, wiggle her toes, talk more clearly. "Can't I . . . be moved . . . back . . . to the regular ward?" Unfortunately, a lot of hometown folks had slipped through the caged bars at the entrance for a visit, checking up on her.

"You'll be going home soon."

"I suppose . . . you'll have to get back . . . to your family."

"Oh, not right now."

Priscilla's countenance used to be as unruffled as an August midday sky, but now some hurt lay behind those eyes. "But . . . how can . . . you be away . . . from home . . . so long?"

"I need the rest. Not see people—the same people, for a change."

Her husband did she mean? Her daughter?

Priscilla seemed to hear those words bounce back from the institution-green walls; they sounded odd. "For a while, anyhow."

The next week Nora was released, discovered the house had been completely cleaned, everything in apple-pie order. "My, you've been busy!" The dog was glad to be sprung from his long imprisonment in the kennel.

"Something to do."

Nora occupied the first floor guest room and Priscilla slept in her mother's bed upstairs. "Good thing we had this bathroom put in—for our old age, we said. As if it'd never come . . . and it didn't, for Tom."

Priscilla shopped, cooked, dusted, spent long afternoons reading library books and listening to fat Beethoven and Bach 78s of long ago. She phoned her daughter, Josie, at Miss Morrissey's boarding school once a week but never placed a call to her husband. Why was that, Nora finally asked.

"He travels . . . isn't home just now. You know, export-import."

"I see." Obviously he'd another life with some woman. Poor girl! How could they speak of it? Should they? She longed to comfort Priscilla, throw her wreck of a life into the churning trouble, if her potash bones would be of any use in the compost, get something growing again in that marriage. But perhaps Priscilla was tempted to chuck it all, give up on matrimony and all the dreams envisioned as a child. Tuck right in again here at home, the roof ample enough to cover her life if she'd diminish it to the size of a dime, her needs shriveled to nothing. She wondered if Priscilla *wanted* the excuse of "mother's illness" in order to do just that— but what madness! It shouldn't be. Both their lives would be throttled, serving each other here. She must make a move to show her independence—that she didn't *need* her daughter any more.

"I've a hankering . . . to see the bridge club girls."

"Sure—why not? A coming-out party! Let 'em see how well you're doing."

A few had already called, for the minister in the church bulletin reported favorably on her progress. Nora hadn't been able to say much, but she did quite well now with her speech, only a little slurring, and she was okay with names. The squeeze-ball exercised her fingers back to life, so her handshake didn't feel like a dead fish.

They'd serve coffee in the Haviland cups and crumb cake with powdered sugar on top—a bit messy, but it'd force the women to take care they didn't spill, put *them* a little at the disadvantage. Ha!

Really, it was almost worth it to suffer a stroke if you got your daughter back close this way, intimate as they'd *never* been before. "I'm so happy!" Both knew it was a crazy thing to say—but not crazy.

That afternoon when the ladies approached the porch, Nora at the screen door called out their names, to show them she could. "What a day! The roses never looked better. So glad you came!"

"Oh, Nora, how *are* you?"

"Want to see the garden first? Go right ahead—sure, I'll come with you." She pushed open the door with her cane. "Might have trouble identifying some of the weird flowers growing out there, 'less I introduce you to 'em."

"How good you look!"

"Sure, why not?"

A whooping gaiety arose among them in the garden, for if Nora could be in such splendid shape after a stroke, anything could be surmounted. According to plan, Priscilla remained in the kitchen, for they'd shunt attention to her—the stranger—and bypass Nora if given half a chance. When the guests entered the parlor at last, Priscilla stepped out to shake hands, for if she remained hiding too long they'd think it queer.

"All set for bridge?" Nora asked, joshing—to show her spunk. "Oh . . . not really."

They gave each other such odd looks.

"Bring in the dessert and coffee, Priscilla. Let's eat."

They settled into easy chairs, hose rasping as they crossed their legs. Sighs erupted as they folded their arms and gazed about the room, where they'd spent so many afternoons at cards.

"Those the same drapes, Nora?"

"The room looks different—what've you done?"

"Furniture rearranged, maybe." Nora hadn't noticed. "Priscilla's been keeping house here."

"Amazing how you forget a place—what it looks like."

All the women were somewhat defensive, perhaps feeling guilty over their wicked reports concerning her sanity. But it wasn't that at all. They'd replaced her in the bridge club! "Thought you'd be out for a long time—that's what the papers said."

"If only we'd *known!*"

"Here it's only six months . . . and I bet Nora can play like a whiz!"

The trouble was, they couldn't oust the new member.

Who was she?

The name surprised Nora. "Never thought *she* had ambitions like that."

Oh, she's a wonderful person, they all said.

The interloper must be feeling pretty sneaky, if she had any delicacy of feeling at all. So be it. "Anyhow, I'm not at all sure I ever want to play bridge again!"

Priscilla looked alarmed—a rifle-shot glance.

But you *love* the game, Nora, they all said, as if they meant it. Wondering, rather, if it weren't sour grapes, or possibly an "odd" comment.

"Think I'd rather *talk*, when I see friends. Like we're doin' now. At bridge, we just sit around lookin' at those pieces of cardboard. Really, it's all silly, if you think about it."

They did, and it unsettled them—about her. Priscilla jumped from her chair and threw herself into the conversation to save the cogency of the moment. "Mother's got *other* hobbies now!"

Like what?

Oh, you'll see. Mother and daughter smiled and winked as if they knew the furbelows of a secret.

Afternoon light slanted strong through the leaded-glass upper pane of the bay window, lancing into the parlor, dust motes alive in the air. The women struggled up, as if deep in a wallow, kidding each other over their awkwardness. Farewells were called endlessly from porch to front lawn, until the final car-door slams ended it all.

"How quiet it is, suddenly. I'm so glad they're gone!" said Nora.

Priscilla sat down immediately to compose the write-up for the social column, since the story had to be delivered to the newspaper office by five, in order to make tomorrow's weekly edition. All the guest names were lined up like streets in town, and Nora's life looked squared off. "A celebration in honor of Mrs. Nora Kemp Summers, who has recovered from illness and wished to share her good fortune with her friends."

Next day, when Priscilla said she must return to Connecticut, Nora insisted no housekeeper or nurse was needed. "I can manage, don't you see?"

Yes, there'd been that pot of tomato soup left on the burner, smoking up the house when it boiled over, but accidents happened now and then. "Just because I landed in the hospital doesn't mean I've got to be perfect now, does it? Do I have to be *better* than anybody else?"

Furthermore, who could they get? Practical nurses were hard to find and often gossiped. Only three cleaning women existed, but Priscilla managed to persuade each of them to come one half-day a week—at ten dollars a time. "What you'd pay a practical nurse!" Nora said, shocked. She waited until Priscilla was safely on her way East, then phoned each women and told her not to come, there was no money. "As for company—I've got the dog—and my flowers! Ha!"

Now there was no one to fear, nobody to expect. She drenched herself in privacy with a lilting sense of freedom. The sober wall of respectability she'd been pushing ahead of her all her life was gone; she was giving way, falling into herself. A taste for solitude feeds upon itself. The grocery boy (who also handled her mail), the fuel truck driver, the garbage collector, the meter-reader— these were the only townspeople who saw her, and even from them she often hid, deep in the folds of the parlor drapes, just as she'd once hidden from young David among the dresses and coats in her bedroom closet. On the phone she talked level-headed to the bank manager and never made a mistake in her checking account, for she knew what might trigger a general investigation into her life: anything having to do with money, something *serious* like that. After the hospital, she'd never grown back her layer of protective fat, and now didn't need it.

Door-to-door salesmen weren't permitted to solicit, by order of the chamber of commerce, but occasionally they came knocking at her door: the Watkins man, the Avon lady, or a student selling encyclopedias. She never slammed the door in their faces or gave them cause to gossip to a neighbor about her. Then one day a young bearded man in sandals, with a pack on his back, and his girl friend, also loaded down, wearing jeans and sweatshirt, asked if they could mow her lawn in exchange for a meal or "spare cash." They were polite, soft-spoken, dignified with her. "I'm Jim and this is Sally."

"I haven't any money in the house—I never do. But I'll fix supper if you like."

It was fun having them for company because they weren't anybody she'd seen before. "Where you from?"

"Not any place you've heard of," he said.

"Not around here, I knew."

"Suppose you know *every*body in this town."

"Well, I lived here most of my life."

"Beautiful!"

Why? What was beautiful about that? They were strange in their views, not only strangers in town. Both vegetarians. Wouldn't touch the brown, greasy pork chops on their plates. Their distaste for meat was catching and Nora found each forkful hard to swallow, wondered if *she* were a vegetarian, too.

No coffee, thanks.

Herb tea, alas, she didn't have.

They shrugged, seemed content. A cigarette passed back and forth between them—a funny little twist, the kind farm hands in the 1930s used to roll. They laughed a lot over nothing, kept saying "Oh, wow!" as they roamed the house, pulled out the 78s and played them on the Victrola, cranking the handle hard.

It was dark, and since they'd no place to go, she invited them to spend the night. They suggested unrolling their sleeping bags on the lawn. "We like it outdoors at night," Sally said. "The earth 'n stars."

"But with all the bedrooms up there? Help yourself—take your pick."

"We won't dirty the sheets—don't worry," said Jim.

"I've plenty of sheets."

"He means we'll use our bags."

"Suit yourself. I'm right down here off the hall, 'case you need anything."

Next day they poked around the attic like kids on a rainy day, opening trunks and trying on old dresses and coats. She said "Wear it—it's yours," to any garment they fancied. They "paid" her for it in sesame bars and packages of granola, a jar of unrefined honey.

Here it was June and she hadn't yet planted her vegetable garden? Couldn't they help?

No, the roses and petunias didn't interest them, but her crabgrass lawn would make a fine spot for an organic garden. "Never used any weed killer or chemical fertilizer on the lawn, have you?"

"Not once."

"It looks great!"

"Dandelions, pigweed, crab grass . . ."

"Beautiful!"

Because of the roses, she never had time to look after the lawn, and the grocery boy could only mow it now and then.

"Who gives a shit about the rose garden? It's hopelessly poisoned. Saw those empty bags of dusting powder on the back porch. You've been very, very bad, buying that kind of stuff." His voice was gentle and high-pitched, almost like a girl's, but he didn't mind his femininity, and Sally seemed closer to him perhaps because of it. She didn't shave her legs; his arms weren't covered with a pelt (the way Tom's had been, with big blue veins); their flesh had been equalized in some way, as if it weren't a matter of opposites attracting but a cancellation of polarity, their bodies interchangeable. They could be inside one for today, occupy the other tomorrow. They were in love and together, inseparable, the same person in two halves.

Sally never wore lipsticks because of "Red-two in the dye" and refused Nora's perfume atomizer: "Thanks, but I don't like those chemical scents." They bathed only on Saturday night in the old-fashioned way, for they respected their skin oils and didn't wish to violate nature.

"I'm learning so *much* from you two!"

"We love it here," Sally said. "No hassles. It's beautiful."

They cut the sod, shook out the loose dirt, saved the turf for the compost bin, which Jim constructed near the garage. They planted a sizable garden just before a rain, then rested with satisfaction, at peace with time. They'd joined the world's work, and "it's good, it's good! How tired I am!"

"How happy," the girl said.

Since it was Saturday, they climbed into the claw-footed tub together and had a giggling, splashing, dawdling session in there, the door wide open. "Nora! Nora!"

They wanted her to sponge them down, rub their backs with the luffa. She found this intimacy surprisingly natural, their nudity easy to get used to. "Oh, that feels terrific," he said as she scrubbed his back—the way she'd done with David, long ago. Lean, handsome bodies, the girl's breasts firm and full, their legs so entwined she couldn't tell who was who.

"Come on, climb in with us, Nora," Jim said.

"Oh no, the tub'd run over!"

"We'll let out some water," said Sally.

"Stop kidding me, you two!" She threw the sponge on his belly and wiped her hands on the bath towels. She knew they were about ready to make love—they always did after bathing, and she'd no intention of sticking around. Downstairs in the kitchen as she fixed supper, she felt happy just knowing how much pleasure there was in the house. She listened to the rain, the sound of laughter from the stairwell, and felt blessed. They'd no intention of leaving now—for they had to wait and watch the garden grow, weed it, harvest the crops.

Sally and Jim lived in the master bedroom which had once been hers and Tom's, the whole second floor their province, and she seldom went up. Occasionally friends of theirs would appear, simply walk into the house without shyness, sleep overnight or stay for a week, an ebb and flow that bypassed all the strictures of the old formalities. "You're welcome!" she said at first, but the newcomers looked at her when she said that, as if thinking "Of course—why not?"

The virgin-soil garden flourished with seven kinds of lettuce, rows of carrots, beets, cabbage, squash, corn, and potatoes. Except for milk, which they purchased from a farmer a mile on the other side of the railroad tracks, they lived off the land, relishing the self-containment, proving once again to themselves—and anybody like Nora, from the regular world—that subsistence was possible with a little effort. There wasn't anything in the supermarket they craved; no sugar, coffee, Coke. The grocer phoned to ask what he'd done wrong, figuring she'd shifted her account. Probably the grocer's boy got him to do it, for the lawn-mowing pin money was gone, and the tips for fetching her mail.

"Everything's fine here. Don't need a thing! Ha!"

When the town marshal's car began patrolling her dead-end street, she knew they were watching her. He shouted to her from the driver's seat as she stood with a hoe in the garden. "You okay?"

"Never been better! How's yourself?"

"All right, thanks." He studied Jim and Sally, squatting between the bean rows, picking away. "See you got company."

"Some garden, huh?"

Sally and Jim kept their faces down, the way cows turn their backs to an approaching storm.

"Call if you need me," said the marshal, touching his visored cap.

"Have I ever?"

"You never know . . . when." He drove off.

Nora knew that guy's dirty mind! Because he'd been caught while still in high school and forced to marry the girl before the baby came, he was determined nobody else should have any free fun. No doubt Sally and Jim hadn't bothered with the marriage ceremony to make it legal, but whose business was it? Surely not the town marshal's! The law must have more important matters to attend to.

But the network closed tighter. One afternoon the minister trudged up the sidewalk while she was tying the tomato vines to poles. "Have a minute? Could we talk?"

"About what?"

"A pastorly visit, that's all." But he wasn't looking at her, even. He eyed the hippie contingent slouching on the porch—three friends, with Sally and Jim. They stared back, wouldn't run hide from a man of the cloth. *They* probably read the Bible more often than the minister!

The churchy, reverential spiel began at once: the fine work she'd done in the Ladies' Aid, how she'd never skip church services, used to organize bake sales to raise money for the orphanage. Everyone missed her and wished she'd return to the fold. "The Lord needs his Marthas and his Marys."

What did *he* know of the Lord? "I don't need church any more."

"Everyone does."

"I praise God every day in everything I do. Can you say the same, Reverend?"

He frowned and turned to go. In this town leading one's own life isn't allowed. Such an example is a menace.

"They're taking advantage of you—that trash!"

"Don't you *dare* speak like that. About my friends!"

"But who are they, anyhow? Where'd they come from? What're they doing here?"

"None of your business."

"As your pastor, I think it is. Can't you tell me who they are?"

"Not really." Jim was indistinguishable from his friend James or Joe, and even Sally with her long hair and jeans might be mistaken for one of the boys, from a distance. They had the same personalities, languid body movements, gentle voices. "They're young persons . . . and *I'm* an old person," she said, "what difference does it make?"

Plenty. He left her. In the Kemp house on the edge of town the women had always been odd. Nora slowly removed her gloves and walked into her home, not answering any of the questions about who "the creep" was, proceeding slowly up the stairs to the attic. When Jim and Sally had opened all the trunks they'd spilled out a ribbon-bound packet of letters from Aunt Clara to her mother, written from "the home," and now Nora studied these documents for a new insight into the fabled Kemp malady. The handwriting in brown ink like dried blood seemed jerky, but her thoughts were cogent, her sentences parsed. Inconsequential prattle about the day's activities—nothing so strange. Poor Clara had merely been ahead of her time, for you could be pretty crazy these days and *that* would be sane of you.

Nora opened and read every letter, wouldn't even come downstairs for herb soup lunch. This reckoning—and final justice to Aunt Clara—mustn't be hurried. Reincarnate a maligned ancestor, bring her back to life, put her in a place of honor in the household. Her young friends downstairs would surely be fascinated by Aunt Clara. They might even set the packet of letters next to their books by R. D. Laing. As she descended, rock music blasted full force from the parlor, trembling the woodwork. This bright, aimless, beautiful day had taken a lurch in some direction.

Alive! We're all alive in this house! And now even Aunt Clara
had come into her own.

If this be madness . . .

One night the house was suddenly a flash of light, the windows
burning mirrors, every room glowing with a terrible illumination.
She thought the house had caught fire but in fact it was surrounded by patrol cars with spotlights. Law officers stormed
through every door, back and front.

"We're gettin' busted! We're gettin' busted!"

Policemen with drawn pistols rushed past Nora, up the stairs,
where they herded the five naked youngsters into a corner and
turned flashlights on their private parts. The cops ransacked the
dresser drawers, closets, turned the house upside down—discovered quite a bit of pot and hash, several pipes, and with this
incriminating evidence hauled the youngsters to jail. Nora was
placed under house arrest and would have to appear in court.

She phoned Priscilla to come.

"I knew it! I knew it! I told you to get rid of those free-loading
kids. I said they'd rip you off—one way or another."

"What'm I gonna do?"

With the help of an old Nembutal, Nora slept late, awoke to
the ringing of the phone. A lawyer she'd never heard of informed
her Priscilla had engaged him to give counsel in her present
difficulties. She was to speak to no one about the trouble, do nothing, not leave the house, until he and Priscilla conferred privately
with the district attorney.

Priscilla's plane landed at two-thirty, but with the airport forty
miles away, she hired a taxi for thirty dollars to drive her home
immediately—and arrived before the attorney. "Mother what a
mess! Now you've gone and done it!"

Half expected, in some way. "I'm innocent. The stuff was
planted by the fuzz."

"*That's* always the line—don't you believe it! The garden's half
marijuana, for one thing. Didn't you *know?*"

"There're sunflowers and tomatoes and lots of other plants out
there, too."

"You could be convicted and jailed, under the drug law."

"The minister squealed on us, I'll bet."

"The only way out is . . . to be hospitalized. At least for now."

"But I'm not sick."

"You know what I mean . . . How else explain—why you let those kids take over? My God, the house is a wreck! I thought you told me they were useful and helped out. Didn't they *ever* tidy up this kitchen? What a pigsty! And the smell! How'd you ever stand it? Living in filth like this."

Funny, once Priscilla spoke suburban words, the whole house looked shambly, odors arose. "I never noticed before."

"Of course, you'll have to go voluntarily."

"Where?"

"To the hospital! As a voluntary patient. I wouldn't want you to lose your . . . legal rights."

"You're gonna put me away?"

"Don't be dramatic, Mother."

Obviously, Priscilla thought a clear-headed, unemotional approach would stave off theatrics, but how monstrous she seemed —one's own daughter!

"This isn't easy . . . for me either," as if such a necessary crimping of one's feelings were painful. This hurts me more than it does you. Whack!

The lawyer's shadow in the doorway appeared just as Priscilla's arguments needed further bending. He got down to business at once, before even seating himself, and explained to Nora the plea he'd enter in court. Mental incompetency. Otherwise, she'd face a fine and possible jail term. She'd have to submit to a court-appointed examination, if necessary, "but I doubt it'll come to that."

"Wait—I'm not crazy!"

"Since you've been a party to the corruption of youth—two of them are underage—and found to possess quantities of a controlled substance, the only way out is that you didn't know what was right or wrong. Didn't know what you were doing."

"I didn't!"

"So there. It's settled."

"I didn't . . . I mean, I didn't know there was anything *wrong* doing what you want, in the privacy of your home. What's the harm in it? I still don't understand."

Her words seem to hang overhead, bonging, a confession of incompetence, admission of her sorry mental condition. "Why can't I just tell the judge the truth? Why make up this alibi?"

"It's the truth as we all see it. Take our advice, Mother."

"The hospital? I don't want the hospital. I *won't* go!"

They made no move to restrain her when she leaped up to put at least a stretch of kitchen linoleum between herself and these jailers. "I was too happy . . . too free . . . and this can't be allowed, I see."

The silver-haired lawyer in his pearl-gray suit and red polka-dot tie was unperturbed, hardly looked at her, merely opened his brief case and took out some papers. "First of all, there's the matter of power-of-attorney."

"I won't sign anything."

"Mother, we're trying to help you!"

"Who's helping those kids in jail? Who's *their* lawyer?"

"Don't worry about *them*. They got you in quite a jam."

"I've another appointment—at four—so if you don't mind—" He held out the pen.

They were determined to go the whole way if necessary, have her committed. She could tell by their frozen faces, the cool, steady way they looked at her.

"The hospital's a temporary thing. A way of avoiding jail. Look at it that way, Mother."

"What's the difference? Locked up, either way."

"A month or two in there at the most. After it's all blown over, I'll find a housekeeper to live-in. You shouldn't be left alone here."

"*How* long? A month?"

"Two, more likely . . . say two."

Nora knew she was making a fatal mistake, going along with her daughter's schemes, but she did it, as animals sometimes seem to go knowingly to their death, and nobody's figured out why.

Nora was placed in a ward of eight old ladies in varying stages of dotage. "This the best you could do?"

"You don't have as much money as you seem to think," Priscilla said, "or somebody took it away from you."

"*We* haven't spent anything—hardly a penny!" If her funds were depleted, somebody managing her account was a thief, but to make such accusations would only seem typical of where she was, so she shut up.

Every day her dutiful daughter came to her bedside, walked her out to the sun porch, where they sat and talked. Never mentioned plans for a return East. "What's wrong back there? I can tell—behind your words—there's something the matter. Who're you keeping it from? This is the loony bin. You can say anything now, Priscilla. Why not?"

Her husband was suing for divorce. "Actually, we haven't lived together in years, as you probably guessed."

"I did."

"And you're right to keep wondering how little Josie's doing—only she's not so little any more. Got herself pregnant."

"No!"

"Last year . . . only sixteen. Luckily, with the abortion law, I had it taken care of in a New York hospital."

"She's all right then?"

"I hope!" Enrolled now in a strict boarding school outside Paris.

"Her father paying for it?"

"Yeah, he's okay on that score. Anything else you want to know about my beautiful life?"

"Tell me anything. Tell me everything!"

"I could write a book, believe me."

"What'll you do with yourself . . . now?"

She'd taken up painting again, this time in earnest, and considered leasing an apartment in New York so she could attend the Art Students League more regularly. She spoke about art as if it were a chalice that mustn't be dropped—or ridiculed—or questioned by anyone. Just like Priscilla, to balance a failure with a hope of success! Become an artist, in order to justify all the mess. Poor girl, on a seesaw; still committed to the self-management of her life. She'd never be a willow in the breeze, flow and wave like those kids now in jail.

"You have time to decide things," Nora said. "Everybody's out of the way. Even me."

When visiting hours were over and Priscilla left, her new associates rose from their cots and tried to take her over, make her join the spirit of the ward, cut her loose from the world, aboard this raft of a room, sailing away. Nora kept resisting, though the pull of the environment was strong. She fought the routine of feedings, cleansings, and TV soap-opera afternoons. "I don't belong here at all," she kept saying to her wardmates. "We pulled a fast one, that's all. When the heat's off, I'll be going home."

But her white-haired inmates clutched at her all the stronger, trying to make her "one of us," because they'd lost their independence long ago and meant to take hers away, too. The nurses joined the battle, gave her bright-colored pills and paper-cups of water to down them—said they'd make her feel good. She lay knocked out all night, sometimes most of the morning.

The battle to stay herself began to fatigue her, though she never doubted its necessity. If she'd gotten a shot of renewed strength from a visiting hippie friend one afternoon, she might've kept up the struggle, but Priscilla couldn't say what happened to them and the papers told her nothing. The days, one after another each the same, began to wear upon her spirit drop by drop. "How much time have I done?" she asked. "Three weeks is it?"

"Two, now." And Priscilla showed up for every visiting period. "Only two weeks."

"How much longer's it gonna be?"

"That's for the doctors to say."

"*You* know what I mean," and a wink. Other patients watching nodded their heads, smiled, happy to see Nora almost as crazy as *they* were. "Gonna bring the lawyer 'round pretty soon?"

"He says wait awhile."

"*You* must be tired of this—running back and forth to the hospital. After Connecticut, this life must seem pretty dull."

"I've got the whole house to clean!" Rugs to be sent out, drapes redone, the interior painted and the outside, too.

"Such expense for you!" Nora wondered what it meant. "Maybe we should sell the house instead."

"Oh no, it's the family home."

Perhaps Priscilla thought of living there and never going back East. She could paint her pictures here as well as in New York City. Though only forty, she looked haggard, didn't bother rinsing the gray out of her hair.

She'll be older-looking than me, if she keeps this up!

It became harder keeping track of the days. Sundays a priest came to bless them, so she could peg a week off that way. Despite her resolves, she was getting accustomed to life on the ward and had made friends with her mad cronies, found it almost fun to be with them, though part of herself knew a subtle change was taking place and if she didn't watch out, she might never be released at all. Would give up caring. The nurses had her buffaloed and she feared the aides, for they could remove privileges if she got ornery. And they were so tired of hearing the tale about her fake insanity, the clever ruse which had placed her here, hiding out, instead of in jail.

One night while on her way to the toilet, she suddenly came to on the floor. The wakeful one on the ward punched the nurse-call. She lay sprawled, helpless—bewildered. "I . . . musta . . . blacked out."

A slight seizure, the doctor said next day. "Move your toes, please. Try hard!"

Alas, again she was paralyzed on that side.

Priscilla learned what had happened last night from the nurse's island at the end of the hall. "Now you've gone and done it, Mother." She shook her head smiling, as if over a naughty child. "Guess I'll just have to stick around . . . a little longer."

Most decisions in life are made in just this fashion, Nora knew; she was getting clearer-headed all the time. Her difficulties cut a pattern in Priscilla's plans for the future, one generation feeding the other. "Why not?"

For several days Priscilla didn't show up—or was Nora forgetting from one day to the next, as she now mixed up the seasons? She tried to hang onto conversational bits lingering in her memory, as if these lines were rope ladders to safety. When Priscilla arrived at last, Nora couldn't decide if she should ask where she'd been, and thus reveal her uncertainty, or pretend it was a visit like any other. She might be caught either way.

But Priscilla talked and talked, as she never had before—and wanted only a good listener. Josie had fled the school near Paris and was living with a renegade Italian on the Left Bank, wasn't interested in coming back to America. "Maybe just as well. I can't watch over her any more, she's on her own." Alimony payments provided ample income for Priscilla to keep on living here, days without end, if she felt like it. Did she?

"Good-by, Priscilla . . . come again when you can."

"Don't I always?"

"I don't know . . . good-by." She smiled, pretending the parting was negotiable, good for a day—or a week. It was up to Priscilla to decide what she cared to do about it.

"I won't be long, Mother."

I might be forever, she meant. Living in the old, comfortable Kemp house, happy as could be, taking over where Nora had left off.

"This term I'm serving . . . is open-ended."

No, she meant it'd never end. And she knew it.

When next her daughter appeared for a visit—whenever it was —Nora said, "I notice you seem . . . happier." Or was it the light here which had changed? "They've moved me into this different room. It's got more of—a view."

"Yes, doesn't it?"

Those heavy cares which had tightened Priscilla's face were gone now and her spirit seemed released. "Really, girl, I've never seen you look so well." Surprised she could speak so trippingly and pleased that her wardmates were banished, that the room was private for this meeting. "Come closer, so I can see you better."

Priscilla moved to the very edge of the bed, sat down, though on that dead side her body seemed weightless. Her face was filled with a radiant expectation of the new, free life ahead of her, living in the family house.

"Maybe it's madness—staying on there."

"No, why?"

"For once in my life I'll do what I damn well please, for no other reason at all."

"Good girl!"

"But I wasn't made that way, I know. It's taken me years to come to my senses, be myself. Oh, if *only* I hadn't been such a conventionally pretty girl. I wasted so much time, behind that mask."

"You were a beauty from the start. Prettiest baby I ever saw!"

"But why'd you have to tell me?"

"It was your father spoiled you, gave you those ideas . . . your power over men. How to do it . . . I never learned that lesson, Priscilla. You got it from him, or someone."

"They made me into something I shouldn't've been. They cheated me of my life."

"You did it to yourself, my dear, but you couldn't help it."

"*That's* what I mean! I ran with the pack, did what the other girls did. Started so young . . . once I knew I could . . . that others would follow . . . envy me. Oh, I had such power then, but look how I used it!"

"Nothing wrong, wanting a husband. A house. *Things*. There's nothing bad thinking those are important, if you don't hurt yourself getting them, or cheat others. You're a real Kemp girl if ever I saw one, and we follow our tune in the end. Go our own way . . . now's the beginning, that's all."

She noticed a shadow in the doorway. Not the doctor. "Why, look who's here! *David!* What're you doing here? Priscilla, did you phone him to come? Am I *that* sick, you called him to come right away? Oh, it's been years since we've seen each other. Yet he's hardly aged a bit! No matter how he rushed his life, with babies and marriage and settling, he couldn't *do* it—couldn't get his wrinkles, or a stoop, or gray hair. What'll earn him those hoary marks? What'll do it to him? Come here, David, sit down. On the other side there, across from Priscilla. That's right. Give me your hand. Now . . . I know what . . . I know what you had to do. You had to come and speak about yourself, didn't you? Not just be off there with your tidy life, the door closed to me, no feelings toward your mother, your past. And so you had to show up here and make things right, didn't you? I know *every*thing now, David. So go ahead—talk."

He sat down slowly on the bed and began to speak as he'd never done before, his voice deeper-pitched than she remembered, his words honestly slow and kind. A crisis like illness—like death—brings people to the fore of themselves, their innermost values rise to the surface.

David took her hand, his fingers lacing hers. She still had one good hand and could feel his flesh and blood. He looked deep and long into her eyes—they matched his exactly.

He *is* different—what is it about him?

He speaks such painful, terrible words.

I'm leaving Jeannette . . . and the children. No, Mother, there's not another woman, nobody else. Only me. I've got to think of myself now. The youngest of ours is fourteen and it'll be hard on her, I know. On the others, too. But I'm leaving them so I can find somebody else . . . to love.

No, I told you, I haven't yet . . . found anybody. I want to love a person who'll love *me* in return, not just see me as the husband, or father, not just use me for the role I have in their lives. I want myself again, the way I was when I was a boy, with long hours to think deeply about things . . . when I was still intact and not pulled apart by these people I've managed to accumulate (where'd they come from?) . . . all these things I have to do (but don't really). Is it so unreasonable? Everyone these days is asking himself questions like this. Who can answer? Oh, don't mention my job—there's no more to say about *it* than there ever was. I've thrown it over. Seniority, pension—everything. Why should I spend my days making money for General Electric, so they can pass on dividends to shareholders? What's such accrual to me? Where does it get *them*, even, to have these gleanings from industry? Certainly *I* don't need any more conveniences or mechanical comforts or devices in my life. There're too many of 'em, all over my house, all over town, all over the country. They're breaking down and nobody around can fix 'em. Nobody needs objects like that—they only need themselves! I could've been a good scientist maybe, might've solved a few real problems of our times—not working on the other side, to undo everything in nature—bring on the end. Such aims don't pay, I know. You're only rewarded for shit. Everybody's used to the situation being like it is. They think shit has to cover everything. But it doesn't—right? I want to be clean again and really do what I think is . . .

You *can*, David. It's not crazy to think you can. You'll do anything you want, if you care enough.

The least a mother can do is pronounce such a benediction, give her blessings. Neither Priscilla nor David now looked over forty—but youngsters again, with futures, with hope.

Would they talk this way to me if I weren't out of my head, so near the edge they know it doesn't matter what they say? They can speak as if into the void.

I am their confessor. I listen and nod, say yes. Please do. Go on. Please live for me. Oh, God, that's all I want, *live* for me. I'm passing on . . . passing out.

Shadows, they leaned toward her, a kiss on each cheek. She felt lifted up by them, born away effortlessly, a slow gliding. How wonderful, how happy, thus to have it ended!

Mentor

Professor Cannon was lean as Ichabod, jerky in gait, vulnerable without his glasses as if someone were shining a flashlight into his eyes. Of the twenty-eight languages he professed to know, he taught only French and Spanish at the small Iowa college I attended my freshman year, but I studied neither under him. He hung around the male dormitory of our nearly all-female campus during the waning years of World War II, when all the men were away except a few wounded veterans, 4-Fs, and seventeen-year-olds such as myself.

On the playing fields at four o'clock, in sweat togs that clung to his stringy limbs like union-suit underwear, Mr. Cannon loped by my side in the mile run I usually set for myself, picking up speed when I did, or slowing down. He was available to referee a basketball game or play halfback in touch-football, his hirsute body giving off an unpleasantly pungent odor. He probably didn't like his corporeal self better than anyone else did but seemed to think physical exercise put us on a smelly par and made one forget the flesh antipathy so quickly aroused among members of the same sex. Although he wrestled with my friends in the mat-room, the notion of coming that close to him repelled me. There was something vaguely abnormal about Mr. Cannon which I didn't want to catch.

In the evening, walking with our girls, we'd sometimes notice his office light in the three-story classroom building and hear the violin and cello music he made with an elderly spinster of the English department, the door locked, far removed from our flushed, direct love affairs. That music was a lesson to us, however—of what solace might be left should we need it someday, like Mr. Cannon. We joked cruelly about the musical lovebirds but in the pauses of our talk recognized the sounds coming from the glowing windows as beautiful indeed—a refinement on the crude blood singing in our bodies which kept pushing us toward dissolution in the anonymous stream of humanity. Should *that* happen, we'd become ordinary. From having been on the brink of unusual possibilities, we'd have flung our lives into the orifices that always needed filling (and which we so much wanted to).

Mr. Cannon observed that I was nervous, tense; knew though I wouldn't admit, that my strenuous time with the coeds was always building to a peak but never getting there. Alcohol as a relief-tonic was out, since we lived in a state of dry liquor laws and I was underage even for beer. So there was nothing left, really, except what young men have always been given: a heavy dose of exercise. And it eased me somewhat. Certainly it must have done the same for bachelor Cannon, who alarmed me at times by the frenzied way he'd drive himself to the point of exhaustion in the gym, not to show he was young enough to keep up but to put himself at peace for a while, mind over body, a demonstration of the mastery of life. We were in sore need of instruction along these lines.

He noticed intimate things about us. "Why do you hold your arms so stiff by your side, when you walk?" he asked me. "You look like an ambulatory El Greco."

In library books I found reproductions of El Greco—ghastly

wraiths with emaciated faces and black hair (like mine), arms that weren't loose in muscular ease but tight with metaphysical groping.

So I learned to walk. I let my arms go and felt them swing from my shoulder sockets with the rhythms of my body. "That's better," he said, smiling over my gangly-youth problems, in a resonant voice that came from the twenty-eight chambers of language he could draw upon. "When you were fourteen and starting to stretch, I guess you didn't know what was happening—and tried to keep yourself together. But it feels good, lolling about more naturally, doesn't it? You don't have to hold your arms to account *all* the time."

Not like you, I thought, for he was a walking wire. Come up behind him unexpectedly and he'd jump a foot.

"What in God's name makes your hair stiff like cardboard? Is that axle grease you've got on it?"

No, green, gelatinous hair-set lotion. Daily head-soakings under the shower made my unruly hair a mouse nest, and when abroad upon the campus I might at any moment meet a girl I wished to impress. "You'd look better a little disheveled," he said. I threw out the stuff and tried his egg shampoo, then let my hair fly in the wind. The rugged effect pleased me—but why hadn't *I* thought of it? Mr. Cannon in these little ways was invaluable. Looking out, on our behalf. When he disappeared into the house of the classics professor where he roomed, no life of his own seemed to follow him.

Kendall Cannon spoke in tongues like the biblical wise men, and we'd urge him to "say a few words" in Hindi, Arabic, Swahili, or Hungarian. Words were power, God had created the world with them (I secretly longed to become a poet), and by naming, Mr. Cannon uncovered important truths—about each of us. He analyzed the reasons for the slovenliness of a fellow student (not that it changed his pigsty much); suggested a low-calorie diet for a troubled fat boy; and tutored a desperate chemistry scholar in memorizing the earth's elements.

I avoided signing up for his courses, however, for to be an abject pupil before his overwhelming knowledge would be unnerving. His brainy extracurricular performances were dazzling enough and even included the occult. He told fortunes by studying the mounts and radials of our palms, read the secrets in tarot cards, and one midnight demonstrated his skill as a hypnotist. Lights off, we crowded onto bed, chairs, and squatted on the floor, a single candle flaming on the table, the willing subject seated before it. (He was a nervous, heart-case senior with a taste for new sensations.) In a few minutes he was obeying Mr. Cannon's deep authoritarian voice: he scratched his head, picked his nose, and finally, "When I count to ten you will wake up . . . one, two, three," and the fellow did, upon the stroke of ten.

Mr. Cannon suggested I be the next victim—as I knew some how he would—and chided me for being so reluctant. Didn't I trust him? The experience wouldn't harm me in any way. But I steadfastly refused and finally even left the room rather than listen unawares to the subtle, velvet voice. "There's nothing to worry about—it's like sleeping, that's all." But the posture of passivity necessary for hypnotism to work revolted me. When he saw my refusal was final, he smiled with new respect.

In answer to a conventionally sentimental Christmas card, which he surprisingly sent me from the snowy, iron-sounding Massachusetts small town where his parents lived, I wrote an arch letter full of poses: how the train trip (really the only news I could share, since my family and home town seemed alien to college life) had bored me to death, but I'd suitably recovered and would strive to prepare myself for the onslaught of the journey back. To which Mr. Cannon replied by return mail: "Your letter distressed me for I fail to understand how the railroad travel described could've been such an ordeal. How will you get anywhere if you let such small, insignificant things bother you? Why not take along a good book and shut up about it?"

Shortly after the school session resumed, "My Hair-Oil Quandary," written for the spinster violin-playing English teacher, was such a witty success when read aloud to the class and later scanned with approval by Mr. Cannon, that I now felt I could reveal my ambition to become a writer. I'd hoped my elegant letter describing the tiresome train would win his admiration to such an extent that he'd suggest I *should* become a writer and had been crushed by his corrective—into doing an honest piece of work. I told him my plan to major in journalism, join the school newspaper staff, and later, become a reporter on a cosmopolitan paper. Would that be the way to do it?

"Do what?" A mocking, faint cynicism pulled down the corners of his mouth. His eyes were enlarged by the thick lenses, a well of wisdom filled to the brim—but none could spill over to slake my thirst. How had the question annoyed him? I guessed he didn't like me to speculate about the future years, when I'd have escaped his company, my life outdistancing his. I might, a decade hence, know *twenty-nine* languages.

Teachers like parents were on hand to be used up by us. I took for granted my parents' delight in my juvenile achievements, thought it natural they should boast to friends when I won several college scholarships. I loved most those teachers who seemed touched by the thought of the many triumphs we students were on the verge of. They'd live extended, really *completed* lives, only if we did. That was the burden of their charge to us as they sent us forth into the world. How was Mr. Cannon different, then?

Perhaps he wasn't quite so sure as the other elders who'd hovered over me that I'd make it. One day he unwrapped two pairs of huge, pillowy, maroon boxing gloves, thereby bringing into the open what I already half knew: I needed toughening up. "Remember, you can't be hurt with these padded gloves. They're not the kind Joe Louis uses. Now hit me just as hard as you can." He crouched behind the swollen leather bags held close to his face and began to dance, dance, in the ring manner seen in movies. I aped him. "Come at me now—hit me—hit me hard!" he shouted. After a few minutes we stopped and he suggested how I might keep up my guard better, how to let fly with a sidewinding right when I had a chance. "All set now? Don't hold back! Try to knock me out! Hit me!"

I plowed into him with all the strength I possessed, but he just laughed behind his gloves. Without eyeglasses, his horsy face looked monstrous and gleeful. I felt too pretty, unscarred—hungered for a broken nose or a cracked jaw—and rammd my gloves against his rank-smelling body. Head, belly, anywhere. I was a match for him only when he aroused my anger. How he enjoyed my fury! When we'd gone all the rounds we could and headed for the dressing room, pulling with our teeth at the lacings, his genial good feelings returned, but to me he still seemed the enemy.

Every day we'd tie on those puffy mitts (he always bound my wrists first, then managed his own strings himself) and set to, he coming after me with little jabs and dancing away, laughing, shouting "Hit me, hit me!"—until I tired of his game and wondered what classmate Keith would be like, matched against me, and insisted Mr. Cannon let him borrow the gloves. My coach seemed reluctant but finally got out of the ring and watched the two of us, as if some monitor always working told him he must. A week later, Mr. Cannon gave Keith the gloves outright and never boxed with either of us again. He'd seen us through.

For long stretches I ignored his presence in the dormitory lounge after dinner or walked past a room when I heard his familiar, story-telling voice. He had no hold over me—except, I somewhat feared his prescient understanding of me. I really didn't want to know what he probably knew about me already. I had a right to find out for myself in my own way.

Spring sloped toward summer, my eighteenth birthday, and the time for war. Since these were very likely the last days of my life, I had to cram pleasure into every moment. I'd no need for a schoolmaster, no reason to train mind or body, think of grooming, or go in for preparations that assumed a future. My only life was the nervous present. I let my studies slip, dozed through scheduled exams, was warned that my scholarship was in jeopardy—as if it mattered! I discovered a tavern willing to serve me beer and got drunk as often as my money allowed. On one such occasion I encountered Mr. Cannon "taking the air," cruising the elm-lined streets at midnight. "I hardly recognized you," he said, "what've you been doing with yourself?"

"Nothing much."

"Rather *ubriaco* aren't you? What's the story?"

" 'The world is too much with us.' "

"Aw, come on, self-pity isn't the route for *you*."

" 'We lay waste our lives.' "

"Don't be an ass. You've got better things to do with yourself—than *this!*"

"How do you know? What ever gave you the idea you knew anything about me?" I bolted past him, down the sidewalk, the soft air cool on my hot face.

One couldn't take advice from a man whose knowing-better

came only out of his head. If I'd enrolled in his French course he might've taught me a proper accent and how to conjugate irregular verbs, but what else was he good for? His physical exposure among us disqualified him from our serious regard. Although a grown man, sound in his parts (except for a childhood history of convulsions which kept him out of the Army) what was he doing but hedging ineffectively on the fringes of life? Had he even slept with a girl, or did he merely tell salacious stories to make himself seem regular? If he was all that smart, why was he frittering away his time among us in this small college town? I sensed at last why he'd kept shouting "Hit me, hit me hard!"

The aching beauty of May brought compassion to my soul, even with regard to Mr. Cannon, for all of us were being swept toward oblivion. He too wouldn't be back in the fall; some of the faculty were let go for lack of students. Poised on the brink of joining the war, about to miss each other forever, caught in the cruel but true randomness of fate (we knew what most of our elders kept forgetting about *that*)—it was fitting that Mr. Cannon should join us. He relished his role so much we almost forgot he wasn't enlisting in the armed services next week. His emotional involvement with us matched ours with each other.

My last night in college, returning to my room after my girl had been locked up, I found Mr. Cannon sitting in the dark. He surprised hell out of me! "Did you forget? I said I'd be by to share a beer with you." He reached into his canvas knapsack and drew out two bottles of Schlitz. " 'Fraid they're a bit warm, but I don't mind if you don't. In Europe everybody drinks beer this way. When you're discharged, you'll have to treat yourself to a *Wanderjahr*. Don't be stupid about hurrying the university years. *That's* the only time of freedom for most young men. Usually they don't know it till it's too late."

And don't marry too soon, or commit yourself to a career you might not want. Don't, in other words, sell short the endless possibilities of youth. These liquid years are happy because the disappointments all men eventually face are held in abeyance and needn't be thought of, certainly not accepted. Everything is before you. Make it last.

We drank our beer in cheerful, guarded chit-chat, for this last evening should be consonant with all the others. His taut face and half-old shoulder slump told me how much it meant to him. I was seeing around him and no longer felt awe, only pity of a sort. My roommate and all the rest of us here provided the sole companionship he had. Poor devil.

"You can call me Kendall now," he said, when I happened to *mister* him, and smiled as if he were letting me out of a testing maze into the open air of equality. He was giving me the last thing he had to offer—relinquishing the edge that had won him automatic respect and acceptance into our midst. But if he was just "Kendall" to us, what was there left of him? I said I couldn't . . . couldn't first-name him, not now. "I'd feel funny, you know."

"Say it," he urged, a stretched eagerness in his voice and eyes, "say it just once, anyhow, so that when we meet again in happier times it won't seem so odd."

"Aw, Mr. Cannon, I—"

"Please say it," he insisted, in the "Hit me again" voice.

"Kendall."

My roommate walked in then and Mr. Cannon drew out still another brown bottle. He had a new joke for us. With the door standing open, others on the floor sauntered in, shared the booty, and we soon had a proper party. Somehow, this still wasn't "good-by" as far as Mr. Cannon was concerned; at 2 A.M., when he walked down the stairs with me (as monitor I had to check to see all lights were out), he grasped my hand warmly and said: "I—I could tell you so much, *so* much, if there were only some way—to do it. I could tell you—but there's *no* way . . ." Maybe he also said: I could look out for you . . . could look after you. . . .

In later years I was unable to reconstruct the precise wording of that groping offer of parental protection or wisdom. Did he mean he knew something important about me he mustn't reveal? That he viewed me as a pleasant, mediocre kid who shouldn't have aspirations toward literature? Or, unless I grew a shell over my sensitivity I'd be wiped out before long? Or what? Too tired to puzzle over the matter, I passed off Kendall Cannon's remarks as beery maunderings of no consequence. But I was haunted by the incident as time went on.

One summer after the war, I waited on tables in a small cafe on Nantucket, my first hitchhiking trip East. There I met a boy who attended the college where Kendall Cannon now taught. "He knows twenty-eight languages—he's fantastic!" and yes, he still spent afternoons in the gym. Doing the same things, only with a new crop of students—it was dreary news. "Do you think he's queer?" I asked. *That* would explain a lot.

"Not really, not that anybody knows of."

Several years later I received a pink notice from the Navy Reserve, calling me back into active duty for the Korean War. At Columbia on a graduate fellowship, I was skidding toward a teaching career I wasn't sure I wanted, but since I hadn't appeared in print as yet, perhaps my ambitions in that direction were hopeless. I could only digest bland food, was on the way to an ulcer. Although still "pinned" to an Iowa coed, I was having an affair with a New York girl and hadn't resolved my ambivalent feelings. Meanwhile, my mother had been hospitalized and I was expected to help the family pay the medical bills. I suffered headaches which an optometrist attributed to my reading a book a day; if I kept up the scholarly pace, I'd surely need glasses the rest of my life. He shook his head grimly; it was *my* decision whether to ruin my eyes or cease graduate studies.

I needed help but had no friend wise enough to offer advice I'd accept—then I remembered Mr. Cannon, preceptor of old, who, because I'd been too young, hadn't told me all he might have. *Now* surely he'd hear me out and say bluntly what he thought I should do. I scribbled a postcard to my Nantucket friend, announcing my weekend arrival, and sent another to Mr. Cannon.

When I got there it wasn't hard to find him, because the college and village were even smaller than the campus where I'd known him. We met in the lounge of the men's dorm, and I sensed my mistake immediately, for although he recalled me well enough, too many similar youngsters had swum into his presence. He wasn't sufficiently *personal* with me, and his dégagé manner and bright conversation seemed inappropriate to my solemn, terrible situation. I was astonished to realize that his seeming knowledge of each of us was merely that one young person is much like another. Only the pristine youth himself feels unique.

Having failed to bring him into the dragging shadows of my life, I felt embarrassed and tried to explain why I'd come such a distance to see him. "Remember when we said good-by? You wanted me to call you 'Kendall.'"

He nodded, interest brightening his face. "Yes—of course. Why don't you—*now?*"

"You were about to tell me something but at the last minute held back. I wonder often—just what *was* it? I hope you'll tell me today."

"Tell you what?"

"Remember? Going down the stairs after the beer party . . ." With a mounting sense of my naïveté, I realized how many times he'd gone down a flight of stairs after a beer party. All these years. "You said you could tell me something, then decided not to. I never figured out what you had in mind, why you stopped short."

"I did? Are you sure?"

"I could take your opinion of me now. I really could."

"Honestly, I haven't the faintest clue what you're talking about. You must've gotten the wrong notion, somehow."

Maybe. I looked—for the last time I knew—at his homely, familiar face, enlarged brown eyes behind the very same rimless glasses. Scarcely any gray hair changed his looks, marking the passage of years; few wrinkles. Even those scuffed loafers were the kind he always wore. But a teacher has to be held to account, just like anybody else. If he puts his life on the line, it has to stay there, otherwise what kind of example *is* it?

I returned to New York and solved some of my problems unwisely, but I survived. After a few years I found myself behind a lectern with a subject to "profess" in university lecture halls. But the real encounters with students came in the privacy of my office, where Susie told me she was pregnant—me the first to know, since her boy friend had been arrested in Boston for pushing dope; and John asked if he should flee to Canada because of America's war policies; and Jim, dopey with Stelazine, stumbled to me for psychiatric help which only a hospital could give.

Then sometimes I'd remember Mr. Cannon, but I no longer pondered what it was he'd meant to say to me, now that *I* hovered over the lives of students—paid to be in their company while they went through terrible moments, perhaps to do something for them. Yet what? Did anyone know? How they kept coming up, forever young and in need. But of what?

I couldn't tell them anything. I couldn't tell them anything.

The Mistake

"Daddy!" said Luke's child, running toward me from the kitchen without looking up. He threw his arms around my knees, and in that second of intimacy was extending a trust so deep that discovery of his mistake, I knew, would seem a betrayal on *my* part. I grinned and patted his blond hair. The others, drinks in hand, smiled at the incident and kept on talking. Luke was next door in the TV room, and many of the guests, full of dinner and languid from wine, were sitting on the floor, dreamily waiting for him to begin his first ballad. I could see some of the men, and the girls with their skirts fanned across their feet; but I couldn't see Luke. Even before the boy looked up at me, I had guiltily sought a glance from his father.

"*You're* not my daddy!" He jumped away, bewildered.

"Silly, that's Lyle," said Karen from the kitchen. The boy's mother had seen it all.

"What's his name?" I asked.

"Joey."

"Joey," I said to stop him from fleeing, to keep the tears out of his eyes—to make amends for what I'd done to him. "Hello."

Karen laughed, and we looked at each other. The business lent a queer intimacy to us, though this was the first time we'd met, the first evening Luke had invited me to his home. The tired, stretched look of her face, which gave her mouth such an unhappy expression, was suddenly gone as she smiled. There was something puzzlingly archaic about her: her image of beauty fixed in high school, the first lipstick like raspberry treacle, and curls adorn the head as if the coiffed glory of womanhood had never been discovered before. She was still trying to keep that illusion, and her ruffly sprig-print dress with its junior-miss skirt seemed too young for her. There was also something desperate in her eyes.

The boy scooted into the kitchen, where Karen and two friends were cleaning up the mess made by the shore dinner, which had been flown in from Boston. Since Luke and Karen were both from New Hampshire, they liked to entertain their midwestern friends this way. Anybody who didn't go for lobsters and clams had better stay home and stick to pork and potatoes, confess to being hopelessly provincial.

I leaned against the lintel as the women laughingly comforted Joey and tried to pull him out of Karen's skirt. Luke and I without our mustaches looked alike at first glance, they observed. We were both tall, dark-haired, slim, and tonight were identically garbed in khakis and thick tan sweaters. I wondered if they were chattering away in order to reassure Karen that the kid was normal. I didn't know much about stages of development in children, having none of my own, and although Joey looked about as big as a six-year-old should, there was a timidity about him that made me wonder.

Luke began singing softly, almost in a monotone, as if his Australian mustache strained out the immoderate notes. Karen's helpers went in to hear better, and Karen and I sat down to what was left of the coffee, while Joey put his head in her lap and sucked his thumb. She talked about the mistaken notions children sometimes get—and told of her own early years in Derry, a personal history that had to be related in a flat, well-modulated voice precisely because it had rasped her life into this smooth, dull shape. She hoped to appear eccentric and so revealed to me what would normally have been reserved for a later time and greater intimacy. She described her father, a pompous high school band instructor, her mother's quiet despair. "Our family secret was mother's drinking, and those packages of Sen-Sen around the house didn't fool anybody. Everybody knew. Me, the only child— I got the brunt of it." She set down her coffee cup without looking at me, the whole tale having come out as she stared at an electrical outlet just to the right of my elbow. I'd the feeling she'd performed this piece before.

And what account of *his* childhood would Joey tell, twenty years from now—and to whom? And for what reason?

"I had musical talent from Dad's side, perfect pitch and all, but just because *he* wanted me to do something with it, I wouldn't. I preferred to paint, probably because I had no talent there at all. You understand me now, don't you?" A slow, pulled smile; our eyes met. I knew fully what she was up to, and that we'd already begun with it.

Joey uncorked his mouth and dashed up the back stairs to his room. She scarcely noticed he'd gone. Now would come the disclosures: Joey'd been a mistake, an ironic gift from the gods just as she and Luke were about to split. Luke had sunk away into some remote world of his own; she was left to herself—and it was lonely.

I didn't have to hear the tale. These tense married women edgy with hungers which were seldom sexual to start with had told me them before. I took their opening confessions as part of the gambit, a note of seeming intimacy. It wasn't *me*, my special self, who moved them, but only what I represented in their eyes: a man uncaught by domestic circumstances, who understood the meaning of the covert glance, who was used to sudden sexual opportunities. Lord, it'd been a while! I was eager to get on with it. But for girls like Karen various guilts had to be salved before they could proceed—these "good" girls from respectable homes, who'd carry bourgeois values through life with them, at the same time they cuckolded their husbands, lied to their infants, and stole from the emotional exchequers of everyone in sight.

I was sorry my newest girl-in-the-offing involved my friendship with Luke, however; I've never gone in for kicks gotten through deceptions of this sort. I'd met Luke at a poker game, when I'd been asked to fill in for an office acquaintance who was sick. A group played regularly Thursday nights in Des Plaines, a thirty-minute trip from my North Side apartment. That first night, whenever Luke was dealer he'd call for Black Bottom—whoever had the highest spade shared the pot with the winner—and three times he and I divvied up the take. It was one of those weird coincidences that set one talking and afterward I learned he was a sportsman, too. It was Armistice Day, and the pheasant season over in Iowa had just started; we agreed to drive west to see what we could chase up in the cornfields around Mason City, where I had relatives.

As with so many men our age (late thirties, early forties), the thing never discussed was what we did those nine-to-five days of our lives consigned to the marketplace, days of hostage to earn our leisure. Luke was now an industrial designer, but he'd gone to Cranston and his dream had been to become a sculptor. I'd seen some of his plaster-of-Paris objects, all of them in the modern mode of agony: cowering heads behind bony hands, taffy-limbed figures with ravaged faces set too far back on the spine, and holes all over them. They were embarrassingly secondhand: Henry Moore passed through some Cranston instructor. Anyhow, while living in Detroit, he'd made friends among the artists working for the big automobile companies, and he did some drafting for them. "He liked the money," said Karen to me now, hitting this stage of her story, "and *I* had to remind him that if he really wanted to be a sculptor he shouldn't be seduced by the first commercial paycheck to come his way. I mean, I wondered how deeply he felt *called*—how serious he was, about art."

During their undergraduate days at Durham, they'd talked of just such a juncture: when one reached the point of either living and acting according to convictions or gave up the pretense. They'd been married a year, had a little money; they decided to go to Paris "and really see this thing through." There, in a little hotel off the Rue St. Michel where they lived, and in the Luxembourg Gardens where they strolled, and at the Café des Chauffeurs where they dined as often as they could, they were able to parlay the atmosphere of "promise" for nearly eighteen months. Still, nothing much happened one way or another.

"The worst was, I didn't think Luke really *cared* enough—not like the other artists we drank Pernod with. Finally we went to the Azores because we lucked into a cheap freighter voyage."

I'd heard Luke tell how they'd trekked to a remote island which could only be reached by hired launch. Once there, they hauled fresh water in cans from a spring high up a mountain. They lived in a stucco hut with a hole in the top for the smoke and subsisted on a diet of fish and fruit. Luke soon developed a nasty skin disease that spread all over him. When they couldn't find adequate treatment locally, they packed up and returned to America. He'd had his run of adventure, his artist's fling. "It was the bit, you know," he'd say. "How we all felt." Perhaps only his guitar playing revealed the lingering sense of various undefined losses, but an acceptance of them. He was settled now and no longer fought "to make something of himself."

"And you?" Karen asked. "What notions of yourself have *you* been forced to throw away?"

"Oh, if you're going to put it *that* way . . ."

"I just meant—as part of growing up."

"Come on," I smiled, "that's not what you mean." I lowered my voice. "How's it with me, you want to know. In *every* way."

"Yes."

"Expect me to tell the truth?"

"I won't believe it, if you don't."

"Has Luke ever said anything about me—or my past?"

"You're absolutely safe!"

"That's not the point." I turned at the scurrying noise on the back stairs.

"Joey! *Now* what is it?"

"Where's my mannikins?"

"Oh, that mannikins! Can't you be *any*where without him? Look in your toybox. Though I suppose that's the last place he'd be. Sure you didn't take him up to bed with you?"

Joey was already undercover of that excuse, peeking out from it —half forgetting it—as he observed me. "Nothing's happening," I said. "We're all still here. You're not missing anything, Joey. You can go back to bed."

"*There's* your mannikins—in the magazine rack."

Joey ran into the midst of the party, retrieved the rag doll, and, just as a murmur of greeting rose to meet him, escaped up the rear stairs again. Karen poured us more coffee. The very act, so homely and simple, seemed to strengthen her bond with me: she was already ministering to my needs, softly opening herself—I was moved. Perhaps we shouldn't talk any more, just let ourselves feel the closeness of our skins.

"And we were saying?" she asked.

"Not much. Luke told you I was divorced?"

She nodded, tried not to show how much this interested her.

"An early marriage, didn't pan out. Four and a half years, to be exact, and I must admit, generally happy ones for both of us, though the whole thing was pretty much a mistake."

"What happened?"

"Who's to say? We met in Beirut on holiday. I was in the foreign service stationed in Morocco—she was a secretary in Abadan. It was a kind of spur-of-the-moment business. But I've never felt the calculated moves, when it comes to the emotions, are to be trusted. If you can't act on impulse, what's the use?"

She flushed. "Go on."

"You know, the Secretary of State himself had to give his okay on the marriage—personally? That surprised me. You'd think he'd have more important business to attend to. Maybe it was just to flatter me, make me feel part of one big diplomatic family. I wangled another tour of duty in the Middle East—Marrakesh, then we packed up and left for Washington, to wait out the next assignment, which was likely to be South America. Things started going rocky for us when we got to the States. She wanted a permanent home, a continuity of life she'd never have with me—in that job."

" 'She,' only 'she'? What was her name?"

"Dorothy."

"That's better."

"Well, there's no use going into it. I'd only give you *my* version, which over the years has been pounded pretty smoothly into shape."

"Why so?"

"Because nobody lives with the ragged edges. In memory, at least, things have to be firm and in place."

"Oh?"

"Only the future can remain blurry and unformed—never the past."

"You *are* a philospher."

"No, but I know what I think—and *why*, alas."

"It's more a question of hope." She put another lump of sugar in her coffee. We could hear Luke singing a chain-gang ballad, one of his favorite hammer songs. It was not about hope.

"Dorothy wasn't happier when you quit government work and moved to Chicago?" This much of my story she knew: that I was vice-president of a management consulting firm specializing in foreign investments.

"*Hated* the city—I mean, that's what she thought was the trouble, so we tried it in Wilmette. When I got my first really big assignment—to Turkey, and the company didn't of course allow travel expenses for *her*. We'd just bought a house and didn't have any spare cash. The trip was not supposed to last more'n a month. We thought we could last. Maybe both relieved to have the decisive break taken out of our hands—you know? She as much as me. Our first letters were sent off daily, but as time went on, our lives did too. The stuff we wrote seemed more remote from the actual skin of our affairs. One night there was the inevitable wild party— I took a German girl home. . . . Didn't set much stock in it, being drunk and all. At least, not at first. As a matter of fact, I didn't see the Fraulein again . . ."

"But there were others?"

"You know how these things go." She met my gaze with a flash of interest, or was she alarmed that I was on to her this quickly? Had she been unfaithful to Luke before, or was this to be her first mistake?

"But you kept writing letters home, 'from your devoted husband,' and all that?"

"Wouldn't you know, pretty much the same thing was happening to Dorothy. She met somebody—went off with the guy—the divorce went through three months later."

"And she lived happily ever after?"

"I won't even give you three guesses on that. One will do."

"You don't see her?"

"Lord, no."

From the next room we heard Luke singing, his baritone thin but clear:

> Didn't know what to do with their big barefeet,
> Didn't know what to do with their big barefeet,
> Oh, didn't know what to do with their big barefeet!

He whacked the guitar and shouted:

> Shame, shame on the Johnson boys!

There followed immediate laughter, applause, and a burst of talk. In a few minutes the little boy, in his white flannel sleeping suit, pushed open the door of the back stairs and ran up to Karen. "What's happening?"

"Nothing but the singing. What's the matter with you tonight?"

He looked at me queerly. Wasn't particularly interested in a drink of water, though that's what he got, and he drank it earnestly, staring at me over the rim. Karen pulled him onto her lap and he straddled her knee. Only children can look this judgingly at adults, I thought. Life hasn't clouded their pure gaze, their expectations of perfection. Joey surely sensed nothing between his mother and me, but I couldn't help supplying that blue-eyed stare with meanings it might someday bear.

"Did you love her?" she asked. "Your wife, Dorothy?"

They were always so interested in that first sister of theirs, eager to know what she looked like, how she dressed, what she said—wanted, in fact, to line her up with some dormitory type from college days. Karen acted as if she were confidante to a harried male who'd come to her with love problems. It seemed to have nothing much to do with *us*. Except that once the mood of revelations belled out into silence and half smiles, we'd have reached the point where one of us might say something about fate or the powers-that-be, and how our small histories constantly weave in and out. Strange that we should now be put together here in the kitchen, coffee cups between us. The marvel of it was true enough, and the nod to the cosmos was surely for luck—and perhaps justification. "Let's go downstairs and put on a disc," I said.

"Off you go!" She gave Joey an affectionate slap on his rear as she sent him away.

In the basement they had a large, vinyl-floored rec room with a bar at one end and a library at the other. She put on a record, but our immediate embrace had little to do with the music. We moved slowly around the big empty room, her pelvis against mine, a good fit. "You didn't answer me. Upstairs," she said.

"About loving her?"

"You don't like that word, do you?"

"Do *you*?"

"Don't switch me off that way."

They always wanted to be sure I'd been deeply in love, the wound sharp and unassuageable, all these years . . . until this very night when something miraculous was about to happen, a new-found love, and the healing could begin. "Yes, I loved her, but I was new at the business then."

"What do you mean?"

My lips were on her temple. "I didn't know how easy you could be mistaken." I liked the smell of her hair and the perfume she used—just the scent I'd expect: something kitchen-cookery, nothing too musky. Dainty and clean. Was this her idea of herself, or what she thought would please Luke? The sad thing was, perhaps she didn't know these were separate questions.

The songfest upstairs began to break up and the mob descended the narrow stairs. I held her firmly and we danced till the music ended, though she wanted to flee at the first sign of people. Immediately, I knew Karen wasn't used to this sort of thing. The revelation unsettled me. I didn't like to think of myself as a home-breaker. If I hadn't come here tonight, if Joey hadn't taken me for his father, would any of this have happened?

Luke hurried up to us. "I've got to bring down ice, Karen. Everybody needs a drink, and now the kid's screaming. Didn't you hear him? Practically drowned me out."

"He's *terrible* tonight. I don't know what's the matter with him. You'd think he'd never seen strangers in the house before."

"Let *me* go up," I said. "You've both got plenty to do. If I can't quiet him, then one of you come to the rescue."

So, I put the two of them together again; even at the time, I wondered why.

I expected a blast of alarm from Joey when he saw me loom in the stairwell—the chopper-come-to-chop-off-your-head, mounting toward his room. But he seemed pleased to have commanded an adult's attention, his mother's favorite guest at that. "What's your name?" he asked.

"Downstairs—a while ago—you took me for your daddy. Remember? Your mother said I was Lyle."

"Do you know how to play marbles?" He said it with a look of guile, as if he'd cleaned up the block.

"Sure." I stretched out full length on the carpet while he poured black and white marbles from a mesh bag. "Where'd these come from? A Chinese checkers game?"

"No."

"All black and all white. That makes it easy to tell sides, anyhow. Mine are the black, you're the white, okay? Now let's each give up eight marbles. We'll make a circle, like this. Now you take one of yours for the shooter—and try to hit one of 'em out of the circle. Your shooting line is *here*." I drew my fingers across the rug, upending the pile. "Mine's here. Is this the way *you* play marbles?"

"No."

"Well, it's like this. You can start shooting. As long as you hit, you keep on shooting. But if you miss, it's my turn." I lay back and watched the easy way he slipped into a concentrated playing of the game. Then I began to mull over what I was getting into, in this household, and the first heavy feelings of unhappiness came over me. But was I to blame? Any other man who came along would find what I'd found, do what I'd been doing—and was about to do (tomorrow afternoon, in a nearby motel?)

I hardly noticed that little Joe was cheating, shooting from a point way forward of his line and copping marbles he hadn't nicked or knocked out of the circle. The longer I said nothing, the more bold his deception became. At last he'd won all the marbles. "Well, I guess you're too good at this game. I never even got a chance to play."

He laughed greedily, a wicked look on his cherub-soft face.

"Maybe we ought to try a different version of marbles. What game do *you* know?"

He let me shoot once, then said I'd committed some serious

error, which cost me five marbles. With marbles worth a nickel, I now owed him a quarter. "If you don't hit anything this next time, you owe me a dollar."

"I do, huh?" I shot but missed entirely.

"Now I'm supposed to get a dollar from you." He'd established a third-person authority, submitting both of us to some impartial law. "If I hit, then I'll get five more dollars from you. That's the game."

"But you're making up the rules as we go along!"

He grinned. "We can play something else, if you want."

I tried to stave off a growing dislike of the sly brat. And here I'd thought all children his age were innocent and charming!

"Pick any number between one and ten—and you'll win five dollars."

"Okay, seven."

"That's not the number."

"Didn't think it'd be." Why did I feel so annoyed? "Five."

"That's not the number."

"Not surprised." Joey had hugged my legs as if I were his father, and *that* had been our best moment. "How 'bout number two?"

"That's not the number." He looked at me with Karen's eyes, he was having me on. I heard Luke tromp up the stairs. He paused at the top step, not wanting to disturb our game, smiled, delighted to find me having such a good time with his son.

"Joey, I'm tired of this numbers racket."

"Pick another one. Pick it!"

"Three."

"*That's* not the number."

"What about four?"

Joey shook his head, lips ballooning over his teeth as he kept from exploding into laughter. "There isn't any number!"

"Then I *didn't* make a mistake, and I win!"

He rolled on the floor in convulsive laughter.

"All right, Joey, back to bed," said Luke, swooping down. Joey didn't protest his capture; he fell limp into the arms of the family. "Enough of this gambling with strangers." And to me: "Did he teach you some new games?"

I couldn't think of the right answer.

When we returned downstairs, Luke asked what I was drinking, where was my glass. I said I'd leave now but didn't want to spoil the party by breaking things up. "Good night to Karen for me, huh?" My coat was right there in the hall. Yes, easy to find my way out.

It always has been if I start in time.

White Blood

Bernice volunteered to move out of the black dorm her senior year because the college was in trouble with its federal funds, HEW claiming reverse discrimination. On the top floor of the Manse, living with Kathy and the other whites, she was the only currant in the oatmeal. Tokenism, all over again. She hoped they wouldn't give her the Citizenship Award at commencement for her act, booby prize for the girl who should receive *something*, but nobody could think what.

Provided she graduated at all, didn't flunk the finals in biology.

What kind of animals were dissected in lab, Kathy wondered, in a rare moment of polite concern for her roommate's problems —perhaps because term was almost over. "Crayfish? Frogs?"

"Started with mussels—bad enough!" The smells made her nauseous and she felt squeamish about killing specimens, cutting them up.

"Fresh water or salt?"

"I didn't eat 'em, Kathy, I sliced 'em up!" She'd no aptitude in the very subject her parents excelled in, both physicians, and wouldn't have enrolled except it was required for foreign service schools.

"Know what you mean about mussels," Kathy began, pausing at the window to look at the distant piece of Long Island Sound in the strong May light. She described mussel gathering on Vinalhaven, where her parents summered, away from the heat of Washington, how she'd pull the purple shells from rocks at low tide, the mussel lips closing just as she reached to pluck them.

"They'd *watch* you? Never saw eyes in any mussel. I *must* be flunking biology!"

"Blood in 'em, too."

"Oh, they don't! Come on, Kathy, I may be stupid in lab, but I know blood if I see it."

'It's *true*, Bernice, they bleed so! Colorless—you can't see it. But when I eat mussels . . . or oysters, I think of it all the time. Blood all over 'em—when I tear into their flesh."

"Ugh! I'll remember that . . . I truly will."

In the dining hall for lunch they served a synthetic meal, which arrived at eleven-thirty by refrigerator truck. Sawdusty Swedish meatballs—bad enough—but the bilious green Dairybeat dessert did her in. Lots of intestinal gas and finally a bowel explosion. Later she felt kind of wet and odd down there. My God, have I shit in my pants sitting here over *U. S. Foreign Policy in the* 1950s? Running to the toilet . . . and yes, wet but not stained. Odd . . . what kind of diarrhea *is* this anyhow? But if mussels could have white blood maybe *she* could have white shit. Brown skin but white shit.

All afternoon she felt tired, lonely; finally wrote a poem—a haiku, sort of.

Above the fenced reservoir
On a Bronx hilltop
Long Island Sound in view
A single gull
Perfectly aligned
Hangs in the wind

I long for salt diminishment
Nothing a bird ever feels
I need the sea

Something wrong with the next to the last line. How'd *she* know
what a bird felt, any more than Kathy knew what a mussel felt,
bleeding white blood from its wounds?

Don't even know what a black feels, only know myself (if
that), not what I'm supposed to know.

In mid-afternoon Kathy met her literature teacher, whom she'd
gotten to accept "a *verbal* essay" on Walt Whitman. She'd
conned him into it by writing: "In the future I'd like to
remember an afternoon of sharing—an event of two people, living and not divided by sheets of paper needlessly. In Whitman's 'I
Saw in Louisiana a Live-Oak Growing' he said, 'But I wonder'd
how it could utter joyous leaves standing alone there without its
friend near, for I knew I could not.' And, Professor Seligman, I
know very well I (can) not. Please accept my invitation . . ."

Bernice watched from the third-floor window as Kathy served
tea on a little tray and talked with Professor Seligman about
Whitman, God, and the Universal Force of Love. He removed his
suitcoat, lay back, then pulled off his shirt and undershirt. Not a
very fetching sight, flabby white skin and a lot of black hair on his
chest. "I'll miss this crazy place," she thought, gazing upon the ac-
ademic tryst. The gulls coming inland with heads down, looking
about, casing the joint, gave her a feeling of the temporariness of
her existence anywhere. You were supposed to laugh, she knew.

Next day the school of foreign service at George Washington
sent her a letter of final acceptance (she'd been on the waiting
list). When one's wishes came true they seemed as empty as the
look in the gull's eye. Here there; here, there.

"Bernice, don't look so sad!" Kathy threw her arms around her
in congratulations. "You'll be the first black woman ambassador
to . . . Nigeria!"

"Oh no, baby, aimin' for the Court of St. James's."

"Of course!" Kathy blushed. "Or Paris, maybe Rome . . . And
I'll bet you'll meet somebody in Washington who'll really . . .
That town's full of possibilities."

Droves of blacks, she meant—at Howard, Georgetown, American U.—ought to be able to find some man who'd do, for there

hadn't been a male in her life for six months, since Ronald, her Harvard pre-med friend, took flight.

"Bernice, I wonder—you got any plans for the weekend?"

"Look at my desk!"

"I've gotten in a mix-up, see—"

"Oh no, wait—"

"Please, Bernice. If I can't count on you, who *is* there?"

"Thought you were in close communication with God."

"This last time—I need help." In Washington during Easter vacation she'd run into a childhood playmate who'd grown into a nervy young man, just as disdainful of cocktail chatter as *she* was. They left the party early, zooming down the streets in his father's Mustang, stopped at two bars. In the parked car outside her front door he made a pass, but she managed to escape. Next morning her mother said Billy was only a high school senior. "Might be taking an acting course at Catholic U., but he's seventeen—because I remember the day he was born."

"She was right—there *is* four years between us. So Bernice, I *tried* to cool it but Billy kept following me around town in the Mustang . . . phoning . . . making a stupid nuisance of himself. And now he's coming up here this weekend. But I'll be out with James, and I don't want a hassle over this—and have to *deal* with Billy—or have Mother find out what's with me'n James . . . and get a lot of funny ideas that aren't true."

"Where's this Billy gonna stay, if he comes?" Didn't want the kid hanging around the suite till 1 A.M. curfew, playing records and making his presence felt. She'd gotten Kathy to agree: no more male house guests.

"Fordham, he said—but he's coming *here* first. Didn't believe me when I told him I'd be gone."

"Well, count me out. Not interested."

"Because he's from home I can't just—ignore him. I shouldn't have encouraged him—that night—but I was so bored, Bernice. You've no idea! I missed James so much . . . missed having my *own* life."

"Tell Billy you made plans. He got no business crashing."

"You don't know Billy. He won't accept a straight answer."

"Say you're out for the weekend."

"Then if Mother hears . . . she'll want to know where, who with."

Because of last fall. Lovers arrived at Kathy's bedroom door at any hour, day or night, and she took them all in. Using the senses instead of being at the mercy of them (Kathy said) was one way of reaching through one's bodily bindings to God and eternity. But when Oscar the night guard took his turn, Kathy began to see that things were leading to disaster, not Deity. A fortyish one-time greaser from the back end of town, he turned ugly, slapped her around for being so immoral. Bernice didn't know whom to call, since Oscar himself was the nightguard—then phoned switchboard and asked Sylvie to ring Oscar out of Kathy's room on an emergency-rape in another dorm. Kathy got off with a broken rib, a black eye, and after the infirmary notified her parents, two weeks with her psychiatrist back home in Washington.

Now Kathy had a quote from St. Paul pinned to her bulletin board: "For I know that in me (that is, in my flesh) dwelleth no good thing . . ." So religious, she wore a yellow button, JESUS LOVES ME, even on her Van Raalte nightie. Never went to bed for anything but sleep—or ever got stuck by that pin. In James she'd found a soulmate who shared her religious bent. All very chaste and holy. Since Kathy had no brother and James no sister, they were euphoric about a pseudo-sibling intimacy that never strayed below the belt. Bernice knew they were building up to something wild, that's all, and saving themselves for it. The Bible they hauled around with them would eventually turn into a pillow. On the lawn behind the Manse, those warm April days, they sunbathed and played I-Ching with the Holy Scriptures, chancing through the Old and New Testaments, falling upon this verse or that and reading their futures in the cryptic lines. He'd rub suntan lotion on her arms and legs as if anointing her for sacrifice upon some high altar; then she'd do his back for him. They lay languid and full in the hot sun, naked limbs entwined; now and then have a prayer together. Any fool could tell they were in love —but they were so righteous they didn't know.

"Gotta keep Billy from coming, somehow . . . I'll send a telegram." Kathy printed the message in kindergarten block letters. FRIEND KILLED AUTO ACCIDENT BOSTON MUST GO AT ONCE.

"What a violent excuse."

"The only thing he'll understand, Bernice."

Saturday morning just as Kathy was leaving for Manhattan, where James coming up from Princeton would meet her, Bernice yelled: "Hold it! Telephone!"

"You didn't get my telegram?" Kathy wailed into the phone.

"*Mailgram*—of course not," Bernice muttered.

"But I *can't* see you here this weekend, Billy, and I don't know why you traveled all this way . . . don't you have any sense? About people's lives? Here my friend's been killed . . . yeah . . . a head on. Mass Turnpike somewhere near Natick. I don't know, not for days, I suppose. There'll be a funeral or something. *I* don't know how I can help, but . . . I mean, he's my friend! No . . . no, not *that* kind of friend. Just a friend. Somebody I liked and now—now he's . . ."

Bernice saw tears running down Kathy's face. Lying was very moving to her, one of the most personally felt experiences of her life.

"If Billy comes, tell him to go back home," she said after she'd hung up. "So *his* folks don't—"

"Where'll you be?"

"At the Y—or a hotel—or somewhere. James will have an idea."

"Wouldn't be surprised if he *does!* About time, with you two."

"Oh, not *that!*" An almost fanatic look on her face.

"'Scuse my dirty mind."

By seven o'clock the Manse became eerily quiet, splendid for work. A high mark in sociology was essential in order to offset biology. Every black was supposed to do well in it, the subject matter firsthand stuff—the text merely informing you your life was an open book. "You're too passive in attitude," the female instructor said, almost like a psychiatrist, so tough and straight-shooting. The whole drift of the reading involved mistreatment of women in American society, especially blacks. "Stop avoiding the material with irony—unless you use that sly humor to score points in your argument."

What was needed, Bernice knew, was a sudden burst of "creativity," but her note cards bore statistics on the underpayment of women, low positions of females in corporations, and the use of

cheap labor for the secretarial pool. Dry facts, without the life of
the mind to give them propulsion. Her professors liked the fresh
approach, no matter how outlandish, because audacity was a virtue in itself and might someday lead to sound criticism and useful
action. Bernice could knock out a properly documented, modest
term paper for any scholarly course, but she'd be shot down.
Those microfilm hours in the library and her packets of five-by-
seven cards—all useless. Her grasp of the subject was pedestrian
and the paper she'd write wouldn't interest the teacher, a former
New York social worker.

She slumped into a chair to read the *Times* once more: nothing
left except the back end of the second section—the want ads.
How crimped the language, when every letter was paid for, and
how cold the call for human lives in the marketplace! Suddenly
her term paper presented itself. She jumped up and began writing
at her desk:

> Sealed bids only. Obligated under code 4437 of the city of New
> York to accept the lowest bid, unless the City Council rules that
> in the city's best interest a higher bid be taken.
>
> All bids will be opened on May 15 at 10 A.M. in the office of
> the Commissioner of Public Works.
>
> Females may be viewed prior to the bidding, but touching,
> probing, testing manually in any fashion is strictly forbidden.
>
> The veracity of claims regarding said females' proportions and
> capabilities must be guaranteed by the offering agency. Any com-
> plaints will be honored by said agency.
>
> *This* specimen is particularly well turned, perfect for machine-
> parts manufacturers, tool-dye companies, drill-punch operators,
> and hardware proprietors, who seek an image of frivolity in the
> midst of their too solid-surfaced enterprises.
>
> She will give the proper zany touch, which instead of discredit-
> ing the product manufactured by the company, will actually en-
> hance it—since no one would imagine that such steel, acids, and
> durably tempered real goods might be corrupted in efficiency by a
> pliant, willowy creature of this sort, a girl who suggests in every
> way that steel is fun.

The telephone rang—and rang. Angrily, her spurt broken, she
picked up the receiver and even before saying hello: "Kathy's not
home!"

Switchboard wanted to know *where*, then. "God damn it, Bernice!" Sylvie, her black sister, working the weekend shift on the plugboard. "Didn't sign out—where'd she go?" The old parietal sign-out system was reinstated last year because a girl had married her East Village Indian guru and before anybody knew had been gone to the Himalayas two months.

"Kathy's in New York somewhere."

"What'll I say to him?"

"Who?"

The next voice was male. "Bernice, this is Billy."

"How do you know my name?"

"Kathy told me. Listen, I have to come up and talk—okay?"

"I'm in the middle of—"

"Won't be a sec." He broke off.

"On his way," Sylvie said. "Ring if you need help."

Of all the mother—! Too late to lock the door? Where the hell was the key?

Billy appeared, a six-foot beanpole in soiled raincoat and racing sneakers; long-fingered hands and a face that seemed all profile. "That's Kathy's bedroom?"

"It's not ready for company."

"Look . . . her slippers." He drew forth her yellow mules as if he'd found the grail. "Does she always keep them under the bed?"

"Yeah, it's a good place for 'em. Then her toes don't have to feel this cold, cold floor."

Billy noticed the pen doodles on her notepad, very feathery, oriental-rug-like. He ripped off the sheet and tucked it into the shirt pocket over his heart. "So this is where . . . she lives. If I could be you, Bernice, for a few days . . . wouldn't that be—"

"Ridiculous! Who'd want to be me?"

"Suppose I could snitch one of her . . . things?"

"Like what?"

"Underthing." He began pawing through her dresser drawers.

"Kathy ain't neat, but she knows the shape of her mess. She'll see you been in there."

"Ah!" He drew out a pair of lace panties and tucked them in his hip pocket. "When you think she'll be back tonight?"

"Not till tomorrow, maybe not till Monday. I don't know."

"Could I stay here till then?" He glanced at her empty bed.

"They won't let you, sorry." She didn't sound it. "Had a lot of

trouble last year with anybody and his brother dropping in. *Five*
rapes—I'm not kidding. So now they make a check and kick out
anybody who don't belong. Figure, if a dude's really fond of his
chick he oughta be able to take care of her properly—with a
motel room."

"I could hide in the closet when they come by, inspecting."

"Sylvie's on switchboard—remember? You been spotted."

"C'mon, Bernice, let's level. Kathy didn't go to Boston, did
she?"

"Should've seen her cryin'—she felt so bad, about her friend
killed in the accident."

"Huh! Accident! You won't betray Kathy, or anything—you
can be straight. Ever since me and Kathy were little, she's been a
liar—but I'm a bigger one, see. Now tell me, what train you think
she'll be back on?"

"She ain't comin' back tonight, Billy-boy, Billy-boy."

"Who's she with?"

"I'm writin' a paper in sociology and it was comin' along fine
till you bulled your way in."

"I'll wait downstairs, then. Sorry, Bernice." He slunk away,
feeding on his love wounds. He really didn't want to know the
truth about Kathy.

That brilliant, creative paper never got up off its hind legs again.
Dead, dead. She threw in nuts, bolts, automatic typewriters,
chains on slave girls, and described the auction itself, in the pit of
the New York Stock Exchange. Everything was far out of hand.
When Sylvie phoned at eleven, Bernice was half glad to be
rescued. "He didn't find Kathy on the ten thirty-five and he's back
again. What'll I do?"

"Oh, send him up."

"Bernice, you need some sisterly advice."

"Thanks, Sylvie, don't want it."

She fixed instant coffee and shared her half jar of chunky pea-
nut butter and sesame wafers. He paced up and down the
dormer room, talking about himself, ducking his head just in time
so as not to hit the sloping roof. He'd acted in *Murder in the Cathedral*, several Shakespearean plays, and was promised a summer
stock job in Bucks County. He corrected himself—"the possi-

bility" was there, through somebody he'd met at a Washington cocktail party. "If she'll *just* remember!"

Always a good listener because people knew they could impose upon her, Bernice figured even now her dark skin served as a backdrop. His monologue on the subject of himself finally took a music-hall turn, and he sang a little German song learned in acting school. Such cheerful narcissism! He hit the highlights of himself frenetically, as if pitching carnival balls. He was a Taurus, on the cusp. Loved Tolkien, hated David Bowie, liked Frank Zappa. Punching holes—computer information applied to himself.

He met the midnight train, though Bernice warned of muggers and weirdos who hung around the station, making dates and picking up strange kids. When he returned alone, despondent, she said: "You only got till one o'clock curfew—then you'll have to leave."

"I can't think . . . mind if I take a shower?"

She handed him a towel and showed him the bathroom shared by everyone on the floor. Since they were entirely alone, there was no danger he'd annoy anybody. Before closing the door he announced he'd meet the one-thirty train: "It's the last."

"*If* she was on it—then what? You couldn't come upstairs with her. Have to say good-by at the gate—soon's you've said hello." By tracking her down he figured he'd make her know how much he cared. He turned on the water and began to sing.

Returning later, he called: "Hey, Bernice, look!"

Stork-white, naked except for Kathy's lace panties. "Exhibitionist!" He had no meat on him at all. "You look less like a girl than anybody I've seen."

Careful not to zip the trim, he drew the trousers on, cupping his crotch. "Feels good! I like having her close to—this part of me."

"Billy, you're really something else—Kathy was right!"

"What'd she say about me? Come *on!*"

Couldn't tell him she'd scoffed at the memory of the high school boy, so Bernice began lying. Fibbing's contagious, can't seem to stop. "What time's that train?"

Billy grabbed for his watch.

"She won't be on it, Billy. You might as well head back to Washington."

"Missed the last Metroliner anyhow. I'll sleep on a church lawn in town. The Unitarians are good that way."

"Far out! It's the night patrol you gotta worry about, not the Unitarians."

"Church ground's sanctified. The law's secular and can't interfere."

"Since when."

"Custom of sanctuary goes back to the Middle Ages, Bernice." He drew on his shirt like a deacon, buttoning the top at the collar.

"Tell *that* to our cops! Ever since New Rochelle began spilling its troubles up our way, they've been on red alert. You'll land in jail."

"So? Maybe—if it's going to rain tonight—that'd be best anyhow."

"Suffer!"

"I'll take my chance—on the lawn."

"Yeah, you'll suffer for her!" But her mocking fell short of him. She pulled from a closet the camping blankets Kathy used sunbathing with James and dumped them in Billy's arms. He left waving cheerfully, as only a seventeen-year-old boy in mad pursuit of an idea can look. Nothing in the world stands in the way. They make such good soldiers at that age, too. Kill me, go ahead and kill me! See if I care! And they get killed.

Bernice couldn't sleep. At two-thirty she finally rose, dressed, and slipped quietly out of the Manse. At the concentration-camp fence gate, the surly guard insisted she sign her name and write down a statement in his book. "Emergency. Friend killed in auto accident. Taking train to NY—will phone in by tomorrow noon." If she put in writing that a seventeen-year-old boy in lace panties lay on the Unitarian church lawn and might get himself raped or mugged unless she saw he was okay, they'd not believe her anyhow.

Billy'd found a nice spot close to an arbutus, beside the illuminated bulletin board announcing tomorrow's sermon. They bundled up, though the ground seemed awfully hard. The earth's cold came through the blankets like the demand of the grave. She thought of past soldiers in trenches and imagined herself on a field of battle. With Billy you could be anybody but yourself.

If I'm caught out here, will they still let me go to graduate school? Can I ever again be the good citizen they thought me, doing a thing like this?

They lay back to back, warming each other. "This is awful, Billy. I'm gonna catch cold and die of pneumonia. Why're we doing it?"

"Shut up, Bernice. We're doin' it for love."

"So *that's* why I can't go back to the Manse tonight," Kathy said. "This Billy . . ."

"We'll find someplace to stay, don't worry." James took both her hands and held them, next to the plate of piroshkis.

"You're not . . . sore at me, for spoiling the evening?" They'd planned on Reno Sweeney's but switched to the Russian Tea Room because long conversation was necessary, and they could spend most of the evening here without nasty looks from the waiters.

"No . . . it's kind of exciting."

"Couldn't we maybe stay in your loft tonight?"

A few months ago he'd rented a room in Chelsea for storing paintings, hoping gallery dealers might look at his work, though none had. Sometimes he stayed there overnight.

"Too grubby, Kathy. Roaches, rats—not even a toilet. I use the alley myself, but *you* can't."

"I can't?"

"Suppose we *could* wash dishes here—to pay for supper—then between us we might have enough for a hotel room. For you." His flat, uninflected Minnesota voice was beginning to have an eastern overlay. "Or why not borrow a violin and fiddle away in front of Carnegie Hall? Velvet case open . . . with a sign, FOR MORE LESSONS?"

They laughed, more united than ever. They'd been in a few tight corners, but not the crucial one of no money. Always a credit card or a personal check to rescue them. Kathy closed her eyes and let herself float free of anxiety, putting herself into a prayerful attitude, though she didn't want to use up her credibility with God by actually uttering a message, a plea for solution. Not to a mundane problem like *this!* She used aspirin sparingly, too, never for just a headache or menstrual cramps; saved it for a really awful pain, so that the possibility of relief wouldn't become outworn. She kept a large reservoir of prayer and salvation for all the trouble that might lie ahead. Let James figure this one out.

He left to telephone a Princeton friend whose parents lived on Riverside Drive, lots of rooms, but as he slowly returned under the Christmas-tree tinsel of the chandeliers, she could tell nobody was home. He offered to bodyguard her all the way to the Manse door, if *that* would help. "Or let's pick an all-night movie on Forty-second Street. They let you sleep if you've paid to get in. I've enough for *that*."

"I'd prefer a sleeping bag, on the floor of your loft."

"No, Kathy, that's out." Not providing for her properly wounded his pride and to bring her into his pitiful lair would only make him feel worse.

In an all-night movie they'd be down and out with a kind of gay honor, but she'd never sleep and Sunday she'd drag around town feeling miserable. "Oh, *why* do I get into these messes, anyhow? I'm sorry, James."

"I beg your pardon," said the gray-haired gentleman one foot to the left of her on the banquette. "I couldn't *help* but overhear. If you don't mind my intrusion, I *do* have a solution for you—about where to spend the night."

Startled, James shook his long, newly washed hair. "How's that?"

"I say . . . if you can forgive an old man for being interested in the conversations of the young, you might consider what I've to suggest."

Was he somebody famous she should recognize? He had that awfully rich look: Custom House shirt, Italian silk tie, and cuff links of lapis lazuli.

"I live on Central Park West, and you're welcome to one or more of my bedrooms. Plenty of room." He smiled, cherubic.

"Well, it's awful nice of you, sir," she began, "but we couldn't possibly accept an offer like that."

"We couldn't?"

"No, I don't see how. I mean, we *do* thank you for—the generous offer. But we'll work it out, don't worry."

"Kathy!"

"There're no strings attached, my dear, if that's what you're thinking. I don't expect a *thing* in return. And I've plenty of help —so you wouldn't be any trouble." He smiled, pleased with himself, the kind of expression New Yorkers have when they help you find the right bus. In the city it's so hard to do things for others and have it accepted at face value. *Why* did she have these suspicions? Except ye be as a little child, ye shall not enter the kingdom of heaven. Yet here she was at twenty-one, cynical and closed-in.

"Kathy, maybe—maybe we oughta . . ."

"Name's Hawley Pennell," and he handed them each an engraved card. "Were you next door tonight, too—at Carnegie?"

"No, you see we've got this *problem*," she said.

"But it's solved, so enjoy your borscht before it gets cold. Then we'll take a taxi home."

"Never heard of anything like *this* before," Kathy said, slowly dipping her spoon into the tomatoey soup. Mother'd be horrified! But fun, maybe—and a tale to tell afterward.

As James introduced himself, flashing his great smile, Mr. Pennell shook his hand. Kathy cautiously gave only her first name, but he didn't press. When they'd finished the soup the waiter removed the plates and handed them menus for the next course, though James protested, aware of the flatness of his wallet. Mr. Pennell said he'd take their bill and they should order whatever they wished. James chose shashlik, the most expensive entree; she settled on chicken Kiev. With the bottle of burgundy Mr. Pennell provided, they settled back to enjoy the whole affair. "To Mr. Pennell! Just in time!" James lifted his glass. Three *clinks* and the bargain was sealed.

After they'd eaten everything, Mr. Pennell offered a Gaulois. "No thanks," she said, "I don't smoke." But James accepted without hesitation—the cigarette was European, something not yet tried.

They respected their bodies and had a policy against smoking, not even a joint now and then. Perhaps James was merely being polite now, or maybe he slipped into defilement of his body more often than he admitted. A little wine with food was all they allowed themselves, so that their senses were kept alive, naturally alert, not all hyped up. Those poor acid-heads of the sixties—

minds blown and gone, only dimly aware of what'd happened. Lost to themselves, the world, and God, in that order.

"Do you live anywhere near a church?" she asked.

Mr. Pennell smiled. "Not *very* near. Some bells might wake you tomorrow from the Lutherans, but the Ethical Culture is decently quiet Sunday mornings—and about every other time, too. Why?"

"James and I will be going to church."

"What denomination *are* you?"

"It doesn't matter. God doesn't have a denomination."

"You two don't look all that religious. *Are* you really?"

"Kathy, show him your Jesus button."

She turned, her braless bosom in a tight, glittery-purple evening sweater. Mr. Pennell looked long and appreciatively at JESUS LOVES ME. "I'm sure He *does* love you, Kathy. How could He help it? He made you, didn't He?"

"And we love Him. That's why we'll be going to church tomorrow."

"Kathy, just this once we could miss."

"No . . . no," surprised by his easy siding with the stranger.

Mr. Pennell quickly asked sensible questions about their coursework. They answered but got little information in return, except that he was a patron of the Metropolitan Opera and had a heavy booking of concert subscriptions. Where his money came from or why he was alone on a Saturday night in early May, they never found out—and didn't ask. They didn't know how to. *She* might have, but James seemed excited by the fragile acquaintanceship and apprehensive lest the whole thing fade. He didn't want to offend Mr. Pennell by any impertinences.

When she met James at the Valentine's Day Mixer (a corny take-off on June Allyson collegiate movies), he was a cheerful atheist armed with Bertrand Russell answers to the important, eternal questions. She nudged him into agnosticism, and before long he'd become an out-and-out believer in Our Lord and Savior, Jesus Christ. He needed the Supreme Being because a certain despair suffused his well-being whenever she asked, "But James, *why* must you succeed and become a famous painter?" His answer, "Because I want to," seemed hollow even to himself. With new humility, he viewed himself as one of God's Elect and took no credit for his usual good fortune. Commitment to religion drew them together, but she never revealed her actual uncertainty about her true relationship to God. She couldn't, once she recognized how James seemed completely infused with the Holy Ghost —the most mysterious segment of the Trinity—his unerring luck testimony of his spiritual good standing. Even Mr. Pennell appeared just when needed.

She sought the peace "which passeth understanding." Having steadied her life with Jesus, James, and sexual abstinence, her goal was to be taken up by God one of these days—ravished by a certainty of faith. James respected her chastity and agreed that the Lord would make it known when the moment was right for them. She wasn't holding off because she thought sex out of wedlock sinful; afraid, rather, that sensual pleasure might precipitate the awful slide and confusion of last fall. She feared losing the only true support she had: God the Father. If only He knew—that was the trouble. She still felt so out of it

"Here's the Lincoln Center mob," said Mr. Pennell, nodding toward the line-up near the bar. "If you're finished . . . Waiter! Check please."

James squeezed her hand under the table, his hazel eyes raffish —just over the impending adventure? If he spent his currency with God this freely, the treasury would soon be bare. Tonight they hadn't needed to be rescued all *that* much!

She felt odd walking out of the Tea Room with their rich pickup leading the way and hoped nobody around would recognize her or ask to be introduced. Two cabbies screeched to a halt at the awning. They chose the Checker for comfort and settled back, Mr. Pennell talking elegantly about nothing, a little like a salesman who's afraid the holes in conversation might drop a sale through. James answered Mr. Pennell with inane social small talk, playing his sophisticated game as only an out-of-towner from the Middle West could, convinced everybody else has either played earlier and won or is presently at it. Chitchat—oh, *really! No!*

Mr. Pennell kept his course somewhat off the banks of the personal. In this way regularity was established, a kind of neutral sea based on city interminglings, changeable identities: a fluidity of style that denied the specifics of names, places, parents, jobs, how-long here, how-long there. They made up their biographies almost in the moment they created their own histories. James posed as a great though undeveloped painter. Tonight Mr. Pennell would show him *his* extensive art collection and perhaps tomorrow buy one of James's. On the strength of that sale, a Madison Avenue gallery would take over dealership and there'd be a show with rave notices in *Art News*.

"Here we are! Driver, a U-turn, please." The liveried doorman rushed forward when he recognized Mr. Pennell in the cab. His dark Puerto Rican eyes looked over the passengers curiously. What's he thinking? Kathy wondered. Who's he seen with Mr. Pennell other evenings?

The marble lobby, denuded of furnishings, had a leaded glass skylight glowing with concealed illumination. They stepped into the mahogany-and-brass elevator, elegant as a rich man's coffin, and ascended at a stately pace, as if St. Peter were up there but he could wait.

"Go right on in." Fifteen-foot balcony windows overlooked Central Park. Here anybody could worship before the candelabras across the park—the blazing Pierre Hotel, the General Motors building dimly seen through the trees; and the communion-host platter of the Plaza Hotel.

Mr. Pennell stooped to light a well-laid fire, and almost immediately the fresh aroma of *piñon* scented the room, special logs shipped from New Mexico. They squished down in black leather chairs, were served a sweet liqueur in solid gold thimbles—strange-tasting stuff from Morocco. With this insidious, warming beverage, added to the wine, James began to talk; mostly about himself. He kicked off his loafers, rubbed his toes in the deep-piled rug; he told of his humble Minnesota origins, the cow in the backyard and the mother who took in laundry. He knew the salient points that would indicate a young man's eventual success, what would impress.

"Like Julien Sorel," Mr. Pennell said, "the handsome youth from the provinces . . . rising, rising. To what heights? What might happen to such a young man? Especially since he's only—how old did you say? Twenty-two? Fabulous. And so talented." Furthermore, good artists were usually physically attractive. "An inner beauty permeates the flesh, until finally one sees nothing but grace! Look at Byron, Keats—or Hawthorne, Melville, Delacroix."

Kathy immediately thought of ugly Toulouse-Lautrec, mentioned him. "Isn't it often as a compensation for deformity . . . that an artist devotes himself to—"

"In some cases, *mine* perhaps. These paintings—I did."

"Really!" said James, ingenuous.

On the high walls each canvas was aglow; pinpoint ceiling lights playing upon them from the open beams revealed clouds of color: underbelly of an overcast New York sky at night, suffused purples, violets, reds. James scrutinized each picture, offering professional opinion in that peculiar language art critics use—which never made sense to her. On a teak platform in a nearby corner a fat, gilded Buddha possessed the solidity she needed just now. The four-foot-high Chinese vases presented themselves to her in a massive form that required no commentary. The Jacobean table had carved faces up and down each leg, gargoyle visages asking her what in the hell she was doing here.

Why would Hawley Pennell be interested in a couple of kids like us? Jowly cheeks hung from his face, white hair growing thin, portly body going to stomach. He was old and they were young; he'd done everything and seen it all—they were innocents. Hadn't been abroad or anywhere on earth worth telling about. A natural meeting, opposites attracting. Mr. Pennell had lived a gratifying life of sensation but was paying the penalty with lonely Saturday nights, no wife or children for comfort, no embedding complications—but would he want them? Or was he bachelor-happy in his solitariness, as he now pretended? She almost asked the simple, necessary question: Mr. Pennell, are you pleased with yourself, do you approve of your life? It'd be a lance thrust into the sophisticated talk, as leveling as if she'd uttered, *"lo, I am with you alway, even unto the end of the world. Amen."*

Instead, she rubbed the Jesus button for luck, happened to touch her nipple, sensitive under the slithery cloth, and wondered if James would insist upon making love tonight. Yet *why* should they give themselves to it now, when accident had shuffled them here? To succumb in Mr. Pennell's apartment would be like giving up their will, their responsibility for themselves. As a consequence, maybe she'd fall back to where she'd been last fall, screwing anybody; never getting close, the closer she came to people. She brushed her nipple again and immediately felt a strong current of desire. No matter what her mother said, she wasn't a nympho and these months of no sex proved it. The psychiatrist said her need for love had gotten confused with pamphlet-promises of gratification. She ceased taking the pill, which re-established the old caution—fear of pregnancy; then she felt the true message of the gospel, and her life had changed. She'd hate to have tonight's adventure send her back to that dismally hushed Washington office—and all the ways Dr. Schuman got her to say things he didn't want her to think he was putting in her head to say.

Mr. Pennell noticed Kathy wasn't drawn into the conversation and kept trying to address remarks to her. "Passage to more than India, O my soul!" he said, looking at her intently.

"You like Whitman, too?" she asked, bewildered.

"'I sing the body electric,'" James said, looking at her excitedly. Too much drink? They'd lost their closeness, acting out their youth in front of Mr. Pennell. She felt outside their relationship.

"I think I've had enough of that queer drink." Again she'd failed to hear what Mr. Pennell asked her.

"The *kelson* of creation."

"I thought that was the name of a racehorse."

"Kelso! Kelso!" James leaped up and pulled her from the deep chair. "You're ready for bed, my girl."

Mr. Pennell marched off grandly, as if thinking: *Now comes the good part.*

"But I don't like this movie. Let's go to your Chelsea loft."

"You crazy? Not *now!* When we got a pad like this."

"I don't *want* to sleep with you, James. We're not ready yet."

"All right, all right. I won't touch you, I swear."

"This way, children!"

The bedroom walls were gray silk damask and the bed a fluffy white moored cloud with a mirror behind and above it. All of Central Park twinkled at the windows, the East Side a stage effect just for them. "Think you'll be happy here?" asked Mr. Pennell grinning, sugarplum cheeks.

"I'll never want to leave!" said James. "Wow!"

"You don't *have* to, my dears. You don't have to."

She glanced up at the mirror on the ceiling over the bed, her head an egg and all the rest a stalk. What a way to look up to heaven! How could Jesus come through, when all you saw was yourself? A naked buttock view. "We don't want to miss church tomorrow, Mr. Pennell. Have your butler or somebody wake us at eight."

"Oh, not *eight*, Kathy!"

"Nine then."

"With breakfast . . . as you wish."

"If I want another bedroom, where is it?"

"Kathy—I promised you I'd—"

"Mr. Pennell offered his whole flat—didn't you? With lots of rooms."

"There's a fine bedroom just down the hall."

"And where'll *you* be?"

"Upstairs. I've *really* got a view."

"I'll bet!" said James, grinning.

Of us? That mirror a one-way window?

"The bath's *here*," said Mr. Pennell, opening a door. "Everything you need. Spare toothbrushes, even. Now I'm going to retire, my dears . . . happily, I might add. It's good to have . . . young people around again. And I'm most relieved—grateful even —that I didn't have to explain *why*."

"You chose a pretty sensible couple, when you come right down to it," said James.

"*I'd* say so. Good night, Kathy. Good night, James."

"If—if we need anything—what'll we do?"

"Go find it, Kathy, if you can. My man's deaf as a post, with his hearing aid off. There's no rousing him." He closed the bedroom door firmly behind him.

James walked into the bathroom, flicked on the light. "Oh, wow! Kathy! Come *here!* Look at this! A Roman bath."

"Not surprised."

Purplish marble like porphyry lined the walls; the sunken tub was black marble with great golden spigots, and the entire floor was covered in white lambskin. "I'm gonna make myself to home, Kathy. That's what this place is *for!*" He peeled off his clothes, down to his white briefs, and hung them on hooks. "Well, come on, Kathy, let's not be shy. The tub's built for two."

"Or more. Mr. Pennell, too?"

"Sure, he's some kinda queen, but what difference does it make?"

"*We* make the difference! I thought you agreed . . . what's sacred. Here you're ready to profane yourself at the first flash of marble and the sight of a few gold faucets."

"I'm getting tired of your religious games, Kathy. Come *on*, you're a big girl. A graduating senior. Let's put the fake innocence away for a bit, huh?"

"Fake? What do you mean?"

"Gonna be my girl, Kathy, you gotta *be* my girl."

"James—I don't understand." Afraid she did.

"Who you think you're kidding, besides yourself? I mean about not letting me touch you. I'd like to be just with *you*, Kathy. Rather have *you* than any of those others."

"What others?" She'd never seen him so purposeful, deliberate —there in his jockey briefs, saying at last what needed saying.

"Course there're others, Kathy. What'd you think?"

"*I've* been true to you, James!"

"I don't like those words, Kathy. 'True to you.' I don't know what the hell they mean, even." He bent over the tub and turned the spigots, adjusting the hot water, then poured from a vial of perfumed liquid soap. A surf foamed up. "Kathy, let's face the facts of life—what the hell! You know damn well what I'm talking about, and frankly, it's really kind of sick, playing this bunny game or whatever it is, brudder'n sister. I mean, it isn't like you'd never done—"

"Stop it! I only told you about that period of my life because I thought we shared each other's trust—and love. Where do you get off *using* it against me?"

"I'm not *using* it, Kathy. Just touching bottom, getting to reality. All I'm saying is, there were guys before me—right? So what the hell? What're we waiting for? You know I've had a few girls, too. And frankly I'm glad we got whisked up here tonight by Mr. Pennell. Confront the truth a little. Face reality."

"*Reality!* This is reality?" She opened her arms and spun on her heel. "Good God, it's Satan's dream."

"Be honest, Kathy, come on," he said softly, taking her hand, standing there in his vulnerable underwear, with a yellow stain where he'd peed. He began unbuttoning her blouse. "Kathy, I *love* you!"

"I don't want to take a bath." She drew away.

"I need somebody to scrub my back. Play a little, Kathy. Let's enjoy ourselves. Come on, join the script—I need you, man!"

"I don't like only being needed *that* way."

"Other ways too, *all* the ways. I don't know, Kathy, you've gotten so Virgin Maryish! It's time you came out of it."

He pulled the blouse slowly over her head, magicianlike, transforming her into a half-naked girl standing before him. He kissed her breasts slowly, reverently, each a station, then helped her out of the rest of her clothes, while she stood there, unable to muster a good line of argument, aware that her defenses were falling as fast as her garments. She heard the rushing faucets, saw the waterfall black pool under the purple ledge. She felt removed, stunned by his information that he'd been going to other girls.

She looked at the mirror on the ceiling over the tub and tilted her face back, breasts showing below her head, like those angels riding wings on the cornices of old buildings. James stooped to remove his shorts, the dorsal fin of his backbone a straight line, then he stood up. His red turkey's gobble bobbed in front of him. They were Adam and Eve after God had left them to their own devices. James saw her looking heavenward and joined her in the tableau on the ceiling, throwing his head back, mouth wide open, a satyr laughing; his hands on her breasts felt rough, and he was hot and hard against her flank.

He led her gently to the pool and they stepped in together, she on one end, he on the other, their legs entwined in a foot of suds which smelled of sandalwood. She'd given up hope of avoiding intimacy and allowed him to soap her all over. She closed her eyes; after all, he said he loved her.

"Now come on, Kathy, it's my turn." He handed her the bar and she lathered the hair on his chest and rubbed his arms and back. "Here, too," he said, closing his eyes as her fingers clasped round him. She was really touching him now, his very blood, hot beneath her hand, violently red in the white lather. He groaned as she stroked. "All right . . . all right . . . stop," he said suddenly, rather tightly, and tried to move himself out of her hand's way, in the slippery tub, but she had him firmly now in her soapy hand

and kept going faster. "Kathy! Kathy—my God!" His face turned deep red. "Oh, Jesus!" almost in pain or anger, and then he exploded into her fingers, warm pulsing gushes like his very blood stream. "I'm sorry—Jesus!" He scrambled away, half rising from the tub. "I really . . . forgive me, Kathy!"

"What's there to forgive? At least you won't have to go to somebody else tomorrow, will you?"

He flung one leg out and tried to remove himself from the pool. "Aren't you getting out of there?"

"No, why? Where're you going?"

"Well we oughta run a fresh tub, don't you think?"

"This one's fine!"

"Kathy—you don't want to sit in that water, now I've—"

"It's in *all* the skin creams that cost twenty dollars an ounce. You think there's something *dirty* about it? James, you really surprise me. Such a Puritan. Don't know where it's all gone anyhow, in this mass of soapsuds. What difference does it make? It's pure blood or something, isn't it?" Her biology lesson came back a little vague, or did she have it mixed up with a porno movie on the subject of nourishment by mouth?

"Blood?"

"I forget. It's a pint of blood, or something like that. And a beefsteak thrown in."

"I never heard it called blood."

"Sure—that's what it is . . . white blood."

"And the kelson of creation is love," Whitman wrote; she lay aglow with it as the sun flashed into the silken room. They'd danced and romped about the room last night, the great open space of New York before them: naked and natural in the universe of man and God. She didn't imagine they'd rise for church today. They'd praised Him sufficiently in the glory of His creation; furthermore, her limbs were too languid, she couldn't move. For all of James's swagger about having gone to other girls (who were they?) he must've been saving up for a long time.

She slipped off the peach satin sheet without waking him and used the bidet again, this time getting the water temperature right before squatting, as he'd demonstrated last night. She'd never used one before. It was a fairly safe time of the month, but if she got pregnant they'd marry according to God's will. She had no particular plans for the rest of the year anyhow. Their baby would be fantastically beautiful! She could see how God might be tempted into a bit of mischief. With the warm water gurgling under her, she sat on the little fountain a long time, carried upon a river of forgetfulness.

Voices interrupted her revery. The butler with the breakfast tray, just as Mr. Pennell promised. Quickly, she dried herself on the blanket-towel. James sauntered in, naked, sleepy, classical-looking —hair Renaissance aswirl. She watched him pee, the Brussels boy himself—probably because of that champagne they'd discovered in the little fridge next to the bed. "What's the butler like?"

"That was Mr. Pennell."

"It *was?* What'd he want?"

"Bringing orange juice, croissants. Big pot of coffee. Must be nine o'clock. Come on, Kathy—I'm starved. I've lost all my white blood. I need replenishing."

"What'd he say to you?"

" 'Good morning'—something like that."

"James—I heard all that talking in there. What'd he say?" She ran a brush over her hair again and again. In the mirror she noticed her nipples looked unusually rosy and full—just as the mother cardinal's beak turns red in spring during mating season. James nuzzled her neck and pressed close; she felt his throb, he was growing strong again. She broke away. "After breakfast— come on." She led him back to the bed. They left the large white wicker breakfast tray where it was within reach on the bedside table, stretched out upon the sheets and munched the flaky croissants, bits falling everywhere. They began licking each other's crumbs off and were making love before the second cup of coffee. He lay face down in her hair and she looked over his ear to see him naked on the ceiling, buttocks rhythmically rising and falling, shoulders tense in the rocking. She shifted, watched her legs in the mirror come over his thighs like arms to embrace him. The angle had changed and she felt him deeper now, all the way to the baby.

And I don't care.

He lay slain for some time, though she managed to rise and use the bidet once more. After so many times all at once, there wasn't supposed to be much sperm left, but she sat upon her altar for good measure and knew perfectly well that if it had happened, nothing she could do now would change things.

Later, over lukewarm coffee, she asked about Mr. Pennell's reappearance this morning. No, he wasn't dressed in a white butler's jacket. He'd explained his man wasn't feeling well. "Said, 'I see you've not been alone here,' or something like that. 'Loneliness is for old people like me, who've grown accustomed to it.' Sort of sad, really."

"Was he leering at you the whole time?"

"Not particularly."

"You let him look, though, didn't you?"

"What're you getting at, Kathy?"

"He wanted a peek, I'll bet. You said yourself he must be gay, and you deliberately let yourself be—on display. Without any clothes on."

"I'm open-minded. If that's what he gets out of it—okay, so what? I'm going to play it cool. Mr. Pennell could do a lot for me, you know? He wants to see my paintings."

"Oh, sure."

"Kathy, he might *buy* one of 'em. You realize what that could mean?"

"I've a few ideas."

"For Christ's sake, cut the snide remarks. He gets his kicks this way, and we—get something out of it, too."

"Everything *I* got seems to be fading."

"Kathy!" He clutched her hand and kissed her cheek. "I've never been so happy! Only, we shouldn't't've wasted all these months. We shouldn't ever do anything like that again—I mean, *waste* ourselves."

"I don't like Mr. Pennell . . . ogling . . . and bringing your breakfast tray." She ran her thumbnail slowly across the narrow pelt of yellow hairs on his white stomach, pausing at the belly button, that holy reminder of his connection to his mother and all women. His balls began to heave and roll over. She looked closely at the veiny, membraned sack, like a bunch of baby robins in a hairy nest. "I don't want anybody looking at you but me— and nobody at *me* but you. I'm old-fashioned. We're lovers now in the eyes of God, not man."

"Perfect! We won't have to go to church this morning."

"I suppose this once . . . we could skip it." Something religious had gone astray, she wasn't sure what.

"We've the whole day to celebrate!" He sat up and kissed her quickly.

"I better look at train schedules sometime."

"Not now."

"Suppose Billy's been hanging around Bernice, acting foolish."

"Poor kid."

Lover's triumph—certain of possession, in the wake of conquest. But the truth was, opened again with all this love-making, she was vulnerable as never before. By tomorrow—by midweek for certain—she'd be in an agony of desire. And him a hundred miles away in Princeton! How difficult it'd be to keep her mind off it, but she *would*. She'd have to! This time there'd be no crazy flailing about—with a psychiatrist's couch awaiting her, and her father's fierce disgust, her mother's educated, weary hysteria.

Her parents would approve of James, though; *how* they'd approve! Unless his art aspirations got in the way of his capacity to make a living, which Kathy couldn't imagine. James would always find Pennells swimming toward him through any sea of difficulties, attracted by his grace if nothing else. Was this God's gift to him or a curse? He knew his powers over other people but was blind as yet to any moral accountability for it. He could revolve slowly in the eye of the beholder, using them in his cheerful, calculating way. Using me, too. Because his baby robins were stirring, that's all. He murmurs *love, love*, but what does it mean?

"Do me a favor, James, promise you'll never get in touch with Mr. Pennell again."

"Why?" Then he smiled. "I won't let him . . . *do* anything funny with me, is that what you're thinking? Homosexual stuff? Oh, Kathy, not for a long time—since jacking off with my buddies in eighth grade."

"But you *are* leading him on."

"He loves us *both!* It's the idea of us together that turns him on, a youth-age thing."

"So I'm part of this voyeur act too? No, James, count me out." The sun felt warm on her skin. "There's still time to make the eleven o'clock service. Let's go."

For a minute he didn't answer, clearly trying to choose between pleasing her religious whims and the possibility of brunch here with Mr. Pennell, with all that might come of it for his career. "You said *no* church, Kathy."

"That was earlier."

"We've had all the sacrament here we can take."

"I *thought* so—before I realized it'd be for the good of your soul."

"My soul? What's that? Where is it?"

"Don't say any more, please!" She couldn't bear hearing him admit he'd lost his long ago. "What do we know about salvation, anyhow? Only what we hear."

"Amen."

The pealing bells from the nearby Lutheran church fell in cascades upon the morning, silencing them. They could not look at each other. They dressed and left the apartment quietly, softly calling good-by. Nobody answered.

Bernice woke up again; the clipped arbutus on the lawn looked like a company of hooded monks praying. What the God damn hell am I doing here? Even as she cursed on sacred soil, she remembered it was only Unitarian turf. *They* were so liberal it didn't matter. How could she stop herself from all this doubling around, never being straight with anybody, especially not herself? If she could just believe in the Sisterhood, like Sylvie. Especially these days, with everybody's part clearly known by everyone else, and they told you in so many words! Unity was bliss, soul-warming. "Blackbirds flock together." Living and eating with the Sisters meant not becoming acquainted with any new white girls and losing the friendship of those once known. In a seminar with only fifteen she'd been caught having to address someone ("What's-her-face?"), didn't know her name—though they'd been sitting together at the round classroom table half a year. The instructor only smiled, didn't admonish her for being so self-concerned. Even the insulted student looked more ashamed than angry, figuring perhaps it was a reverse put-down whites deserved. "Can't tell 'em apart . . . Whitey looks all the same to me!"

With their all-black table, everyone in the dining hall had to remember the years of "back of the bus," "balcony only," "Colored drinking fountain." Digestive juices beware! And the Sisters eating there imagined slights and rebuffs, campus intrigues; politicked for more power. She hadn't participated, but she didn't bolt; she sat there with them morning, noon, and night. Thank God the U. S. Government broke it up, said federal law prohibited segregation.

Now she'd spent her last year in the old mixed way, privileged like Kathy and all the others whose parents could afford six thousand a year to keep her in college. She was the only black student not on scholarship here. When she rode the New Haven back to college from Brooklyn Heights, after a weekend home, she'd sit there watching all the maids for Westchester pile onto the train at the 125th Street station. They'd look at her so friendly, comfortable. To be mistaken for "one of us" and not really *be* made her feel she ought to stand in front of the coach and utter some statement.

What would it be? "I'm not and never have been . . . a black like you? And I'm sorry . . . Can you forgive me, please?"

The closest she'd come to such public self-revelation was one morning last month in Grand Central, the train far down the long pier in semi-darkness. Passengers had the sleepy quietness that makes you think the world's work is hard work and this is the hour you know it.

She was startled by a woman's loud voice, right behind her. "No smoking in here! Can't you read the sign?"

"Oh . . . yeah." She'd only lit up, trying to get herself awake.

"I said put it out! What makes you think you can smoke— can't you read?"

"Yeah, I kin read," borrowing a voice and an unfamiliar anger. The gray-haired, babushka-headed nuisance was clearly happy shooting off her mouth, and she clutched her shopping bag as if she thought Bernice might take it.

"Think you can just disobey the law, if you feel like it. Nobody's ever going to say anything . . . well, *I* am."

All heads in the car were turned, every *Times* set aside. "Think you can get away with anything you please."

"Oh, shut up."

"Listen, I'll call the conductor and he'll throw you off before the train even gets started."

"The cigarette's out." She felt an adrenalin rush of anger. The old bitch's hostility had nothing to do with the cigarette, everything to do with the color of her skin. Nothing to do with *herself* inside that skin, who wasn't the kind of person the woman saw at all. "Leave me alone, you old fool."

"Takes a fool to call a fool."

"I tol' you I put out the cigarette. Now shut your mouth—hear?" Darky as could be.

"You people get away with altogether too much. Think you can run over everybody. Get this, get that—without having to work, the way the rest of us do. Every one of you on welfare to boot, and who's payin'—"

"Now wait a minute!" A student across the aisle jumped up. Ropes of bright beads on his chest, long black hair. "I don't have to listen to that kind of talk from *you* or anybody."

Here was this Yalie or whoever he was, big liberal, standing up for the cause. "One more word out of *you* . . ." Jabbing his finger in the air.

"Oh, what're you butting in for?" A male voice from the rear. "Two women are having an argument and *you* have to butt in." An elderly man, slightly German accent.

"How's that?" The student stalked down the aisle.

"What're you coming to *me* for? You going to hit me? Is that it? Free speech, huh? You young people! Settle everything by force—but talk of peace. Two women having an argument, but *you're* going to start violence. That's your way, huh? I saw your kind in Hitler Germany before I left."

"You're callin' me a Nazi?" He grabbed the man's lapels. "I'm a Jew, I tell you!"

"So am I! Take your hands off me—you punk!"

Bernice felt as if she'd gone through the machine that puts plastic over your ID card. The passengers sat stunned, immobile. The conductor's wee signal whistle blew—to the gateman far down the ramp, at the station. The train began to roll out of Grand Central.

"Tickets please . . . tickets."

The student tapped Bernice's shoulder. "I'm so sorry . . . I apologize for the terrible people on this train with you."

She almost laughed—hysterically. "*You're* not responsible!"

"I know what I'm talking about," said the German in the rear to anybody listening. "In the schools they came then . . . the Hitler Youth . . . These self-righteous young people. They said to us, *we're* in charge and you must do as we say."

In the forest of pillars before the tunnel run under Park Avenue the lights flickered, went out—causing an animal stillness in the car. Bernice wanted to shriek, just to ease the tension, but she couldn't do a mad thing like that. She never could.

Not even now. Finding herself on the Unitarian lawn at 6 A.M. —college pranks, that's all!

Billy stirred and she studied his white face. Such passion for Kathy inside him, but leached out by sleep. "Billy . . . Billy boy . . . wake up."

He did a beautiful thing: he smiled! Before anything else. Only tiny babies did that. Most people—mouths foul as rancid wash-cloths, pains in their joints—groaned or sighed, unable to speak till the cup of coffee. But not Billy.

"Shoulda been in my dream, Bernice." He stretched and folded his arms behind his head, crossed his legs.

"*That* good, huh?"

"But when you think about dreams, there's nothin' there. Gone! Only got the glow left."

"Least that's something! I only got a hundred aches and pains." She stood up slowly to see if her legs would move, the blanket a shawl.

"Kathy loved me, I think. We were happy."

"Please, Billy, don't start *that* so early."

"Bernice, what am I going to do?"

"Let's head for Pat's Diner and have breakfast."

"—about *her*? I'm not getting anywhere this way, hanging around and all. She sounded awful pissed, on the phone."

"Upset. The death upset her."

"Bernice, I don't believe in that accident. I told you."

"You better believe it." If he didn't, he'd have to believe something he'd hate to hear, and *that* might undo him. She spoke the phrase with cliché ease, the way everybody grabs off sayings these days. "You better believe it." Saying *some*thing while saying nothing.

They strolled slowly down the fresh streets, passed houses as asleep as the inhabitants. The morning smelled of rain, and they possessed the whole town. A breeze blew softly off the Sound, oceany in its freeing, wide implications. Billy strutted beside her with the touching self-assurance of someone newly come into adult life, having just found out how much fun it is not to falter or lean back upon childhood. But he'd never, never make it with Kathy. Not because of the four years she had on him, though it made a difference, but Kathy knew better than to mix with this kid's ego. A magnetic field surrounded him; anybody close wouldn't be free of it. He had to have a satellite, not another sun. Or the dark side of the moon—*me*.

In the diner, four middle-aged male patrons looked them over disapprovingly as they entered, rumpled, obviously having been together all night. How could she get herself straight with the world if these mistaken assumptions kept flying at her? Forced to deal with misconceptions lest they become valid. Look the fuckers in the face dead-on, Sylvie would advise. Be proud. Billy hardly noticed the men at the counter, didn't see the elbow nudges, the way their eyes hung heavy in the sockets. Swiveling intelligences that would black-girl her if anything could. She usually managed to find some Billy hanging around who helped throw her light-years back into a sweetness she knew she mustn't believe, a trust in goodness that had no place in the world, an aura of kindness that would ultimately do her in. For remembrance she should take a Polaroid of those truckers' faces over their waffles and maple syrup, looking snarly at the black girl with the white boy, wondering where their daughters were and what their sons were up to; wishing long ago they'd done a little mixing themselves to see what it was like, so now they'd know from experience and wouldn't have to sit heavy on the swivel stools and imagine it all. God, ain't it time somebody in this country put a stop to it? Sunday morning, yet! You see anything, any hour. Only usually it's the black guys who've got the white girls because everybody knows their pricks are big.

"I'll have number two," Billy said to the waitress, pointing to the soiled breakfast card. "Scrambled."

"I'll have the same." Bernice looked up into two blue, disapproving eyes; a bleached blonde, curls all over.

Church bells began to ring, solemn peals, Catholic mass.

"Kathy'll be going to church somewhere, least I know that."

"She's very religious—about some things."

"About God."

"Kathy needs God to keep her steady."

"You know about last fall, then?" Bernice was surprised. Surely the thought of all those lovers would tarnish her image.

"Couldn't handle it there for a while, she told me. Had to come home. She's very sensitive . . . high-strung."

So that was all he knew. "Rough . . . on *me*, too, that whole time." Why had she ever put up with it?

Billy threw down the orange juice like a shot of whiskey. "I can really *talk* to you, Bernice. I like that!"

"It's cause we slept together."

"You scared hell outa me, coming up like that in the dark."

"Dumb thing to do, sleeping out in a town like this, you know? Must think it's a small suburb like Chevy Chase or something."

"*Small!* Chevy Chase? Guess you don't know Washington."

"I will . . . next year." She still couldn't quite believe in her future.

"Hey! We might see each other, then. Unless I get a part in that show I'm auditioning for—I mean if it moves to Broadway."

"What role is it?"

"This kid who's dying of leukemia but nobody knows it. They dump on him, see. And he's got to figure out how to save them from feeling guilty, later on, when he dies—because they'll remember how rotten they were. His girl friend keeps stringing him along, all the time she's making it with another guy. And his buddy does him shit, too. And his old man keeps layin' it on him. His Mom twitters away and can't see *any*thing any more, like she's some character out of a 'Lucy' show . . . I like the part."

"You're the hero, I take it."

"Nobody wins."

"Terrific."

"Otherwise . . . I'll be at Catholic U."

"Good theater department, I hear. But isn't it awfully Catholic around there?"

"That's just the name. Nothing's very Catholic any more. Even Cardinal Cooke got stuck in an elevator and never once prayed to God. You read that?"

"I'm not much interested in Catholics. Now since we're through here, guess we better walk to the station. You'll be heading back to Washington."

"Bernice! You're not being very diplomatic. Could this be Ambassador Bernice speaking? I don't think so. I know you've got a paper to write, so why not ask if I'd help?"

"You might say yes."

"While I wait for Kathy I could—"

"Billy, you don't know *anything* about my paper. We don't grind 'em out. This one's more like a poem, a mixture of facts and feelings. Has to be *personal*. Like me."

Billy made no move to go. He dropped into a dreamy fantasy all by himself on the yellow plastic bench, humming a tune, imagining himself a folk singer. But he'd never lose the distinction between himself and these other selves ready to be put on like costumes for a show. In that way the part, though interchangeable, never owned or consumed him. *She* kept fading back and forth, in and out of the various expectations the world seemed to have of her. Role-playing, the sociology teacher said, her mouth going round on the hub of that word. For some, like poor Diane, her suitemate in the black dorm last year, the roles suddenly became real—Diane and her dude playing a street game, with a little heroin thrown in for kicks. "Skag's not much different'n hash—really it's not!" donning a red Afro wig, got up the spangled style of a night-club star. But Diane and her man were busted, both now in jail, all of it started from a need for drama, a drawing-on of interesting roles.

"More coffee?" asked the waitress, aiming a Silex at them.

"Yes, please. I like your hospitality." He wasn't a good enough actor, his voice not quite sincere-sounding. With a hate-look she swirled away. "Okay, okay, who wants coffee anyhow?"

They sat two hours, ignoring the woman's glares and the unpaid check, the last thing left on the table after all utensils and breakfast ware had been removed. They took turns going to the toilet so as not to lose their booth. "Now c'mon, Bernice, tell me more about Ronald." He wanted a full account, fair exchange for confidences poured forth last night.

She tried to speak off-hand. "He was beautiful, Billy, but he split—my Ronald." Harvard pre-med, son of her parents' friends from their Chicago days, delighted to take advantage of the new opportunities for blacks. ("Old crimson-and-white Harvard—can you believe it? Turning black!") Never sucked into thinking *he* was worth all that much, though he scored fairly high on the College Boards. Attended to his books, he'd do good *later*. "Agitation's not my thing." But she couldn't imagine him ever practicing medicine in Harlem or Bedford-Stuyvesant, where he was needed. He had his sights on a good research post, probably in cancer, at Sloan-Kettering.

She'd go up to Cambridge weekends and stay with him in his Hicks Street flat south of Mass Ave. Saturday night excursions to Roxbury, where they could eat cheap (seafood, not soul-food), take in a movie, and ride the MTA back late, walking home from Harvard Square, arms tenderly about each other. Street-corner dudes there in the black section of Cambridge would whistle and stomp as they passed. Their hot fanfare over sex exceeded Ronald's, who was matter-of-fact. In the beginning, since she was a virgin, it helped. Then the absence of impulse and passion, the jar of KY gel on the night table, made their love too routine. If she ever let go in bed it might shock him—so she never felt the urge to. He was gentlemanly, "Does that hurt? You okay?" and wanted to know each time if she'd come. Shouldn't a man *know*?

He warned they mustn't fall in love. With five, six years of schooling still ahead, he had to "keep control of my feelings." A peculiar thing to say. Wasn't flattered, as he seemed to think she ought to be, that she was such a temptress he had to watch out or he'd swoon and be gone. No, he meant he was reserving a small piece of himself for *her*, and gradually she understood which part it was. She had all of him down there, but not his head or heart, and without *those*, what good was the rest of him? Typical scientist, he'd cut himself into measurable portions in order to "understand and be in control."

Like her parents, Ronald embraced science because it was committed to reason, free of illogic, prejudice, and half-truths. In a laboratory nobody could argue with the results of an experiment properly undertaken. While they inhabited medical corridors, they could almost forget the trauma of the ghettos—except when the maimed and bleeding stumbled in from the streets.

She went on the pill as soon as they became lovers, a prescription advised by her mother (who'd introduced them). With gynecological good sense, she approved the termination of Bernice's virginity. Her father, fortunately, said nothing, indulged in a little old-fashioned reticence and pretended he didn't know what was going on. Her parents were so practical and adapted to their world, able to undertake their lives with satisfaction, doing good and at the same time well paid. What black couple had it better? They'd thrown their lives into medicine, but it'd narrowed them. "They're incredibly remote to me, Billy, but I sure don't want 'em to know."

"You're lucky Ronald drifted. He'd've been more of the same."

"Nobody's lucky to be passed over, in preference to somebody else."

"She was white, I'll bet. Threw herself at him."

"How'd you guess? Barbara Ann Halper, a medical student, too. Informers told me."

"*They* thought they were being good friends."

"I asked. Couldn't stand not knowing . . . what happened."

After leaving Pat's Diner, they strolled to the beach on the Sound with its sign, NO SWIMMING, WATERS UNSAFE FOR BATHING, and looked at the brown, polluted water lapping dismally at the shore, much of the sand washed away in winter storms. Four years ago, arriving as freshmen, she and the girls hoped to swim here, hot September afternoons, but were forbidden by the town fathers. Only taxpayers and residents could use the beach; the college, being tax-exempt and full of transients, had no right to this strip. Now, who'd want it? Behind them the village had a New England look: white-painted houses, great trees bright with new leaves, and the sound of church bells.

"Let's go back to *our* church, Bernice."

"Only the Unitarians would have us, looking the way we do. You need a shave."

"I do? Really?" Smiling, he rubbed the patch of stubble on his chin. The rest of his jaw and those baby white cheeks looked completely adolescent.

No other blacks sitting in the pews, when they entered. "Pew" was probably the wrong word. Benches. No candles, lace altar cloths, gleaming cross, velvet runners, or stained-glass windows. Just a plain oak table with a small stack of collection-plate baskets, and a large Bible. The congregation had the frumpy, intelligent look of college professors and their overly bright wives. Two couples actually *were* from the college and, recognizing Bernice, smiled and nodded. History and French, both men sharp-witted, with big student followings. Surely they hadn't come here to *learn* anything! What was the point of their going through old rituals, following a manner of worship but substituting reason for faith? At least her honest, atheistic parents stayed home Sunday mornings and watched Camera Three at eleven o'clock, imbibing culture instead of religion.

The ungowned organist in a pink Easter outfit sat down to play a little Bach, crisp, precise in her attack; no swooning seas here, no bath of religious emotion in that music, only a fearful symmetry. When she let up on the last chord, she rose with a look of satisfaction, as if the logic of the music had again convinced her all's-right-with-the-world, Bach's in God's heaven.

Emerging from the wings, the clergyman to her surprise was Kathy's literature teacher, Mr. Seligman. A Bahai, Kathy said (*"The* only universal religion"), but no doubt Unitarianism had to do as second best. Mr. Seligman, grave as a rabbi, read a long passage from Erich Fromm about respect and love for oneself, the necessary preliminary to love from others. Why did she find his earnestness so funny? Only because she remembered his flabby, black-haired chest as he lay on Kathy's blanket in a swoon, on the lawn of the Manse? Transcendental in his talk, full of the Oversoul, he was better at fathering babies than as spokesman of universal forces. He had two adorable little boys, miniature reproductions of himself.

Hymn book in hand, Billy belted out a song like a paid choir soloist. We're making their Sunday, by God. If Billy just didn't get *too* carried away. The sermon concerned corruption in high places, Washington politics, and Mr. Seligman avoided mentioning God as if the deity were inoperative. The point was, *Know thyself!* Thank you Mr. Emerson, Plato, and Socrates. Someday we shall discover the true navel of the world; and while we're looking, where the hell am I?

Blanket folded neatly as a poncho, Bernice followed Billy out of church and waited in line to shake hands with Mr. Seligman, who remembered her because she was one of the "good" blacks at the college. Billy chatted away. A few more bushy-tailed questions and they'd end up invited home with the Seligmans for chicken dinner. Maybe not a half-bad idea—no, a *terrible* idea!

"You sure enjoying yourself," she said as they pulled away.

"That's my act, Bernice, don't you believe it. Inside teardrops are fallin'."

"The act over now? Didn't all that Washington talk make you think of going back home?"

"There you go, tryin' to get rid of me."

"What do *you* think we oughta do?" Not that she'd go along with it.

"I—I don't know. I was just . . . wingin' it."

"Hate to be the one—to shoot you down."

"Bernice, what're you looking at me like that for?"

She felt unfamiliarly certain. A stroke of illumination bright as the shaft of heavenly light hitting the Virgin in Christmas cards. She knew exactly what she was about. "Billy, there's something *I* know, you don't. And it's not fair. Kathy spent last night . . . with a Princeton friend, James. Ever mention James to you? I mean, she's been goin' with him for months, but nothing heavy. Maybe *that's* why she never said anything about him. Or maybe Kathy's like that."

"She's like that."

"Just friends, Billy—till this weekend, with you coming up here and—anyhow—she decided to stay the whole weekend with him. Don't know where they ended up . . . or what happened . . . but it's funny how it worked out—I mean, that you put 'em together that way. I mean peculiar, ironic, or something. Oh, Billy, don't *look* at me like that! You said yourself you didn't believe in the auto crash—and you were right!"

"Wow! Guess *I've* been totaled!"

"There's a train-on-the-hour, come on." She grabbed his arm.

"I *knew* she must be with somebody . . . suppose that's why I threw myself on the ground last night?"

"Come on, you can make that train."

They moved quickly toward the station. In the aftermath of her sudden burst of honesty, the landscape seemed laid low; there was nothing left to be said. He looked as if he wanted to take his hurt out of her sight, to feed upon his unhappiness by himself on the

long train journey home. They arrived at the depot just in time
for him to buy a ticket and climb aboard. He pecked her cheek in
farewell, his lips cold.

He'd be a better actor for it, since wounds that don't kill make
you stronger. Strange, though. Where'd the sudden vicious streak
of honesty come from? So easy to be destructive. People are doing
it all the time! Should anyone ask—if there're repercussions—just
say the Devil made me do it.

Kathy can go to hell! But oh, Lord, what've I done to that kid?

They arrived at the Cathedral in time for the ecclesiastic procession, the robed choir a magnificent troupe of the Lord's
Crusaders, marching, marching, in the stone-slab aisle, followed
by priests in princely gowns, their faces sternly aglow with the
religious importance of this moment. Prickles flew down Kathy's
back like the tongue of the Lord. She almost swooned, her face
felt hot. She pressed close against James and felt unaccountably
sexy; awakened by him, she was susceptible to anything. God
would have to understand.

The vast interior was suffused with a murky light from the
brilliantly glowing stained-glass window high over Harlem. All
sound became part of another dimension. Shuffling footfalls on
the stone; the organ and choir song blended, died away. How the
priests swung their censers this way and that! The high groinings
seemed to capture the clouds of God.

"O Lord, I believe!" she murmured fervently, eyes closed. She
was only saying it to herself, she knew, though God's habitat lay
somewhere near, if she could just attach herself to that place.
Walt Whitman had imagined himself marching into the bodies
of the lowest prostitutes, bricklayers, sailors, and farmers of the
land, breathing a spiritual force which was as unseen though present as blood in clams and oysters, the juice of a cut flowerstalk—
all that holy nectar of creation. Even now she hadn't quite gotten
all of his semen out of her and a little from way up somewhere
came down while she sat there. "I love you, I love you God," she
said again, thinking that if He listened to anybody here, surely it'd
have to be her. But how could she tell? What was faith but an acceptance of never being able to tell and yet *knowing?*

I don't know, though. I want it to happen, but it hasn't yet, whatever it is I'm longing to feel, about becoming part of God's universe.

They rose, spoke the order of worship, sat down, knelt, listened, and prayed. "Surprise me, God. Don't make me have to work this hard to reach you, when I already know that nobody climbs into heaven. You've got to be lifted up and taken away."

After the service they stood to watch the religious mummers leave the chancel and flow down the Red Sea division of audience, out into the real world at the rear. "I think Catholics—Episcopalians—really've got the right idea," James said as they walked out. "God wants style in it all."

His flipness bothered her. She couldn't smile and dismiss religion this easily—remembering his fake piety.

In a drugstore she waited while he phoned Mr. Pennell to ask when he might view James's paintings. "Wants us up for brunch. More champagne and Beluga caviar—how does *that* sound?" He cupped his hand over the mouthpiece as if strangling somebody in the phone booth.

"No, no . . . *you* go if you want. But I don't—"

"Kathy, *please*. It's important to me."

"I know, but not to *me*, see. If we go to Mr. Pennell's—I don't know—he's getting us involved with him somehow. We can't be our own *persons*."

James squatted in the folding-door booth, light gone; in the shadows his handsome face brooded. Was she making him choose between career and love-life?

"Mr. Pennell? We—ah—talked it over . . . and Kathy feels, I mean, she's got to get back up to the college . . . I mean, there's the problem of this high school boy following her around—remember? But maybe we could come up for a *little* while . . ." When he noticed her fiery glance, he closed the door.

She rushed out of the drugstore, down the street to Broadway, slipped into a cigar store which also sold newspapers and found a phone booth like James' cubicle to hide in. Taking down the receiver, she pretended to be talking and expected James at any moment to open the door and drag her out, into his arms.

But she'd been too clever and quick in her escape—or he hadn't tried very hard to reach her, if at all. She'd never know. The city itself had lost her and when she emerged fifteen minutes later, she took the 104 bus to Grand Central. A tense helplessness consumed her, as if she'd been put on a grooved track. If he were determined, he'd think of capturing her before the next New Haven train departed. She lingered outside the entrance grill to the ramp, but when he didn't show up, she walked slowly down to the waiting locomotive, every step removing herself from possible rescue by him. Had it been sexist of her to force him to choose between his painting career and their new love life? Perhaps one couldn't have both God and a worldly lover—maybe St. Paul was right. Now she had neither.

Bernice scribbled quickly, with a new ease about her ideas.

And one among the slave women at the marketplace for American merchants knew the devious ways of managing but shunned those methods—for forthrightness. A feeling of one's worth, or lack of it, in the eyes of the white beholders, had so left her with a doubt of her value that she'd placate, scrounge, bend low, just to be thought well of, knowing even as she spinelessly did this, that respect for her was gone. Submissiveness only brought out the brute in the triumpher. Should she ever catch her White master in some mistake, she'd be quick to point out how easily and understandably such a mistake could have been made, in order to fend off the White's anger toward her for having discovered a weakness, an error. The ways of deviousness were infinite, and to a remarkable degree accomplished a certain power.

Wasn't amusing, however, and this didn't go with the preface already laid out.

Now the slave-women were on exhibit at the Manhattan market, like that housemaids show in the Bronx which used to be available to upper middleclass housewives. They could actually come and say, "I'll take *that* one!" because her skin matched the color of breakfast coffee, or because she didn't *look* like a Nigger's nigger but had already taken on the sheen of the White world in some subtle way every White recognized and which meant: "This one will work hard, ask no favors, and accept the wages I pay." Might even be *honest*. Honest as any of 'em are.

Now this new slave-woman has just suddenly decided to speak

her mind, but the moment she opens her mouth, out fly the old blackbirds, and who can ever call them all back again from the trees and skies or wherever they've gone? Her trouble was

The phone rang and Bernice rushed out to answer it, desperate to be rescued from a sentence she couldn't end. "Is this you, Bernice?" Kathy's mother, calling from Washington.

"Kathy's out just now."

"We're terribly worried about her."

"Oh . . . she's okay."

"But—where *is* she? If she's not there . . . I'm afraid we're heading into another period . . . like last fall. You know . . ."

Insidious pull of the confidante. Keep your distance, White Washington lady, this is Bernice here, and I'm a black column. I'll not be toppled.

"What's happening up there? Where *is* Kathy?"

"She had to go off real quick. . . . Friend killed in an auto crash near Boston." Only said that to fill the wire with some cargo, but immediately a cottony deadness, a strain floated along the telephone line, all the way from Washington, D.C. "Somewhere near Natick, I believe it was."

"It's sweet . . . and loyal of you, Bernice, to cover for her. But I've been speaking to Billy's mother, and we know *he* went up to see her this weekend."

"Then he *didn't* get the telegram?" Fake surprise—any straw to grab. "About the funeral in Boston?"

"Came after he'd gone—so naturally they opened it, and called *us* . . . rather concerned. After all, Billy's only seventeen."

"Mrs. Meeker"—she summoned her newfound strength—"you happen to catch me in the middle of trying to write a term paper, so if you don't mind, I'd—"

"Bernice—oh, Bernice!" Now the hidden hysteria came out like a sword. "*Won't* you help?"

"I can't follow Kathy's truths or untruths. Just do what she asks —when it comes to her personal life—if I have to, because we live here together. She told me she was off to Boston and that's all I know. This boy got hisself killed in a head-on near Natick."

"I'm afraid I've hurt your feelings."

"No, ma'am."

"I'm not *blaming* you in the least. It's just that . . . I feel rather responsible for Billy—I mean, to his parents. Kathy got *so* involved with him, over Easter."

"I try to keep out of her affairs."

"You any idea where Billy is?"

"At the moment . . . exactly . . . *no.*"

"Did he show up—there?"

"Oh yeah, he come here all right."

"Ah! Now we're gettin' somewhere. And what did he do?"

"Why—I spent the night with him. What d'yah think of that?" Sassy as could be. A funny intake of breath on the other end. "He's on his way to Washington now."

"Thank you, Bernice." She got off the line immediately.

"And good-by to *you*, Nosy Bitch," she said into the dead phone. "About *time!*" The sociology paper on her desk was a defunct tract compared to the fun of drawing real blood. Too bad she and Billy *hadn't* made love, if he'd been the least interested. She giggled at the idea but caught herself immediately and wondered why such glee possessed her, why she found her power so refreshing. Intervention meant control. Now she could move them all like chess pieces from this square to that. Obviously the foreign service was the right career for her. She'd say one thing to the Arab representatives, another to the Israelis. She'd move through them all, dark, beautiful, and dangerous. All these years her latent powers were undeveloped, never exercised, and they loved her that way.

> The present market is rich and ripe, eager for black limbs and halos of black hair. In hot, summer New York, the colors are right for them. Every merchant wants one out front to show his proper attitude toward the change of times. Another move on the chessboard. Of course! Advance the rooks!
>
> Black man, under your yellow steel hat, hanging from that steel beam out there, what're ya lookin' in here at me for? I got me a desk, telephone, and a fresh, candy-colored blouse each day. I know your high wages, man, I know what's on your mind. Can we meet in the air, though? Somewhere twenty floors up, where the fall could be fatal. I'd hate to go only halfway, wouldn't you?
>
> With our new opportunities, we got a lot to lose, so how do we play it? I think we both like to win, it'd be such a change! Throw me a rivet while you're at it. Put me in place forever. I'm maybe

more loose than I can stand. Only stop lookin' at me that way. Anybody ever tell you, you look good in a yellow steel helmet? Nobody *needs* to tell you! Here comes the crane for me now— I'll be swinging right over.

Bernice rose from her desk and threw herself wearily on the bed.

Kathy burst into the room. "Bernice! Wake up! Oh, God, wait'll you hear what I've been through."

Bernice rubbed her eyes. "What time *is* it, anyhow?"

"We split! James and me split!"

"Had my doubts about him, Kathy. If he was willin' to wait *this* long, I figured he'd be no good in bed."

"No, no, that part was great."

"So?" Bernice yawned and propped herself up on pillows.

Kathy removed her clothes as she told of meeting Mr. Pennell and how James was so busy making contact "he couldn't think of me or anything else. It was disgusting!"

"Didn't plan to marry anyhow, did you?"

"But I thought—we were in love. Oh, why does it sound so foolish even to say the word?"

"So tomorrow when the placement office opens . . . you can go line yourself up for some interviews. Gotta think of the future."

"I haven't the strength!" She'd once told Bernice she craved a job in publishing, an apartment of her own.

"Be independent—of him . . . and your parents."

"Yeah . . ."

"Free yourself from parental bondage." A wicked, mocking smile.

"Bernice, are you laughing at me or something?"

"No, just dead tired. You woke me up."

"The Cathedral of St. John *was* divine! Your soul seems to expand in there . . . lift up."

"Heard a rock concert in that place once."

"It's big enough for anything . . . and there *you* are, puny and helpless, while the organ sounds bigger and bigger. Before you know it, you're in the right perspective . . . with eternity." She stopped because Bernice looked amused, doubted God had *any*-thing to do with it. She drew on her robe to hide her naked body from those cool, watching eyes.

"Before I forget—your mother called."

"She *did*?"

"Told her about the auto crash and all that shit. Cut me down, though. Billy's mother'd phoned *her*."

"Billy! Bernice, did he *come* here?"

"At last you remembered to ask."

"I was so—"

Bernice told how she'd watched over him, actually spent the night on the lawn of the Unitarian church. "And that's what blew your mother's mind . . . when I said I'd slept with him."

"She didn't understand what you—"

"Why make myself clear? It'll do the kid's reputation good at home, won't it?"

"How?"

"At seventeen it's time for a white boy to dip his wick—isn't *that* what everybody'll think? His dad will hand him a cigar and slap him on the back."

"Bernice, you seem . . . different."

"I am. Something weird happened to me at church this morning."

"*You* went to church?" She knew Bernice shunned anything to do with hand-clapping and soul-song, just as some blacks refused to eat watermelon.

"Well, we'd been *out*side all night, so we figured . . . Anyhow, it happened to me there . . . I feel . . . like I turned my skin inside out. Been born anew—don't I look it?"

"You look the same, but you sound changed."

"I'm into *truth*."

"Truth? You mean it's some sect—Christian Truth? Those people who pass out leaflets, like the Jehovah's Witnesses?"

"I mean I'm tellin' the truth." She gave it a Topsy turn and it came out *truff*.

Kathy pulled her challis gown tighter. "Bernice . . . you'd better tell me . . . what it is . . . you're tryin' to say."

"Billy knows you spent last night with James."

"Did you *have* to tell him? Oh, God—now you've really done it! So Mother's heard already—that why she called? They'll jerk me outa this school so fast I won't . . . won't even graduate!"

"Hold it—*I* didn't tell your mother. Now did I say that?"

"But if Billy knows—"

"He might be noble about it, who knows. Maybe he's more of a man than you think. Anyhow, there's no sayin' he'll tell your mother."

"But wasn't he furious—about me and James?"

"It wiped him out—at first—but he'll survive. And think of ways to get even, if I know Billy."

"Like . . . like how?"

"Better save next weekend for him, honey."

"He's gonna come up here again and cause trouble?"

"Trouble? How much trouble to you would it be?"

"He still *wants* me?"

"His turn . . . next weekend."

Ridiculous! Kathy walked into the bathroom to start her tub. Surely Bernice's sex notions were just the sort of easy answer blacks were said to have for every romantic problem: jazz, jellyroll, and everybody feels good again. But it wasn't like her!

Transformations . . . first James and now Bernice. *He* wasn't what he pretended to be either. Knew his own lost-soul but wasn't sorry, just as mad people keep telling you they're perfectly sane. Maybe you couldn't get near heaven merely by having a longing for the Lord. Something always has to make the issue urgent. That astronaut who walked on the moon also saw God out there and ever since he has been on the preacher trail—hardly what he imagined when he was shot into space. If she put on saffron-colored robes and marched on Forty-second Street with the shaved-headed Hare Krishnas, nobody would believe her faith was real. Her parents would nab her off the curbstone and haul her to Washington, turn her over to Dr. Schuman, who had that way of fixing his eyes upon her, so that *his* glance was to become her own.

Bernice knocked, pushed the door. "Before you get in the bath . . . I gotta pee."

Kathy returned to the bedroom, glanced at the term paper on Bernice's desk, and began to read.

> Nobody sees the manacles under the office desk, where her ankle is chained to the floor. Her paycheck is just enough to cover her pussy. I'm a woman, she says, naked except for that narrow

green diaper with the Mason's eye over the pyramid, and George
Washington half winking—you got to believe it!

George Washington now says, you come on down to my university, Bernice, and I'll teach you a thing or two.

Bernice speaks: You know, if you prick me I shall bleed. Only
you can't see it—you don't even try! Just because you can't see
blood doesn't mean it's not there. Black is the absence of all
color, we know. And white the presence of too much—so there
seems to be nothing there at all. I speak of the flowing, invisible
wounds, juice of our lives. Blood all over us.

At nine o'clock next morning, Kathy's Community and Society
class left for its last field trip to the Bronx, where it had been in-
terviewing an Italo-American family. "Kathy, you look so . . .
bored! Or are you sick?" asked the professor at the steering wheel,
as they turned into Fordham Road.

"I can't relate to this experience very well."

"You're doing beautifully with those two little Italian girls—
they love you! They'll tell you anything."

"Yeah, but why should I hear it?"

"Because you're . . . an educated woman . . . and you can put
facts together those girls can't."

"But what's the value—of it. To anybody?"

"Listen, Kathy, when all our notes and reports are assembled,
it'll be an amazing study."

"'Fraid I've nothing to say about that family *they* don't know
already."

"Maybe, but the world should know, too."

"Why?"

"Oh, now I get you, Kathy. You're one of these who think science is soulless, getting us nowhere. We should all go back to
magic, Tloth, and tarot cards."

"Before we left, I was reading the Bible, and—"

"Why not turn on a little religion when we arrive? It'll help our
image."

The other passengers came to her defense, as she knew they
would, just to be contentious. But the professor had been through
such playroom rebellions before; he merely smiled and shook his
head.

Why should *she* hover over the lives of those two adolescent

Italian girls and begin the first peck-pecking—when they'd break
the shell of their innocence easily enough themselves in one violent stroke. Fall from grace in one way or another . . . with the
pimply-faced boy next door . . . or sucked into some disastrous
adventure.

We of the Community and Society class hereby proclaim the
discovery of a family in the Bronx possessing two teen-age virgin
girls, still dewy-eyed and in a state of God's grace. Only a matter
of time, however . . . and nobody can predict *who* or *what* might
initiate the falling, when it'll come, or how they'll respond. My report on these two girls is now complete: nothing whatever to say.
It's exactly as we've thought all along.

But the day in the Bronx distracted her; no time to think.
When she returned to the Manse at four, Bernice was still at her
desk.

"Wish *I'd* taken a course that went into the field. Tired of sit-
tin' here on my ass."

"Thank God, I'll never have to take another of these trips."

"Italian family throw you out?"

"No, they loved it! Talked their silly heads off. And we all got
diddled, I think. I'm not sure. I don't know . . . anything any
more."

"James called . . ."

"I can't talk to him—good thing I wasn't here."

"Billy, too."

"Not Mother?"

"Not yet anyhow."

"I think I'll go into a nunnery."

"Do that . . . we'll have 'em send your diploma there."

"*Seriously*, Bernice, you know of any—retreat—or someplace
like that?"

"What would *you* do in a nunnery?"

"Where I can meditate for a while . . . on everything. That
sound so awful? I lost my soul somewhere, and if I don't find it
pretty soon . . . I'll go crazy!"

"*Soul!* Don't you know it's *us* who got soul?"

"Please, Bernice, don't black-face me—not now."

"Then why'd you ask me to room with you this year? Wanted
nothin' but black-face the whole time."

"You mean it?"

"Kathy, you don't know *nothin'* about me."

"Maybe not." She remembered the strange wording of Bernice's sociology paper.

"Think I'm good ol' Bernice . . . who'll take shit from anybody, but one day I'll surprise you."

"You getting militant *now?* After all these years!"

"Gettin' to be myself. The alternative."

"*Yourself?* How do you know? And if you answer, I won't be able to stand it. I just want a nunnery, a monastery—anything—a place away from it all. I've done my Whitman, and now I've finished Community and Society. There's only Panaceas and Principles left. Maybe I can get by, turning in my diary . . . reading notes, really they are. It's legitimate, sort of."

"I *did* hear of some kind of nunnery . . . near Harmon, I think."

"Really?"

"Read about it in the paper. The bishop is trying to break up the place, don't know what for. They're going their own way . . . defying Rome, Cardinal Cooke . . . I don't know. It was all in the *Times* not long ago."

"Can you find out?"

"Look it up yourself, New York *Times* Index."

But since senior work had to be completed this week, Kathy first had to find out if her professor would accept notes on Tolkien as one of the Panaceas.

"How original!" he said, smiling, but he couldn't read her childish handwriting, so she spent the next three days typing it up, adding passages where her thoughts seemed too skimpy.

On Wednesday, a long letter from James:

Dear Kathy,

You ran out on me—won't answer phone calls. What am I to think, after our beautiful time together Saturday night? Why are you angry? What have I done?

I made love to you, my God we made love! I told you how I felt. Everything was okay until you got jealous or something, when I began thinking about my work—instead of you. The more I considered it, the stranger it seemed—and then *I* got sore. I went to see Mr. Pennell again—"Hawley" I call him now. He looked at my paintings and didn't buy anything. Does that please you? He thought it was "pretty good for student work"—does that satisfy you?

Here I go falling into your traps, your games. I suppose it was foolish to expect a sale just-like-that! But one good thing might come from it all. He told me who to send my slides to. A SoHo gallery where they're interested in new painters. So we'll see.

I'm only going into all this because you should know right now I love my work. If I could get started in what I really want to do —if I just could!

I know you think there's something crass in the way I go after things I want. You're jealous. Figure I should cut out everything in my life—now that you're in it. I hope you realize by now how impossible that would be. Also, it's being sort of old-fashioned possessive—or do you expect me to be flattered?

Painting is my real love, too. It's a spiritual activity—right? Up there with the God you're so busy thinking about. Maybe I shouldn't have strung along with you, reading the Bible and praying, but I thought there was something beautiful in our times together, doing it, so I didn't mind. I wasn't as false as you think— I really hoped I might get somewhere with it.

Isn't that what you hope, too? Unless you see religion as a kind of state of existence where it's possible for you to approve of yourself. I wonder sometimes. That puts *self* first and isn't religion at all.

I got that idea because you labeled it *self*-interest when I suddenly tried to further my painting career. I wasn't thinking so much of *me*, or getting money, or having a reputation—all that career stuff—just whether or not anybody'd ever look at my work and say *go on*, it's getting somewhere interesting. The work is what I'm thinking about, not *me* doing it.

Don't know . . . if I'm making this clear, what I mean. There's a certain *self*-less-ness in it all, I can't explain. I'm very humble about it—not just throwing my ego all over the canvas. I'm not thinking about *myself* all the time, only whether I'm doing a good painting.

Maybe *you* shouldn't think so hard about yourself and God. Try being more naturally open—a different way. I don't know, anything, any more.

Are we ever going to see each other again?

> Your lover,
> James

She burst into tears and stuffed the letter into her bag, hurried out of the mailroom. Everything he said was right, but how could she correct herself—and be worthy of him?

Except—he still didn't explain his duplicity in sleeping with other girls all winter and not telling her he was doing it on the side. Not confiding in her, only pretending to be intimate. However, what claim did she have on him then? Saturday night made the difference.

What do I mean by that? Sex is sex, isn't it?

She'd squeezed out twenty pages of typed reading notes and, since the professor had gone for the day, slipped the paper under his door. School was now over for her. She returned to her room, careful to avoid running into anybody she knew, closed the door, and then read James's letter again. It was so beautiful and sincere. Somehow, she felt dreadful. How could she ever face him again? What did she have in her life to counter this . . . testament?

Bernice heard Kathy's sobs when she entered, blubbering so typical of spoiled white college girls traumatized by life's experiences. She'd heard their whoops of despair over the friend who'd taken an overdose, although the screaming-siren trip to the hospital, and the stomach pump, managed to salvage the would-be victim for society and future life. She'd witnessed the plummeting dismay of girls left stranded when their parents split, took on new mates, produced babies to supplant them. She'd seen the betrayals and roommate deceptions in the very moment knowledge dawned . . . the grief of one girl whose friend was picked up as a pusher in a Cornell clean-up.

Cry your eyes out—go on! Nice and clean you'll be again—after an emotional curettage like this . . . ready for the next impregnation. Who says I'm flunking biology?

"Bernice?" Waver-voiced.

"What's goin' on here?" She walked briskly into the room, tough as a nurse's aide, read James's letter, heard Kathy's story all over again. When the phone rang, red-light signal flashing in the room, Bernice went to answer it.

"Glad it's *you*," Billy said. "I need to know what's happening."

"How should I know?"

"Kathy's there?"

"Yeah, but she's . . . indisposed right now. You better not try talkin' to her."

"I've got to find out when I can see her."

"Billy—what's the point of it? What do you expect to get out of it?"

"I can't help myself." A sadness in his voice, he sounded older, less likely to crescendo himself into oblivion.

Something could be made of this kid yet, if the honing were done right . . . if done in time. "Anyhow, you're goin' about it the wrong way. Asking *my* advice and all."

"But what do you think?"

"If I was you I'd just call up from the Paradise Motel on Route 13 and say, God damn it, Kathy, you let me see you in Washington, and if I was good enough for you there, I'm good enough for you here. So you come right over to this motel, and we'll have it out."

"That's an idea."

"Too late, Billy . . . you put yourself in the junior department, hanging around last weekend."

"I always get it straight from you—don't I?"

"Do you?"

"Even if it's shit from a fan. So maybe I'll take the shuttle—if I can lay hands on some bread."

"Billy, don't listen to me!"

"So long now."

When she returned to the room, Kathy had dried her face and was combing her hair. "Wasn't for me?"

"Yeah, it was—Billy—I put him off."

Kathy leaped up and embraced her. "Oh, Bernice—thank you! Thank you!"

"Don't *hang* on me, Kathy. Don't *count* on me."

Our problem is, their reality isn't *our* reality, and that's why black skin or brown skin, or *dark* skin—what have you—should, should what? The blood is as red under it, in each case, and no transfusion centers in hospitals make any other distinction than Type A or Type O, etc. Wherein lies the difference then?

Dear white liberal Jewish intellectual lady reading this: if you got this far, you know I been shitting you. Like always, I try to tell it like you *think* it is, not like I know it is. And somehow I can't help it. Stop me before I kill more! In my sweet black heart my old red blood keeps pumping away. I sit here, like it's the only thing to do—to think about it all the time. No way! I tell you, I'm one black woman who knows the difference but cannot speak it, and can you guess why? No, not because my head's screwed on different, or that I've stopped taking my daily dose of Black Sisterhood propaganda (which I have), it's that nobody can fill me with substance or refine me with opinions until I've become Bernice herself—until I come into my own. Nothing much has happened yet to make me real. I'm just like Kathy and all these other chicks, don't you see? I'm waiting patiently (not so easily) for an awful fix, for the bleeding, and then the healing, the scars. After that I can be a battered old know-it-all, and you can argue with me, and I'll give it back. Right now I'm just a dusky backdrop, but I promise, I won't always be only that. I'm trying even now to throw myself into some trouble, see if I can wiggle out.

I don't call this a life. I can't even feel it. At least when I lived with Sylvie and the Sisters I could hide my emptiness in their rage, in doctrine. You see, I haven't acquired individuality as yet, and that's the assumption everyone around here begins with: that you're some body at least. Therefore, I have no preferences, and I certainly can't be counted on. Usually I give way, which is why the Citizenship Award will probably be coming to me at Senior Honors. I'm needed by Kathy and her friends, but they'll never guess *my* needs, for the pure reason I don't have any. Maybe *that's* why Ronald replaced me with Barbara Ann Halper. Couldn't figure out where I was, even when I lay right next to him in bed.

I know, dear Professor, Teacher, you'd have a lot of advice for me, and that's why you're never going to have a chance to give it. I don't need it from you. I ought to just listen to my inner blood singing its old song, and fit my own lyrics to it. God knows what they'll be. I cannot surely misspend many more years of my life without tripping over my own black feet. Then I shall pick myself up and walk on. Let me do it by myself, please.

I hear you talking, Teach—and I know why you're saying it, but don't you understand? The words fall down through these great big cracks in me. Disappear, never come to anything. I should think knowledge of the futility of helping me would discourage you from trying. Maybe you half realize the situation—and you're careful never to know what a waste your efforts are. I believe you're in the teaching-bag for your own health, sanity, and emotional kicks. You practically tackled me at the door of your office, the first day I dropped by to inquire about Sociology—you wanted me in the course so bad. One black girl. You needed the queen of spades in the midst of all those heart-queens. You know the girls wanted me there to make them feel right about themselves and these times. One hour-and-a-half seminar spent shoulder-to-shoulder—with a nigger.

They think I'm beautifully black, and I know from the mirror I'm not half bad, but I wish they didn't glow with advance approval of me. They shoot right past, with those looks, not even coming near. Let me keep my distance from that blonde who's making it with the cute black dude I see hanging around the Manse so much. Why in the world would she think she had a special relationship with me just because of *that*? Will they never understand? I wish he'd pay attention to *me* and really dig us up some trouble, bad trouble even. Not drugs or ripping off things from stores—but something I can't imagine—completely absorbing, the way it is for Kathy, with her problems. Something so terrific I have to turn to God, even though I know a prayer won't get me out. But that's how the lines'll be made in the Mississippi mud, how the smooth brown skin of me will get punctured and my blood under the thin epidermis will flow just like your blood or anybody's. Type A. Type B. Type O. (Which am I?) And others less known. My transfusion awaits me (please, no sickle cell anemia or hepatitis). I graduate from college the end of next week. Look for me under the Mortar Board. That's me with the fringed tassel in my eyes. I don't know how else you'll spot me, though they've put me for show in the very front row. I'll step up smartly to the podium and accept the B.A. scroll, my hand out to the president. He knows my name and he'll smile, for I've been one of the good ones. There's hope for society, I dearly believe—

In nothing.

"Hello—Kathy? Look, I want to see you—" She almost hung up the phone in reflex, hearing Billy's roosterish, strong voice, insistent in her ear.

"I'm *here* again."

"You're where?"

"Just down the highway. Paradise Motel on Route 13, and that's our lucky number, Kathy. Having dinner sent over for us—you like Chinese, I remember. They'll deliver."

"What're you doing in a *motel*?"

"Ain't a restaurant for miles around—far as I can figure."

"You drove all the way from Washington?" In a stolen car—his father's Mustang, without permission?

"No, no—took a cab here from the station. I ain't got wheels, Kathy."

"But you were just here—last weekend . . ."

"Who needs wheels? I'm sending a cab, so you can join me."

"I've—I've got other plans, Billy." What though?

"James again?" Matter-of-factly. "Well, I got here first, didn't I?"

"I didn't invite you up. I don't know anything about it—why you came all the way up here again."

"You said last month you'd—"

"Oh, that was in Washington! And I said *some*time, not *any*time—there's a difference. My life's pretty complicated right now. I can't take on anything more."

"I'm only asking you to come over—share a meal, if you can't stay all night."

"All night? Why'd I do that?" It came out ingenuous—Billy was practically her kid brother, after all. "I'm surprised they'd let you *be* there."

"Oh, my parents don't mind."

"I mean, the motel owner—letting you *be* there without a car." Considering your age.

"Why'd he care? You don't do anything with a car except park it in front."

"Just . . . just wondered."

"I've signed up and paid for the room—tonight and tomorrow."

"The *weekend*, in a motel!"

"Not by myself—I expect you'll want to see me—don't you?" A slight faltering at the end, unable to carry it through. "I'll send a cab to pick you up—in, say—half an hour?"

"Billy, I—"

"I'll pay the driver in advance."

"Oh, I know you've got money, but you see—" What was the point of it? Unless they fell back into the innocent companionship of youth. Of course he had other ideas, but they could be quashed in no time. If James called and hoped to see her—argue with her—she could have Bernice say "Kathy's gone for the weekend . . ." To Dartmouth, Williams, Amherst . . . to the May

Fling, the Spring Hop, the Relays Ramble. One of those prom events they'd been reviving all over New England, couples dressing up like Fred and Ginger. "I'll have to think a minute, Billy."

"If you think—you won't!"

True, she longed to escape for a while, and with no nunnery in the offing, maybe the nursery would have to do. Long ago they'd slept on a Washington screened-in porch, playing house. Trouble was, in a nowhere landscape like the Paradise Motel, Billy'd have nothing to hold onto except his fantasies. Could she handle him if he got ardent? Of course! "Billy, you're not getting me into trouble—with your folks and mine. I mean they *do* know where you are?"

"Where do you think I got the bread?"

"I don't now . . . just asking." It seemed unlike them, that's all.

"Sweet-and-sour okay? It's Szechuan coming—you go for Szechuan, you said."

"Oh, sure." Safe with him, surely. No phone calls could find her, nobody could ferret out her intentions or spy on her. Let James wonder where she'd gone, let him worry. "A double-minded man is unstable in all his ways," the Bible said, and surely his pretending to love God was a clue to his way of loving her. He tried to mix art into it, but the fact remained, "Whosoever . . . be a friend of the world is the enemy of God," and no friend of mine. But why did she still feel this awful ache of love in the bottom of her stomach? Stabbed by him, his white blood now mixed with hers and red as could be, inside her skin, two lives in one.

"You'll be at the entrance gate—for the cab to pick you up?"

"How'll I get back?"

"There're two beds in this room. You don't have to go back tonight."

Making love with him would be like going to bed with one's brother—but why didn't *he* feel the same about her? She could be having her period. He'd have to understand a basic fact of nature like that. But would he believe it? In a motel room, cooped up close, couldn't he *tell*? Hard to guess the extent of his experience thus far, he was so good at pretending.

"Half an hour—for the cab? That'll give you enough time? The Chinese are due an hour from now."

"And egg roll—that's coming too?"

"The whole chink bit!"

"Well, all right then. Just a visit, understand." A fine private supper and a good night's sleep. Since he cared so much about her, he'd do whatever she said. "Like old friends—we'll be—right?"

"Sure, Kathy, you know me."

She packed her white leather overnight case with toothbrush, Dr. Lyon's powder, a nightgown, sweater, nail polish remover and a bottle of polish, pantyhose, and packet of Tampax, for it was nearly time. Her things seemed poignant, rather pathetic; she felt sorry for herself in these meagre manifestations, shut up in a mirrored box. Bernice, fortunately, wasn't around to leer and not-believe the story of where she'd be for the night, should anybody call. She closed the lid. The good-luck JESUS LOVES ME button rattled in the bottom like a medallion for her journey.

Not until reaching the sign-out desk did she realize she'd made no lie-provision for a name, address, and telephone number—which the new college rules demanded. All the girls fibbed about where they'd be, but the administration didn't care so long as *they* were off the hook in case the girl got murdered. She signed Hawley Pennell's name ("Uncle") and gave the Central Park West address, drew a line through "telephone" and wrote "It's in the book." The taxicab waited just beyond the barbed-wire barricade, and she nodded to the driver. The guard on duty looked her up and down with lust-heavy eyes. Was her motel destination so obvious?

No, the guards here had sex on the mind all the time, from their chastity-belt function, as she knew from her experience with Oscar last fall. She hated to remember that binge of promiscuity or even try to justify why she'd done it—such a time of confusion. Now with God the center of her being, all had changed. He didn't know it yet, but He was with her.

Since Billy hadn't given the motel room number, she wondered how to find him at the Paradise without brazenly inquiring of the manager, but as they drove up she saw him pacing beside the tulips, hair blowing wild in the wind, dressed in a black turtleneck, dark denim trousers, pointy cowboy boots. He rushed forward as if the golden coach had arrived, paid the driver, tipping so generously the cabby got out and opened the door for her.

"Room seven, right there," Billy said to him.

Her case in the driver's hand looked silly, like a large purse; he walked ahead and placed it inside. "Now you kids have a good time—hear?" Unable to keep the grin from his face, a lovely, happy, voluptuous grin.

After he'd driven off, she asked: "Were you waiting out there long?"

"Kathy, you look terrific! Better'n I remembered, even." Beanpole body hard against her—the embrace sudden and too charged with stagy effects. He combed her hair with his fingers, like a Ronald Colman or Clark Gable. If only he wouldn't *try* so hard.

"Oh, there's John Chancellor," she said. "Don't you think we oughta watch?"

Billy broke away, sorry to have forgotten possible intrusion from the TV. It was seven-ten and NBC had already moved from Washington to the world. "Want a drink?"

"What've you got?"

"There—" He pointed to a fifth of Johnny Walker, two-thirds full.

"You drank all *that* already?" He didn't *seem* drunk. His mouth tasted of anxiety, lips rubbery cold.

"I grabbed this bottle before I left."

He must've raided wallets, too. Money for the shuttle, train trip, taxis, and this motel room, with its sinister chemical-flower disinfectant odor and Mediterranean-style furniture, pictures of flamenco dancers on the walls. Would Billy's folks blame her for ruining him—causing him to do desperate and dishonest deeds?

Billy poured her a strong one over ice cubes, in honey-comb plastic glasses; they sat on the edge of the bed and watched John Chancellor. Billy put his arm around her waist, while his eyes remained fixed on the screen. She felt terribly distant from him, took a big gulp of Scotch for comfort. "This is great, isn't it?" he asked during a commercial, still not looking at her.

"Yeah." Seedy elegance. Twenty-one-inch color TV and turd-colored wall-to-wall "sculptured" carpet. He'd probably shelled out thirty bucks. Easter vacation in Washington at those stupid parties, he'd been biting, irreverent, good company. They felt superior to their setting, a little bit up out of childhood. Now all that home background vanished. He was just seventeen-year-old high school Billy trying to be big time on Route 13 with a girl he might guess was somewhat experienced, comparing his perform-ance with others. How vastly maternal she felt toward him! If she could just fold him to her bosom and comfort his wretched anxi-ety, without their *doing* anything.

The whisky got to him quite quickly, and he giggled through David Brinkley's Journal, though there wasn't anything funny about SALT agreements regarding missile-counts. "We *are* get-ting some Chinese food, aren't we?"

"Hungry? Me, too."

Just after "And good-night for NBC news," knocking on the door. She flicked off the set. "What perfect timing!" Eager to praise something.

"Right on cue." He almost stumbled on the bas-relief rug as he moved toward the door.

They sat down to eat. Clear plastic utensils, limp paper plates. The Szechuan sauce was so hot it seemed to eat right through the picnic ware. "Think what it's doing to our stomach walls!" she laughed. As long as they could be doing something, it was all right. But after supper, how would they spend the evening? "San-ford and Son" would help, but she was loath to mention it. "More tea?"

"I've had enough."

"There's still a little rice, Billy."

"*You* take it." He strolled over to the TV and turned it on, slumping into a chair nearby. Familiar noise of heavy studio laughter. They succumbed to Redd Foxx, found relief in pro-gramed reactions; normalcy flooded the room.

She's eaten too much rice and bean sprouts, felt bloated. When she went over to the twin beds, Billy was too busy looking at the program to entertain ideas because of her sudden move to recline. His neck just under the black hair, which hung down like a cowlick, seemed awfully vulnerable and thin.

"More tea?" he asked, rising as the program ended. He made no move to shut off the monitor of America.

"No thanks."

"Water's cold anyhow. We're through, I guess. I'll just dump all this junk into the garbage can."

"It was very, very good." She felt at home now with him. TV set blaring, they could be two kids anywhere together, in a situation which had nothing to do with wild sin in a motel room. But after tossing out the canisters, he sidled over to where she lay and cupped her left breast in his hand, rubbing the nipple. "Oh, Billy, I'm so full, please!"

He left her immediately, as if he'd done nothing other than take a trip to the fridge for a beer during the commercial. He plopped down in front of the set and watched the next program, mesmerized by it; he could always find home base right there. At nine o'clock he fixed himself a highball, though she declined. She pretended absolute fascination with the TV, as if their bodies, personalities, and thoughts had been evacuated for the evening. "Isn't this nice?" she said smiling, so he'd not worry. Eventually they'd settle back and sleep like old friends, completely relaxed. What a fine, restful night it'd be!

Accompanied by remote, snappy TV dialogue, Billy loomed over her single bed, lay down. The saggy spring-mattress threw them into a sandwich. Even while running his hand up and down her bare leg, he kept looking at the screen, as if the program had produced him, lobotomized but animated.

The ceiling was sandblown plaster, Sahara-colored, a wasteland of unevenness up there. She stared and stared at it while his probing hands roamed everywhere on her terrain, an explorer who didn't know the region. "I'm so full yet!" She lay cowlike, passively feminine, as if she'd no idea what his masterful notion could be. The TV light played upon the small rocks and crags of the ceiling, and she kept gazing up there. He rolled her over slightly to unfasten her skirt zipper and unbutton her blouse, his fingers like chopsticks, bony and quick, yet clumsy in their task. Still she wasn't alarmed—could stop him at any moment. When she felt his hands on her bare back she cried out. "How cold!"

All that beanpole body and not enough blood to fill the extremities. Maybe scare had chilled him. Now the commercial concerned acid indigestion, and the stomach-sack in the diagram looked the way she felt. He palmed her cheek to kiss her lips again, his mouth cool as plastic. His love-making was merely acting, but to speak her thoughts would only drive him to prove her wrong.

When he got her blouse open the sight of her breasts seemed to arouse him. He kissed them again and again, his tongue warm and slippery. All this was like a secret seduction in a back room, the family watching video dangerously nearby, with no idea that while simulated life on the screen absorbed them, real life was happening just a few feet away.

His hands were still icy, and she pushed his fingers away when he started probing down there. "Can't we turn up the heat or something?"

"Yeah—yeah, sure." He leaped from the bed. Still all in black, he was like the puppet manipulators in Kabuki theater. He pushed up the thermostat and the radiators pounded.

"Maybe a hot shower—would help?" she said.

"You want one?"

She mustn't respond at all except in this lumpish way of lying back and *letting* him. Up to a point. "Why don't you go first?"

"Okay." He closed the bathroom door securely. She heard the shower running a long time. Probably not getting warm so much as shiny clean. Propped upon an elbow, she watched a panel of somber, bespectacled men discuss urban transportation problems.

He emerged, towel secure at his waist, and rushed over to the desk for the scotch. "Want a drink?"

"No thanks." What a stork he was, all thin white limbs with a rib cage like a carcass in Death Valley, picked clean by the birds. "You'll catch cold, Billy, come to bed." She threw back the covers and crawled between the sheets. He entered from the other side, casting the towel away at the last second. She felt his frosted feet against her ankles, toenails like icepicks. "Billy—your feet! What's happened to your blood? Why're you so white like this?"

He pressed himself tight against her backside, clinging hard with all his regular bones, nothing special presenting itself in the lower regions. After waiting all this time and now naked full length against her bare back, something passionate should be happening to him. She felt a little insulted, annoyed. Perhaps he was too terrified. "What's happened to your blood? Where'd it go? Isn't there enough for all over you?" She smiled, motherly in her concern. "That's all right, Billy, let's just lie here awhile, till the blood comes back."

He hid his face from her, nuzzling hair behind her left ear. She carefully did not move a muscle. His determination to succeed removed him from her. He'd nothing to do with her except that she was to fulfill his as yet untried idea of himself as a great lover. She kept thinking his problem had to do with not enough blood. He'd grown so suddenly there simply wasn't enough to go around all the time, especially not the extra half pint needed for an erection. Maybe they had the same blood type and she could arrange some day to give him a transfusion.

Lord, why didn't his hands warm up? She was sweating, it was so hot in the room, but his body felt clammy. He rubbed his legs up and down hers for friction heat, but she tired of it pretty quickly. Grasshoppers, crickets. If only they could talk about the problem until it dissolved into unreality. Or shut off the TV set in order to possess their own selves again. She closed her eyes and accepted her punishment from God. Or St. Paul . . . "If any man defile the temple of God, him shall God destroy; for the temple of God is holy, which temple ye are." She'd discussed that passage from Corinthians with James on the lawn of the Manse, the day her feeling of trust crept far enough toward him to reveal her sexual excesses of last autumn. She'd always had a peculiar sense of what was right because it *felt* right, and she'd defied this intuitive knowledge—completely sullied it—last fall when her holy body was used grossly. "Billy, let's *not*, just now. I mean, let's turn off the TV and just go to sleep. We got plenty of time—even tomorrow! I usually wake up early. We should just . . . just be friends and . . . enjoy our companionship. Turn off the set, will you? I've heard all I want, about emission control."

"*Emission* control?" He looked wild-eyed, hair black on the pillow, neck like a waterbird's.

"They're talking about transportation, aren't they?"

"I don't know . . . wasn't listening. How come you were?"

"Couldn't help it. Two things going on at once."

"I'll shut it off, then." He leaped out and streaked over to the set, turned and raced back, like one of the pack of boys who ran naked around the Manse one year. How could he be so shy of anybody seeing his limp, floppy organs—and expect to be an actor?

Most likely in his first part he'd have to strip before a strange audience every night. He thought he had *private* parts! She began to giggle, knew she shouldn't.

"What's so funny?" Angrily, he pressed his chill, hard body against her.

"Nothing, I—I just thought of the streakers!"

"Oh, yeah, how about this?" He flung himself out of bed again and raced to the bottle of scotch. "Hey—you're not even looking!"

Whatever made them imagine it was so great to look at? "You'll get even colder, running around like that." She'd never seen such a naked-looking male: all white limbs like birch sticks and much adangle in front. "Come to bed!"

He set the bottle on the night stand, drank half a tumbler, gurgle, gurgle. "*That* feels better!" And lay back.

"But your feet don't. It's a long way down there. Those veins and arteries are in the provinces. They reach to Antarctica, I think."

"I'll lie still and send down a message."

"What'll it be?"

"Hello down there."

"That all?"

"Let's hear from you—some time."

"How'll they answer?"

"Kathy, we'll *feel* the answer." He pressed his pelvis against her thigh. "They'll deliver—a certain message."

"Takes a while for news to get here. The distance, and all. Like it takes a tank a long time to fill—a hot water tank or something like that."

"Hello down there!" He swallowed more scotch, drinking away anxiety, getting drunk. "Say something, Kathy. What're you thinking?"

"How'd you get money for this trip?"

Simple. He'd ransacked his father's bureau, searching for spare cash. His mother caught him in the act and demanded an explanation. When he told her, she peeled off a hundred dollars and said go get it over with.

"Cool! Never knew your mother was like that."

"She's not, usually. And she doesn't have much respect for you, sorry to say."

"Oh? What've I done?"

"You're in bed with me, ain't you?"

Why am I doing this? Oh, if only there were some way of fleeing to that nunnery—be alone, get everything straightened out once and for all. In the long pause while she mulled things over, Billy fell asleep. She lay there a silent prisoner; the longer he slept, the warmer he became, until finally his body burned as if he had a fever. She'd have to lower the thermostat or they'd roast. Careful not to jar the springs too much, she inched out of bed. Her hand happened to touch the hottest part on him, now full to bursting, a banister of blood—lot of good it'd do him! Only when his head went off could his blood leave the brain and go down there. How terrible to have double-duty blood this way, so you couldn't operate with all parts simultaneously. His face was very white, mouth open, as if he'd drained himself in order to rise mightily at last in his crotch.

After adjusting the thermostat, she deftly crept into the cool sheets of the twin bed across from him. Closing her eyes, she fixed a message in her head to wake at 6 A.M. Her mental alarm clock would have to get her out of here in time. Billy would break into the morning alone, be on his way. His mother loved him, wanted him to be a man, provided she could despise the girls he had. Curious. A throwback to pre-women's-lib days. She fell asleep trying to figure that one out.

The sun shone brightly at 6 A.M. when she awoke. Billy looked pale and slain, his pipestem arms flung over his head, the hair in his armpits a gentle, maidenhead fuzz, discreet and unbushy as the little ruff on his pelvis, glimpsed last night by the light of the TV set. She packed the overnight case quietly and did not snap the latch until she'd slipped out the door, for she remembered the noise it made.

Bernice awoke when she heard the door to the suite open from the hall. Hadn't locked up last night because Kathy didn't say where she was going or when she'd be back; most likely she'd left without her keys again. Shuffling footsteps out there. Alarm started in her stomach.

"Kathy?" A male whisper. "You here? Don't want to wake Bernice."

"You already *have!*"

Billy poked his head in, black eyes large, skin so white it looked powdered for the stage. "Bernice, where *is* she?"

"What're you doing here, Billy?" She sat up in bed, hugging her bare knees, happy to be found in her new pale green nightshift, which she'd put on before retiring because she felt depressed in the Friday night stillness of the dorm. What a pleasant surprise! One sweet, funny, crazy, wandering kid.

"Looking for her."

"At this hour? You oughta know Kathy's habits by now. She likes to sleep late, weekends."

"What do you mean? Been with her all night."

"You *have?*" Could she believe him?

He strode into the room, paced nervously about. Probably wore black all the time because of his white skin, black hair. Knew what he was doing, all right. Even managed to entice Kathy into his bed. Pretty good start. "What're you lookin' for her *here,* then?"

"She slipped out early while I slept it off."

"Must've been some night."

"Sure was." He grinned, triumphant.

"Where'd she go to—you suppose?"

"Figured she'd come back to the Manse. Where else?"

"Did anything—anything happen—I mean, to make her want to get away from you?"

"Well, Bernice, God damn it, of course things *happened.* I said we slept together down there on Route 13, the Paradise Motel. Like you suggested."

"I *did* . . . didn't I? Can't imagine why."

"As usual, you were right."

"She actually went there, of her own free will?" Wonder of wonders. Must've been really pissed at James, maybe even in love, to be able to do such a thing in anger.

"I sent a cab for her—and she came. Sure—she had to, you know."

"Had to?"

"I mean, after what she did . . . the tricks she pulled, doubling around on her stories. I mean the *run-around* she's been giving me. I figured . . . I figured we had a score to settle, and she knew it, too. Only *she* thought I was still in love with her. *That's* where I fooled her! She thought I was driven crazy! But while I kissed her and all, I thought—you bitch, Kathy. You God-damned lying little bitch!"

"Must've not been much fun then."

"Oh, I don't know . . . Revenge can be as exciting as love—right?"

"Do I really have to answer you, on that one?"

He dropped the mask, his face woeful. She almost leaped out of bed to put her arms around him. "Well, now you can deep-six the idea of Kathy. And don't come knocking on my door at sunrise—so the rest of us can sleep."

"Only came—'cause I wanted to be sure—she didn't get hurt or anything."

"Kathy hurt? She only hurts others. It's why she's so eager to find God."

"I don't follow you."

"You'd better not."

"Bernice, I feel sort of—*awful*, if you want to know. I figured I really got even with her. But givin' me the slip like this . . . I don't know. I feel . . . sort of empty, like *she* is. Maybe she's won after all. Could be I won't get over her so easy, like I thought. Maybe the rest of my life I'll have her—like a barb I can't pull out without tearing my flesh and losing my life, so the barb's got to stay in there, hurting. Oh, Bernice, what the fuck am I gonna do?" He walked quickly over to the bed and knelt beside her, head on her breast. She rubbed his back and kissed his blue-veined, throbbing temple, murmuring comfort in her best Dilsey way.

"We spend our weekend mornings together, don't we, Billy? But this bed's better 'n the Unitarian lawn, I can tell you."

"Sure is," a full-throated, low purr. "Sure is." He kissed her cheek and throat, then climbed right into bed next to her.

She delighted in his quick-change; wonderful, the way he suddenly became somebody else. What an actor he'd make! From tears to joy, new colors like a chameleon. Where was he—*who* was he? Billy had no more notion than *she* had who she was.

He lapped at her breasts like an overgrown baby. Pretty soon he kicked off his pants and boots and there he was on top of her. Good God, he really meant it! All night with Kathy and still *this!* Praise be the manly strength of seventeen! He was butting, urgent. She couldn't think what to do about it, didn't know *why* she should try to stop him. If she discovered herself pregnant a couple of months from now, she'd hurry back to good old New York State for an abortion. Didn't want any half-white Billys hanging onto her skirts, mixing up her blood any more than it already was.

She thought the damn bed would break down, he grew so violent—then suddenly lay sprawled, lifeless on top of her, and she didn't dare move. He wasn't heavy anyhow. Almost the best part was now, thinking about it, him there but quiet. When he seemed nearly asleep, she gently rolled out from under, folding him away into her bedclothes. She found the long-neglected red douche bag and syringe in the bottom drawer and padded off to the bathroom. Took a hot tub, then brushed her teeth. Hungry enough to eat a mammoth breakfast. She felt marvelous, in fact, and looked at herself in the cloudy mirror, pussycat expression.

I should hate you, Bernice, you know that, don't you?

She just smiled back, grinning like sin. What kind of incest is it when two roommates share the same boy? "It's been done before," she said aloud, drying herself on a towel. She plugged in the illegal hotplate kept on a shelf in the closet, got out the powdered Maxwell House and fake cream, found two stale but edible pastries.

When she brought in the breakfast tray, Billy woke up. "Bernice . . . Bernice!" He smiled at the food. "Will you marry me?"

"This is so sudden."

"You make me feel—terrific! Oh my God! Isn't it wonderful, Bernice? Isn't it?" He sat there in his black turtleneck, naked as a jaybird below, a cartoon out of a dirty book.

"Yeah it is."

He reached out a long arm and pulled the hem of her shift, tugging like an infant. "Don't bring me down, Bernice. I'm high! High! Oh my God, I've never had a high like this!"

"Drink your coffee while it's hot."

"Forget the coffee. Come on, Bernice, let's fuck."

"Billy, now wait a minute—*I'm* gonna have breakfast. I'm hungry. And don't forget, Kathy lives here too."

"Who's forgot?" He leapt out of the sheets, naked buttocks as small and round as two softballs. He quickly snapped the lock.

"Now you can *wait*, Billy." She tried to push his groping hands away. "You're making me spill my coffee!"

Fact was, he couldn't wait. He was high, mighty, and ready to go again. He set the coffee cup aside and pushed her into bed. "My God, you're some lover, Billy. I never heard of any lover like this. No wonder you're so thin, Billy. If you do it this often, you're—"

"Shut up, Bernice."

"Billy, I—"

"Bernice, shut up! We're making love." He kissed her quiet.

She let go once, twice. At each cry he opened his eyes but didn't seem to see her and kept on. Ronald had been tepid, discreet, but Billy practically went out of his head. Luckily his flesh saved him. Passion spent, he fell into a swoon. She thought of his white sperm inside her, all those pale chromosomes with messages so different from hers.

Something better be done about it. Nice as it'd been, she didn't want any more. Not even in the future. This was not to get very far, not all the way up her Fallopian tubes—to a shared tomorrow, a new piece of life, a Billy-Bernice black and white chocolate fudge sundae. She rose to use the douche bag once again. Not that these archaic remedies did much good, as her mother warned. Better than nothing. No morning-after pills around. Her mother didn't approve of them, said they were dangerous, and so none were supplied even during the time of Ronald.

When she returned, Billy still lay in bed; big sleepy smile, half-closed eyes. "Come on, get up, lover. Have to hunt you some ham and eggs, real food, before you waste away entirely. Don't want to be responsible for a frazzle . . . Have you so worn out you can't move . . . get outa town."

"I'm aglow, Bernice. I can hear you—but far off. Oh, I'm far *out!* I'm in heaven, Bernice. Feel all burst open. Oh my God, Bernice, I *love* it, don't you?"

"Come on, Billy, you great big lovin' baby, get out of my bed."

He grabbed her when she neared and ran his hands under the

green shift. "Billy—now—wait a minute! You haven't got the strength. I mean, you think you do, but you don't." As he hugged her thighs, she fingered his hair and stroked the ribbed wool of his sweater. This border-state Maryland youth found happiness in love with the umpteenth daughter of a slave from the back-buildings. Someday the pinky-white Kathys would satisfy him, but now he found his best love with the dark meat southern adolescents always went for.

Was this sad knowledge laughable? Or should she be furious, a militant Sylvie? With Kathy he'd no doubt been trying strenuously, only half making it and worrying the whole time, but with Bernice he'd nothing to lose but his inhibitions, no guard up, no defenses. Ontology recapitulates philogeny. In her bed he'd become a master. Both of them flung way back to the beginnings of racial intercourse in the South.

Those bastards! Why did it have to be? She and Billy weren't cast in the old mold and Chevy Chase wasn't Charleston, after all —which boasted a cat-house named the Big Brick, where boys Billy's age dropped their virginity in the arms of black whores. And since she was third-generation removed from Charleston by way of Chicago, her parents wouldn't know what the hell to make of her throwback thoughts just now. *They* believed profoundly in the restructuring of mental processes through science. Behaviorism didn't seem a sterile box of reason but a way to get free of the Big Brick. Reshape mankind, make over the world; there was hope of control. What a deviant *she* was, taking the old route!

But if Lysenko turns out to be right, maybe my blood will carry more knowledge than even *I'm* aware of, and my children will inherit learned characteristics—forget the slave quarters of the South entirely.

"Oh, Bernice, it's goddamn wonderful!"

If only Billy wouldn't go on this way—creamed into oblivion; if only *she* could stop comparing this morning to those tidy sessions in Ronald's bed. Did it have to be this way, then? A whole lifetime of miscegenation on every damn level? Four years at this college wasn't enough? Now she had the prospect of a series of Billys in the future, some of them blond, blue-eyed, others with carrot hair—all with Whitey's bright red penis?

"Maybe we oughta get married and live happily ever after."

"Billy, get out of my bed."

"If you're worried about Kathy busting in, I'll put on my pants and look respectable. But please, Bernice, *please* don't make me get out of your bed when I'm high like this. Blood tingling, every nerve of my body alive. *Alive!* Oh, I never been so *woke up* like this."

How could she send him away so he'd understand he mustn't return? Next year at George Washington would he hang around and try to make it with her again? All she really hoped for the future was some black friend who'd get her going along a new track entirely.

Somebody to kick my ass and fuck me good.

But here she'd let Kathy mess up her life again! *Why* did she allow herself to be used this way—with Kathy's leftovers? Sylvie and the Sisters would view it as white society pressing down upon her, imposing injury, degradation—worst of all, she hardly realized it was happening. Once she left Sylvie she'd been floating nowhere, between a white world and her own dimly understood black self. Alone, capable of anything—or nothing. She'd let herself be seduced merely because she hadn't been able to think of a good reason to say no.

She moved away from the bed and looked hard at the photograph of Malcolm X, her big brother. "Don't you feel—a little strange here . . . I mean, after Kathy?" *She* felt secondhand, ashamed of herself. It was one thing to share a suite with Whitey, another to take on her boy friend at virtually the same time. Pointless, emotionally unhealthy.

Get the hell out of the Manse *today*, back to Sylvie and the Sisters, where things like this couldn't happen. They leaned on each other's strengths ("We're *supportive*, Bernice").

"Sure wonder what happened to Kathy." His voice showed little anxiety.

"Billy, you don't just sleep with one girl and then roll over and take another!"

"I don't?" He grinned.

"*Why'd* I ever let you in here this morning?"

"You know why. Now come on, Bernice, you didn't say no. And then it was yes, yes."

"I don't like to talk about it. I hate that kind of after-talk."

"I didn't start it, Bernice."

"Well, I still feel—odd—about Kathy." Maybe it'd be best to pack up while Kathy was away. *Now.*

"I feel a holy glow all round my body, like I'm a saint, on fire with God. I'm just—lifted up—up!"

"Billy, get out of my bed."

"I smell you in the sheets, Bernice. All funky and mixed up with *my* smell—I love it!" He drew the sheet over his head.

"I guess nobody has to worry about *you*, Billy."

He uncovered part of his face, Arab-like. "It was worth everything, Bernice, wasn't it? Last weekend—all I been through. Maybe I'd never've come out *here*, if it hadn't been for all *that!*"

"Billy, get out of my bed."

"You're makin' me come down—with that tone of voice. Please don't spoil it, while I'm so high."

"You're still in my bed, Billy, and it's nine o'clock."

"Okay, okay, where's my pants?" He jackknifed into them and strode off to the bathroom.

There's my teen-age lover, Sylvie—Sisters! Don't snicker, please don't guffaw. I've learned my lesson. School's over and I can go now, dismissed. Having come full circle, I'm right at the beginning: of my *own* life at last. This time I mean it, Sisters.

She dressed while Billy was out of the room and made the bed for expediency's sake, to conclude the episode, though she knew she'd strip the sheets later. An after-awareness connected herself to him, as if the umbilical cord which had once tied her to another human being had now transformed itself, shifted lower down. An invisible, veiny rope reached all the way from Billy in the shower, right up into her. I've become *two* people instead of one, and until that vine withers, I'm not my black self alone. I can't get rid of him by changing the sheets and putting on my clothes.

The framed photograph of Malcolm X over her desk kept staring at her, that strong, surly portrait from the dust-jacket of his autobiography, a story ending with his almost-discovery that whites could be accommodated somehow. No one would ever know quite how he might have worked it out—just that he was beginning to see there might be some way. Pinned to the curtain nearby was the medallion image of Martin Luther King—a badge just as big as Kathy's JESUS LOVES ME button. God and Love were united in King's world of whites and blacks, with his own blood covering them all in the old sacrificial way—just as Isaac's blood, to Father Abraham's mind, was supposed to propitiate God. How could it? Was there ever enough blood to do the job? *Why* then was it seen to be the only way to try to reconcile the great differences? Make love not war.

I've been bled white.

But she saw herself in the mirror, Afro hair and all; she could gaze and smile, for the image in the glass seemed to possess all the answers. No need to plumb them just yet. There was time.

Billy strode back into the room, barefoot, hair plastered down, looking as if somebody'd tried to drown him out. "Nourishment *now!*" she said. "Billy, you gotta be fed—instantly!"

They headed for Pat's Diner.

Kathy hitched a ride with a fisherman who left her at the side of the road and drove off without waiting to see if she'd found the right place. The gate-bell handle rolled loosely in her grip, no sound in response anywhere, no mastiff aroused. With little traffic on the highway, she'd have trouble getting another lift, should this huge residence turn out to be some Vander-boop estate, not a nunnery at all. Birds sang wildly in the grove behind the wall, excited by spring and the prospect of nest-building. It was God's garden in there, and she wanted *in*. The journeying hero of *Pilgrim's Progress* never glimpsed his goal so near—and yet beyond reach. After considering the logistics of the problem, she decided to shinny up the tree and climb across the strong lower limb. She tossed the overnight case to the other side. Even if the mirror in the top broke, there'd be no seven year's bad luck, since it'd be cracking on holy ground. The rough bark provided a grip, but it was abrasive, too, and she bled slightly on her knee. Bright eyes of blood—the kind that appeared on the brow of Jesus and saints, those miracle days in Naples and elsewhere in the still-believing world. San Gennaro's blood manifested itself surprisingly, suddenly, this way. She couldn't wipe the wound clean. So bright red and alive, such a reminder of the flesh and all that passes; herself there in the beady drops.

She might have remained transfixed by the sight, the way one stares at a lizard on the wall until the eyes of the creature possess all the intelligence of one's own—and neither one can move—but a car on the road passed, slowed, the driver looking up at her. She pushed aside the shorter branches and plummeted into the garden, landing three feet from her overturned case. The contents had spilled but the mirror hadn't broken.

That's good luck! She headed in the direction of the Hudson River, knew the house would command a view, and soon stumbled upon a path.

Sounds of footfalls behind her. She hid as a middle-aged woman in overalls raced past, arms swinging in an exaggerated jogger's sway. Mosquitoes feasted upon her—she shook her arms, slapped her head. Soon the racer approached again. Kathy plunged into the brambles, though not quickly enough to escape being seen. How long could she stay in this swarming jungle, hiding like Ishi, the last primitive man in the U.S.A.? Needles pierced her skin, woke her up, as St. Sebastian must have felt closer to God when each arrow went through him. For the first time—or in a new way—she saw the birds, ants, flies, the luxuriant shrubs and ferns; herself intermixed with them. She sensed the silent insistence of it all. Never had she been the least interested in working a garden, identifying butterflies, couldn't tell an oak from a maple unless it was October. The folly of her blindness to this "book of God's World" amazed her.

She watched a very large mosquito suck blood from the back of her hand until it was swollen like a bladder—then smacked it dead. God's wounds! Blood on her arm and blood on her knee. Her life was on the surface here. Or rather, her body was here but her mind was out there, like God's over the universe. She felt conscious of life, hers and the quiet or insensate lives all around her. ". . . for the earth is the Lord's, and the fullness thereof."

Perhaps she need go no further into the cloister. Instead of removal, she'd been thrown closer to God. This forest would impose universal laws upon her if she just remained long enough to let her innate self feel the way back to primitive times. *Then* she might learn to exist with the insects, trees, and birds . . . but in the end, what would such harmony do for her? She wasn't Ishi— who hadn't been "lost" in his life at all, only seemed so to the Californians who found him.

The truth she was after would only do if it were something she could take back into the world beyond these walls. Something already within herself which merely had to be discovered—the cloister giving her a chance to find it. In her longing was a notion that faith would release her from the awful necessity of trying to understand *why*. Why she'd been given a small measure of knowledge, a nagging wonder, a feeling of almost-knowing—when God surely hadn't done the same for that mosquito, blue jay, or oak tree (if it was an oak).

Again the pat-pat-pat of running feet.

I'll make myself known!

She broke through the undergrowth. "Hey—just a minute, please!"

The woman didn't pause, merely lifted her arm, finger pointing up, a kind of salute. Kathy followed her and soon came to a timber-and-stucco outer building. The jogger sat puffing on the well-curb in the center of the courtyard. "Hello?"

The woman turned a flushed face; sweat all over her, staining the white T-shirt under the armpits.

"Is this the . . . the order . . . of sisters, I mean—"

"Where'd *you* come from?" Her overalls were a fruit farmer's outfit, faded from much washing. Her flapjack dugs were scarcely hidden by the bib.

"Couldn't find the right entrance—so I climbed over the wall. Is this the . . . Catholic order where sometimes a *lay* person can stay?"

"Who told you about us?" Still breathing heavily.

"My roommate, at college. I'm a graduating senior."

"Then what're you doing here?" She'd only enough energy for short questions.

"I need to go into retreat . . . a chance to think . . . sort things out."

"I see."

"This *is* the order of sisters who—"

"Oh, yes."

"Good! I've found the right place."

"Well, I wonder. You hungry for breakfast?"

"As a matter of fact, I haven't . . ."

"Come on then."

They walked slowly through the courtyard, where chickens pecked and scratched in the loose dirt. Kathy smelled a cow nearby but couldn't see her. Unlikely, any horses—the pleasure of riding wouldn't be in keeping with the rules of the order. Near the rear of the house, two German shepherds strained at their tethers when they saw the woman and Kathy approach—but didn't bark, just whimpered.

"I run three miles every morning."

"Oh . . . are you mortifying your flesh?"

"*Fortifying* it."

"How so?"

"The cardiovascular system needs flushing out each day. You know what happens to the arteries after a while, otherwise."

"No, I—"

"Didn't you take biology? What do they teach you people these days, nothing but macramé?"

"There's a big emphasis on individual development."

"Tell *that* to your arteries and heart!"

Kathy heard weird, mumbling sounds in the basement of the turreted mansion. Beyond, green lawns swept down to a wide clearing; the Hudson River lay there as if forever, catching her heart in a strange feeling of transport. She could look at the river and stare herself into eternity. She'd come to the right spot to find God.

They descended narrow stone steps to the basement and entered the cavernous kitchen. "Has everybody eaten breakfast?"

"No, no, they're still at it. Didn't you hear them as we came in?"

A human buzzing, murmuring of a score of voices. "Still praying?"

"Sort of. God consciousness-raising."

"Oh, I see." She didn't in the least but thought she'd keep mum at least until after eating a little food.

All the 1900 kitchen furniture was still here, as if while the two of them crouched belowstairs, some glittering, rich family strode full of life in magnificent rooms overhead. She understood now why so many Catholic retreats were great estates. Walking barefoot on parquet floors, all the things-of-this-world were seemingly set aside by *will*; a constant, living lesson that what's perceived to be the glamorous, good life is actually hollow and means nothing. In this house one could sense the triumph of prayer!

"I did an extra lap this morning, just to make sure I really *did* spot you there in the bushes. And can I feel it!"

"Are your . . . arteries . . . in pretty good condition?"

"One never knows, for sure."

"Since you're close to God—here," she began, oddly self-conscious, bringing up His name, "the physical and spiritual blend together, don't they?"

The woman's face was still fiery red; her eyes had that peculiar mobility and intentness that comes with a pounding bloodstream. "We don't believe one should forget who created the body."

"Oh, I agree."

"We're flesh and blood, with physical needs. Hunger, sex. And there's some purpose."

"But to find the purpose! I only see the world refracted through the prism of my being."

"Very pretty." She smiled wryly. "How long has *that* been hanging around inside your head?"

"I beg your pardon?"

"Bullshit!"

She hoped the nuns wouldn't come in just now and hear language like this. The help here was probably tempted to use profanity, just as cooks in great houses felt compulsions to spit in the soup.

"Have you worked long—in this place?"

"We take turns with the work."

"*We?*"

"The sisters."

"You're *one* of them, then?" This overalled, red-faced old char —how *could* she be?

"I'm the Mother Superior."

"Oh dear! I'm sorry, Mother, I—"

"Don't 'Mother' me, please. It's not good form. Now eat your oatmeal before it gets cold. I hope you don't mind our raw milk, straight from the cow. Healthier for a person."

"I suppose nutrition must be attended to, as well as prayer."

"With the junk food around, we grow most of our own. Fill up the freezer, preserve what we're able to. Lots of storage space in these old houses. And now with our funds entirely cut off, we're strictly on our own."

"I heard . . . there was some kinda trouble. Don't know about what. Some . . . ecclesiastical problem?"

"I don't discuss these things with strangers. How do I know the bishop didn't send you?"

"Do I look like a bishop's spy?"

"Who knows? What're you doing here, anyhow?"

"I said—I need a little peace, time for prayer."

"You want to be a postulant?"

"Oh no, nothing like that!"

"Scared you, didn't I?"

"I've come to a crisis in my life."

"Every day should be a state of crisis. If it isn't, something's gone dead in you."

"But this is a *serious* time of—"

"Graduating, huh?"

"It's not just that."

"Boy friend, then."

"Yes, *that* too."

"Here we don't have time for petty personal problems of that sort."

"I hope to find perspective like that, too. Once I get into a right relationship with God." But as soon as she said it she felt odd. Strange, that in His own household, the Master's name should never be mentioned.

"Oh?"

"A prayerful relation. I mean, I go to church regularly—and all that." She glanced down, for one awful moment afraid she still wore her JESUS LOVES ME yellow button. "But I don't seem to be getting any . . . feedback."

"Feedback! Ha! That's a good one!" She was still too red in the face to laugh more than once, though reaction to Kathy's remark rumbled around like thunder inside, shaking chuckles out.

"My, this oatmeal's good." To say *something.*

"Should be. We raise the oats and grind the kernels ourselves, in our mill. Got one of those watermills turned by a stream coming out of the cliff."

Moses struck the rock and water gushed forth. "Sounds beautiful."

"Useful. But we only really raise a couple of bushels. Now then: how long you plan to be with us?"

"A few days maybe, if I could. I've got a little cash, to leave as contribution."

"It's a deal. Need all the donations we can get. Electricity, fuel oil—with our funds canceled."

"Perhaps you'll be reinstated before long."

"Not likely. Unless by some miracle I'm named cardinal."

"That *would* take a miracle."

"Who needs the church hierarchy? We don't believe in rules imposed by tradition."

"There's been a . . . great change, then, in your aims?" If only Bernice had remembered more from the newspaper article.

"We discovered our emptiness, and it shook us up. Now we're busy finding the true way. *That's* all the yelling you heard, when we came in. Going on all night. The girls decided to hang in there and not let up—until they'd come to a new understanding of themselves."

"Thought you were going to say, 'understanding of God.'"

She studied Kathy with sure, measuring eyes. "For a girl your age, you're awfully interested in divinity."

"Should think you'd be glad."

"Mis-messages come in all codes."

"What's that supposed to mean?"

"*You* better sit in—if they're still going to it. In the Pit. Might learn something."

"I'd love to. Then afterward—I'd like a little free time to meditate."

"Aw, come off it!"

"I'm rather tired, see. I got up awfully early." Memory of herself and Billy in the Paradise Motel brought a swimming unease. How this cynical Mother Superior would laugh. By now Billy would be looking for her—at the Manse, pestering Bernice with questions. If only he didn't notify the police, just hurried home to Washington, tail between his legs. She visualized him naked, loping off, white bloodless penis dangling.

"This was the billiard room, when the Robber Baron lived

here." The Mother Superior slouched ahead, hands stuffed into her overalls. "The men'd go down this little stairs from the dining room, for their cognac, cigars, and pool, their randy stories—well out of earshot of women—enjoying their puffed-up notion of pleasure—and worldly success. A perfect place for us to have the Pit, we thought."

A fetid odor of perspiration, incense, and overly used air rose as they descended. About a dozen women in faded jeans and overalls, most of them in their twenties and thirties, with a sprinkling of gray-heads here and there, lay sprawled on wrestling mats, faces pasty with fatigue, hair mussed, stringy.

"Sisters! We've got a visitor."

They stared with a curiosity and animal alertness Kathy hadn't experienced since childhood on the playground. As she stepped down into the Pit, she thought of Daniel entering the lion's den and put her faith in God quickly, before terror sent her flying up the staircase. *I and my Father are one.*

"I've work to do upstairs. This session can't go on much longer —they look half dead, don't they? Afterward, one of 'em'll show you the guest room." She mounted the spiral staircase, the only exit from the Pit. Kathy introduced herself, pretended this was a rap session, for if she faltered, they'd have an awful advantage. She met Ben and Cess (Sister Bernadette and Sister Cecilia), Marge and Mag (Sister Marguerite and Sister Magdalena) and all the others, whose Holy Order names and monikers jumbled together as the faces rose, balloonlike, on denim bodies. They were "bushed." Up all night "to work it out."

"A crisis in faith?" she asked the nearest nun, Sister Ben—a tomboy in her mid-twenties, the games-girl who has trouble wearing dresses that look right.

"No, more a matter of getting it all together *here.*"

"I suppose that comes first," she answered, puzzled by Ben's euphoria.

"You better believe it!" said Cess, a pretty, blue-jeaned nun, whose delicate features suggested a fourteenth-century prioress in drag. She grasped Ben's hand affectionately and they exchanged warm glances, smiled back at the world together.

"A beautiful night," said Ben blushing, "and we came through it just fine, didn't we, Cess?"

Obviously, they were a pair. Had an understanding of *this*—and similar groupings among the rest—been the object of the all-night encounter session? "None of you've had *any* sleep?" She glanced around at the bedraggled women on the mats, in various slugged-looking stages of repose.

"Got right out to the limits—it was beautiful!" Ben said, hitching her trousers.

"Best shit we've had here in a *long* time." Cess smiled but seemed unused to the strident words.

"You smoke pot here? Really?" She'd thought the smell Pakistani incense.

"We grow our own," said tomboy Ben, "but now and then we luck into some really sweet Acapulco Gold—you know, from our friends in the street."

"I . . . see. What is it you do . . . in the street?"

"What'd'ya think?" asked Ben, squaring off. "Suppose we sit here prayin' and singin' psalms and doin' penance? *That* your idea of nuns? I bet you figure we still shave our heads!" All of them laughed.

"I don't know. I'm not a Catholic."

"You must be, if you came here," said Cess.

"I was . . . looking for a different kind of place."

"A safe harbor, I know." Cess's expression clouded with perhaps a moment's nostalgia for her former self, the shade of the wimple that once enclosed her face. "A place to pray for the world, once you're well removed from it. I know."

"God's in the streets," said Ben. "Lesson number one for you."

"What's your name?" asked Cess.

"Katharine, with a K—after Hepburn, you know, but now I like to think I'm named for the saint."

Ben and Cess probed to find out how she'd gotten here, and as she told them, they seemed to line up her story with their own. For one wild moment, she wondered if she were dead and comparing backgrounds from the vantage point of the afterlife.

"So actually you ran away," Ben said. "Just remember, running goes in *both* directions. You can as easily scoot back."

"Not for a couple of days. After the weekend."

"Mine was a careful, deliberate decision—it's different," said Ben.

"It's a commitment," Cess added.

"I'm just in . . . in retreat. I haven't made any decisions about anything. Somehow . . . can't."

"We'll take you up to the guest room," said Cess, yawning.

"While you're all sleeping, I'll have time for prayer and meditation." She meant, don't feel you ought to be hostesses. I know what I came for. But they both looked at her oddly. "You know . . . worship." It was one of her favorite words: so full.

"Are you puttin' us on?" Ben asked, suspicion and amusement alternating in her berry-eyes.

"I think Jesus said, 'God is a Spirit—'"

"Oh, you think so?"

" '—and they that worship him must worship him in spirit and in truth.' "

"Jesus said that *really?*" Ben mocked. "Where'd you learn such things?"

"I read the Bible all the time, don't you?"

"We *used* to," said Cess, clutching Ben's hand as if to give herself strength. "Used to have the Bible coming in and out of our ears, didn't we, Ben?"

"Mostly out."

"Suppose you know more about it all than *I* do," Kathy said placatingly, the way defeated graylag geese in Lorenz's aggression experiments offered their rumps to the victor.

"Lot better things to do with our time than read the Bible," said Cess as if by rote.

"The Church as it was—is finished!" said Ben. "We're harbingers of the new way."

"I see." She'd stumbled into a rebel camp, the midst of strife. "I'm—I'm looking for a way, too. But I'd hoped to find . . . a place where they'd already *found* the way. So I could see if it might be mine, too."

"We know what you're lookin' for," said Cess.

"Same thing *we* were after."

"When we came—"

"But it's not here?"

"God's in the streets," said Ben.

"What do you mean when you say that?"

"Sing-Sing's our gig," said Cess. "We go up there—do remedial reading, writing, work with the guys. Get real tight with 'em."

"They're like us, really." Ben smiled.

"And then—then you return here to the convent and . . . put everything into context? I mean, with God and all?"

"No, no, Katharine . . . St. Catherine . . . climb off your wheel. Prison work is prison work, doesn't have to be justified or examined, does it? *You* read the Bible, and you know where Paul spent most of his time. In jail!"

Laughter from the others nearby, but most of them hardly listened, the effort was too much. "I guess I've come to the wrong place."

"If what we're doing here is right, you've come to the *right* place," from Ben.

"I thought I'd be given a pad somewhere to lie on. A room to myself, where I could have time for meditation and prayer."

"We don't believe in anybody doing *that* by themselves," said Cess. "We work together, pray together."

"And sleep together," Ben added.

"That's all very well, but I think I'd—"

"We don't deny the flesh in order to reach the spirit," said Ben, reasonable as Jill Johnston in *The Village Voice*. "I'd think a message like that wouldn't be hard for you to understand."

"It's not. I understand the message all right. I just—don't—know if I believe it, that's all." Everything that went on here goes on *any*where, that was the trouble. What was so special about spiritual life then? "I think it's great, your going up to Sing-Sing . . . I mean, good works have their place. But I'm interested in . . . what comes *first*."

"What're you trying to say?" asked Ben.

"I mean it's like Paul—he says somewhere, 'by grace are ye saved through faith; and not of yourselves; it is the gift of God. Not of works, lest any man should boast.'"

"Or any woman," said Cess quietly.

"Amen," Ben echoed.

A bell rang upstairs. "Let's go eat!" The women rose heavily.

"I already have," Kathy told Ben.

"We'll show you the guest room, then," and Cess led the way up the spiral stair.

Kathy retrieved her overnight case in the hallway above and proceeded through the dark interior, rich in carved woodwork but nearly devoid of the furnishings it must once have had. "We sold everything off—to keep going," said Ben. But the guest room still contained a ruffly, canopied bed, gray silk chaise, and tufted chairs. Amorous cupids frolicked on the ceiling; and a large mirror over the marble fireplace extended the cupids into a further distance. "This gives a person . . . some idea of what the place was . . . once."

Here the rich man's wife or mistress spent private hours, weighed down with the baggage of luxury, two hundred dresses in the closets. Would such suggestion of the former owners bother her? Kathy preferred the spare, stripped rooms in the rest of the house. "Funny, this room was left—like this."

"The abbess liked it. Entertained the bishop here—you know. Thought this suited her station in life. Any wonder Sarah took over?"

"Your Mother Superior?"

"*Never* call her that," Ben warned.

"I know . . . she said. What happened to the abbess?"

"Oh, she's president of a college now. That was a year ago, we took over the joint."

"It's beautiful . . . here." The river lay in the distance like a Leonardo painting, calmed her. "Go eat breakfast, Ben. I'll sit right here and think awhile."

After the door closed she curled up in the velvet window seat and stared at the Hudson, until none of the world, not even herself, seemed left. At last she stirred, tried the other window facing northeast, and gazed down at the circle of the front drive before the main door. A metal three-tiered Victorian fountain stood there, not working. The two German shepherds, now loose, galloped ominously around the grounds. Luckily they hadn't torn her apart when she dropped over the wall. But they'd surely be after her if she tried to escape this cloister. Long-sought utter confinement was hers at last, all communication with the outside world cut off. No need to deal with James or Billy or anyone. No way but up to heaven left open. Perhaps her feeling of being pressured was merely a symptom of the "graduate's syndrome," terror at the thought of the "real" world edging near. A silky sickness filled her stomach at the thought of James—was such agony love? Eventually they'd have to have all the arguments out, matching point for point, empty hours of discussion—but about what?

Knock on the door. "Kathy?"

No, they didn't believe in peace and meditation here. She opened the door for Ben.

"We're all headed for the showers—c'mon."

She'd love a long hot bath but obviously wouldn't be getting it. "I'll fetch my towel."

The marble bathroom had been converted into a large shower area capable of dousing all the sisters at one time, since apparently the old rule about a nun's never seeing her own body or glimpsing another's had now been reversed. Their diet, exercise, and sexual releases were all factors in making the body an instrument worthy of serving God. Or kept them happy.

Removing blue jeans and shirts, rolling them neatly like swimmers leaving a bank, they urged Kathy to do likewise and step under the shower spray. Of course they eyed her as she stripped and she was self-conscious about their interest—but covering herself seemed unjustified by any principle she could think of, just as James, naked in bed last week, had let Mr. Pennell look, if he wanted. Was there any harm in it?

Even in high school gym, she couldn't remember being hosed down this way by a dozen nozzles, so many naked women close around her. Water pouring straight over her head half removed her, enclosed her in her own being. Soon it all seemed perfectly natural, as if she were in a South Sea island stream washing herself with the village maidens. She felt curiously free. *She* along with the others had triumphed over sanctions regarding the flesh, in so far as it was an end in itself, something that limited her. Exhilaration possessed them all. They shared a kindred spirit; it moved and dwelt among them, everybody smiling at everyone else.

In the outer room they toweled each other dry, gentle over the sensitive zones, soft-patting in the crotch. Her nipples stiffened under Ben's towel; she closed her eyes. "I'm dry now, I think."

They pulled on terry-cloth robes and retired to the nearby bedrooms where cots were set out in rows, curiously incongruous with the parquet floors, marble-and-tile fireplaces, and leaded glass windows, as if this were a behind-the-lines hospital taken over for the duration.

"We'll sleep till evensong," Ben said. "Meditate and pray all you want."

"Thanks, I—I will."

Like stations of the cross, Kathy took up positions at the windows. She was bored, bored! Instead of thinking about herself and God, herself and James, or trying to pray, she dwelt on events in this convent the past year. Sarah had put together women's-lib and the rebel church movement, taught these nuns to chuck their robes and come out fighting. No longer did they follow Jesus' doctrine that only those who lose the world find eternal life—for if they lost the world they'd lose themselves, too.

Finders aren't keepers, in any case. She opened the door a crack, hearing voices below. The sleepers had awakened and now were assembling in the chapel. Should she join them?

No, the closed door—the silence—would make them wonder, think about God.

If only *she* could! She scavenged around in memory for a prayer suitable but could think of none except "Our Father, who art in heaven . . ." It did very nicely and she felt suddenly at peace.

She'd expected to hear a service begin downstairs, but the talking grew louder; no hymns, chants, or psalms. All night in the Pit, and now another go at each other? Wasn't this carrying Encounter altogether too far? The arguments rose and fell, different voices. Sarah would be for participatory democracy, a full airing of all issues.

"But what's wrong with a shaved head!" someone screamed—could it be Cess?

The answer was engulfed by a wave of speakers at once.

They were discussing *her!*

Loud clapping. "Right on! Right on!"

The Lord's Prayer evaporated at the thought of Sarah downstairs in front of the altar, in her sincere overalls and T-shirt, arguing with her charges to keep the new faith: useful work "in the streets." You couldn't hide in a convent and pretend things out there were okay or that the wrongs of society weren't *your* concern.

Sarah harangued, made her points; her gradually quieter audience didn't prove she was winning. Kathy closed the door firmly when it sounded as if the session below was breaking up. A few minutes later, a knock on the door. "You awake?"

Sarah stood there—strong, dark eyes formidable.

"Yeah, come in."

"We're ready for supper now."

"Thanks—I'm pretty hungry."

"Praying's hard work?" Again that wry smile. She looked around as if searching for some evidence of a diversion other than prayer. Not even a Bible anywhere. "How much more of it, you think you'll need?"

"I'm sorting everything out pretty good."

"I've been thinking, since you won't be along with us Monday to Sing-Sing—you better plan to leave tomorrow. I wouldn't want you alone here in the house."

"Oh, you can trust me."

"It's not that."

"I'll have . . . plenty to *do*, I think," What though?

"Another *kind* of institution is probably what you're after."

"Maybe."

"If we had a car, we could drive you some place. But we don't. We get our rides from a friend in town, but I can't very well ask her to—"

"That's all right. I'm used to hitching."

"Now the Franciscans, they're a good sort . . . and I think maybe more your—"

"Oh, I don't need a nunnery now . . . this was enough. I got what I came for already."

"That was quick!"

"You say there's supper?" She didn't want an argument with Sarah, the hostility was too strong.

"Come on."

Her reappearance caused a sensational ripple of attention. Rest and chapel argument had stirred them alive again. Ben and Cess immediately possessed her, one on each side, and they sat down together on a humble wooden bench at the long bare table. "Our visitor says grace," Ben announced, and Kathy murmured her childish Sunday School prayer: "Bless us oh Lord, for these Thy gifts of Thy bountiful goodness . . ." She knew there was more but couldn't think what came next. The pregnant pause held them, heads bowed, as if no-words were best of all. At last Kathy said, "Amen," and they repeated it, crossing themselves. Bowls were passed, each helped herself. The carrots were a bit under-cooked and tough, but the hard-boiled egg on toast was runny, the way she liked it. "A beautiful supper," she said, to the inmate across the table. "Not too heavy."

"No meat, you mean."

"There never is," Cess added.

"Did Gandhi ever eat meat?" Ben asked. "And look what he ac-complished!"

"Jesus mentions meat-and-drink," Kathy said. "*He* wasn't a veg-etarian."

"True, but we've a problem with stilbestrol in beef that Jesus never thought of."

"Everything—He thought of—then and now," Cess said.

"Kathy, you know what I mean. With quick-curing chemicals injected into hams and mercury deposits in fish . . . and poisons in just about every processed food—who wouldn't want to be a vegetarian?"

"We've got no money for store food anyhow."

"You ran out, just when you got alarmed about the super-markets—what they sold?"

"Almost like God planned it that way," Cess nodded.

"Sarah says—" Ben began.

"Shhhh," from Cess.

The Mother Superior passed behind them with the salad bowl, placed it on the table with a half smile, as if she knew they'd been talking about her but didn't care.

"She ask you"—Ben glanced over her shoulder, Sarah was out of earshot—"to get the hell outa here?"

"Tomorrow . . . because on Monday you'll all be going to Sing-Sing."

"*That's* not the reason," said Cess.

"I know. It's that guests can't *be* here right now."

"No, they should be!" Ben said.

"Singing alleluia . . . alleluia," Cess added.

"I haven't done anything but pray."

"That's enough," said Cess.

Quickly, before they closed her in with a misplaced gratitude, she freed herself—and them. "'It's not me but the Father in me which doeth the work.'"

"Beautiful," said Ben. "We should use that in today's Office."

"So . . . I'll be ready to go tomorrow. All these hours alone— that was enough."

"Maybe *you're* straightened out, but we're not." Ben put her elbows on the table, tomboy style.

A bell rang; supper was over. No coffee or tea—a sparse, simple meal. For the first time this really seemed like a convent.

"Compline, everybody," Sarah announced. "Compline."

"That's some kind of prayer, isn't it? Vespers—something like that?"

"*Nothing* like that," Ben laughed.

"We're sneaking up to the third floor—come on with us." Cess pulled on Kathy's fingers.

"No, no thanks . . . I really need this . . . privacy. Maybe not to meditate or pray—just to think. At my stage of spiritual development, thinking is praying and vice versa. I mean, you *are* what you think."

They looked at her so startled, or in awe, she couldn't imagine what was the matter. "I've got to think about my life . . . my plans . . . I mean, what am I going to do? That kind of thing." Had she made herself mundane enough? Or should she mention James, Billy's pursuit, and her mother's pressure? "After I leave tomorrow."

"Compline!" Sarah called again, annoyed with Kathy for hanging about the refectory.

"I'm going back to my room," she said quickly to them all.

Once there, she locked the door. The river was violet colored; the world lay stretched before her, as if the evening, her youth, and springtime were all in perfect alignment. There'd never be a better moment of promise than this. If she refused to accept such a gift, whatever followed she'd properly deserve. "The world's so beautiful!" she said aloud, walking toward the window seat, sitting down. Only when outside the world could she appreciate it, even though in the very direction she looked, miserable Sing-Sing lay just beyond. Now that she no longer had to lean into the em-

pyrean, having in some odd way *found* God, she wondered what
to do with her idle consciousness, her empty, singing head. The
search for salvation had ended where she always half knew it
would, back within herself.

The strains of De Profundis floated up from below, wavery-
voiced but heavy with conviction. Kathy unbolted the door to listen, realized the singing came from the third floor, whereas in the
chapel someone was making a speech. Sarah again, still at it. The
house had split in two, with faith at the top and good works
below—and herself in the middle. Tomorrow couldn't come too
soon. She closed the door.

Nightlights from strategic corners of the house flashed on, illu-
minating the crumbling fountain with its wedding-cake tiers, in
the center of the front drive. The two German shepherds raced
about under the trees—hunting what?

Totally confined—a prisoner, a maiden in a tower. At least, no
phone calls from a hysterical mother trying to save her daughter
from one more painful fall; or from a pushy neighbor-kid who
wanted to *use* her for his own growing up; or from James, who
knew exactly the measure of her character, who showed her up—
and then said he didn't care—he'd forgive. A warm unease flushed
over her at the thought of him. She'd have to hear his arguments
eventually, empty hours of discussion. To be in love wasn't
enough for anybody it seemed; you also had to have an understanding. She was sick of it!

Knock on the door. "Kathy?"

Ben stood in the corridor—like a bald-headed little old man,
rubbing her skinned scalp, grinning.

"Lord! What happened to you?"

"Come on!" She clutched Kathy's hand, childlike, and led her
to the third floor.

In the slope-roofed chamber, four of the eight women were
skinheads, and the girl on the high stool in the middle of them,
getting shorn, seemed the object of a precious ceremony. "No
electric razors—not for us," said Ben. "It's the shaving brush and
straight-edge . . . just like old times."

So much hair had already been collected in a shopping bag, it
looked as if Absalom's head had fallen in. Ben said they'd sell the
hair to a wig manufacturer on Spring Street. A row of white

gowns hung on a clothes rack nearby, and an ironing board had been set up in a far corner.

Kathy smiled nervously. "Oh, you're getting ready to be angels again!"

"No, just nuns. Just a bunch of nuns, that's all." Ben rubbed her glistening dome, which was as naked as her hopes for eternal salvation. Cess helped her into the newly pressed robes, then fitted the bonnet, hard with starch, over her forehead.

"How'd we ever *do* it? How'd we ever *stand* it!" Ben said in joyous complaint.

"You will." Cess pushed the wimple lower, shoving hard.

"Ouch! For Christ's sake, Cess!"

"*Yes,* for Christ's sake!"

"Must be somebody else's. It doesn't fit!" Ben pulled it off and a wide red band like the crown of thorns on Jesus' brow marked her forehead. Ben studied the welt in the mirror. "Suppose I'm allergic to starch?"

"Try this one," said Cess, like a vendeuse. "It's a little bigger."

"But when you people go over to the prison—on Monday—and into the streets . . . won't it be harder to—infiltrate? I mean, be like anybody else?"

"We're not throwin' out our jeans and stuff," said Cess. "We need 'em for disguise."

"Look at all these wigs we bought once." Ben threw open a cupboard door. "In a thrift shop in White Plains." Now with her face framed in the pure, severe whiteness, all the gamin angularity was gone. She was freshly innocent, sweet-looking, despite her boyish, somewhat coarse voice. "One day I'll be a redhead—another time, a dashing blonde. We'll go out in Levi's and boots but come back here for choiring. Cool, don'tcha think?"

"You'll have more . . . dimension that way, I guess." Kathy still wasn't sure such a double life was possible. Could either be lived sincerely?

"How 'bout *you* bein' next?" Cess asked.

"Oh, not me! I told you, I'm getting out of here tomorrow."

"*Sarah* told you to leave," Ben said. "Not us. You could stay if . . . if we shaved your head."

"You'd *have* to stay—then," said Cess.

"No . . . no, I'd just steal one of your wigs." She smiled, so her refusal could be taken as if she hadn't seriously accepted the proposal.

"We been talking. And we figure you really wouldn't be here," Cess said, "if you didn't actually want to join us . . . for a while."

The scissors opened and shut like jaws, somewhere in the room. "I'm leavin' tomorrow, like I said. Gotta get back to school . . . to graduate."

"School's over—you said yourself."

"They'll be looking for me. Somebody will. Notify the police—who knows? You'd have a lot of fuzz coming in here—and if they find any of your . . . supplies . . ."

"Don't worry—Pam and Penny will take care of the pigs!" Ben nodded, the movement exaggerated in her headgear.

"Who're they?"

"The German shepherds."

Kathy felt herself as much a prisoner as any of their buddies in Sing-Sing. She couldn't run down the gravel path without being torn to pieces by the attack dogs. The lock on a door always works both ways—and protection soon breeds suffocation. "No really, I mean it . . . I've . . . I've come to the conclusion I'm best off—on my own. You know? Working things out as best I can. And then . . . then there's this boy—this friend of mine . . . who loves me."

A musky attention filled the room, she could almost smell it, as soon as she said a boy loved her. She'd become different from them, drawn herself away as surely as if she'd shrieked or spat in their faces. Some of them had been loved by young men at one time—in a different life. She'd declared the power of her estrangement from them and they accepted it without argument. "I'd—I'd better get back down to my room before Sarah finds me up here."

"We'll stand up to Sarah!" said Ben.

"No, I mean since I don't have much time . . . to pray . . . I want to get back at it."

They gazed at her tentatively, slightly hurt. She put out her hands palms up, a St. Francis gesture toward the universe. "Sisters!" she said softly.

They came quickly toward her and touched her hands, fingers meeting lightly, flesh against flesh. They felt each other's blood,

warm and stirring, but at the same moment sensed the spirit—
which couldn't be seen or touched—moving strongly among them
all, revivifying them, transforming them. "Sisters!" Kathy said
again, and fled the room.

The suitcase lay open on the bed, ready for a second load of
Bernice's stuff. She flung aside the flimsy closet curtain for the last
of her winter things. Malcolm X and Martin Luther King were
packed and ready for exhibit in her new cubicle in Sylvie's outer
room, where she'd stay until commencement. The room was entirely devoid of her personality and once again asserted its true
identity. The mattress had that gray-stripe institutional ticking;
the bare, pocked walls were known now in their greenish, board-
inghouse hue; the windows naked except for roller shades: this
was a room like a whore, used to having a lot of different company. It was never mine, thought Bernice. I was never here at all.

Had Kathy shown up Saturday afternoon or evening, perhaps
the old, lying, sly Bernice might've carried off matters. "Yeah,
Billy come, but he gone *now*." Oh, the wicked, wicked deftness of
it all, because Kathy couldn't hear her, had never known her.
"Upset? Billy upset? Not partic-u-larly. He seem his old self to
me." Stop it, stop it! Kathy wouldn't get the irony, catch the
darky tone, see the humor.

But what's so funny? Joke's on me and always has been.

She slammed shut the suitcase in disgust. Now, all set. Except
for the typewriter. Dear talking machine, still with a sheet of
paper in the roller. The sociology teacher had been taken care of
Thursday with a rollicking "oral report," which Bernice justified
by the fact that McLuhan warned of the end of the Gutenberg
syndrome—the written word is no longer important. Everything is
audio or visual—or seismal. "Seismal?" asked the teacher, huge-
eyed behind thick spectacles, eager for data on the ever-changing
contemporary world. "Seismal—what's that?"

"You know, ma'am, anything that *moves*. Things gotta move!"

I'll no longer have the privacy of you here on the page, where
I'm going, but neither will I need a confidante like you any more.
This isn't the meaning of my life, only an expose of some mis-
takes in it. I'm commencing now—something new. I promise, not
the old wandering among Whitey, where I could get away with

anything, everything, and in the end, nothing. Now for a last blooded bonding with Sylvie and her toughies, who still call it the way it is—over there in their staked-out territory, their fierce corner of the dorm.

She ripped the sheet from the machine. "Lies! Lies!" Whatever gave her the notion she was wise or strong enough to put down the truth in black and white? She was crashing in with Sylvie because the Sisters would look out for her. Knew who they were, what they were about. Eventually a little of that definite pigment might rub off.

No, wasn't enough time . . . not now. Again her parents had arranged a summer job for her at St. Luke's, in the personnel department. Good at meeting people, everybody said; easy with the lies. She could project a genuine warmth, interest, and lively concern; such a contrast to the cool, perhaps necessary distance all the professionals maintained who worked there year round.

In the company of Sylvie and the Sisters she'd feel close for the last time to the skin of her problems. She'd truly fucked herself, but good! Remembrance of what happened on this bed turned sour the more she thought about it. Joined to Billy—God! Ridiculous, if it weren't so pathetic.

I stumbled over my own black feet and fell into the arms of a seventeen-year-old white boy. Whee! Catch me, Sylvie!

Better get the hell out of here—fast!

She heard footsteps in the inner room and her heart surged. Oh, Lord, *Kathy*. Now the awful confrontation, the sliding, oozing, white lies.

"Anybody home?" It was James.

"Yeah, what d'ya want?" Furious. Now him, too. They're *her* problems, not mine.

"Where's Kathy, Bernice?" He poked his head in—and it was shorn!

"What happened to you? Stick your neck in a lawnmower?"

"Barber went a little far, I guess." He rubbed his clipped blond hair self-consciously.

"You doin' penance or somethin'?"

"The Europeans started—this new cut."

"Might've known, James, you *must* be in style."

"Aw, Bernice, that's nasty." He said it gently in his old, charming way and walked into her echoing, empty room. "Going someplace?"

"Summer coming. Good idea to cut out."

"You leaving before commencement, even?"

"Thought maybe you chopped off your hair to show Kathy you're sorry. You know, the way they cut the hair and shaved the heads of those Frenchwomen who slept with the Nazis? Came out bald and looking like nuns—there was a movie on it, the Late Show last month—didja see it? Anna Magnani."

"No, I didn't. Now tell me, what the hell's going on? Why're you packing up?"

"I'm moving over with the Sisters—where I belong. I'm going to end my college years right, if it's the last thing I do."

"Kathy around? Hear she's signed out to Mr. Pennell, but *he* doesn't know anything about it."

"Suppose you went and told somebody *that*, downstairs."

"I'm not that dumb, Bernice."

"Who said how she'd signed out—I mean to *who?*"

"Mr. Pennell. Kathy's mother called the Dean's office because she figured something funny was going on again—after last weekend. Then she phoned *him*, real upset."

"Heard about your big weekend, yeah." And one thing screwing does—gives you the appetite for more. Here he was, no Bible under his arm, but a long face and just one idea on his mind.

"What's with Kathy—you know?" He stradled a chair, bluejean legs easy in the curl, and he leaned his dimpled chin on his hands, on the back of the chair. These months she'd been pretty sure she had his number: a phony, because of his good looks and calm, Ivy League assurance. But now he seemed rather open, exposed by his own affections. They'd made it together finally last weekend, and he wasn't soon over it. Too bad.

"Kathy's mother bugging her again! Oh, if that woman really knew what trouble *was*." There I go, acting out the black experience, as if trouble has been heavily mine, I'm part of racial history *period*.

He bowed to her superior claim to travail, as she knew he would. Didn't question what she alluded to, didn't call her bluff by asking just what awful difficulty *she'd* ever been in.

"You met Kathy's mother?" Bernice asked, emptying the dresser drawer, packing the last of her stuff.

"No . . . don't have to. The woman's a tight-ass. Funny how she seems to *know* when Kathy's . . . with somebody. I mean, like last weekend she got upset for no particular reason, didn't she? Still raving. No wonder Kathy took off. Tell me, Bernice, where'd she go?"

You should not hit babies, innocent children, vulnerable white boys who put their trust in you because you're black, who talk to you this way because it never enters their heads to be male/female, only the soothing, confidential distance of black/white, as if the very unbridgeable distance allows for a certain intimacy, an exchange of confidences.

Oh, *why* do you trust me?

James would never want to take me, on this bed. He couldn't be talking soft and easy like this if such a possibility ever glimmered on the edge of his mind. He doesn't even know he's not accepting *me* for what I am, that he's conditioned already just by the color of my skin. *I can't stand these don't-knowers!* It's easier yes by far to deal with the nasty ones like the woman on the train who yelled at me for smoking. That's the way of Sylvie and the Sisters, and it's easy, too, to have everything so laid out and set. You never find yourself alone in a room with a young man who's your roommate's lover and who talks to you like he might to a kid sister. A cozy, *dangerous* ease.

Dangerous for *him*. "Might try lookin' for her at the Paradise Motel on Route 13."

"What'd she be doing *there?*"

"What d'ya think?"

"Bernice! What the fuck are you trying to tell me?"

"*Trying?* I *am* telling you. She's so pissed she's spending the weekend with Billy Dunham, her friend from Washington, *D.C.*"

"That *kid?*"

"Well, he must have *something!*" She excavated the last drawer and slammed it shut. One glance at James to survey the damage. He looked as if he'd been pistol-whipped. "You got what you deserve, didn't you? For treating her that way last Sunday."

"She ran out on me."

"After you abandoned her—for creepy Mr. Pennell, and your precious career. I heard."

"She didn't understand."

"Well, that's one of life's little problems, isn't it? Not understanding."

"Are you shitting me, Bernice?"

"No, baby, I ain't got the time." She snapped the suitcase lock.

"You can't lift that," he said quickly, rising to help.

"Yes I can—go away!"

He wasn't so dumb, saw the flare of anger.

"Okay, okay . . ."

"Sure, you can help me, James. I got books in there and it weighs a ton."

"Even if she *is* with Billy, where do you get off—telling me—about it, that way."

"You asked and I told you."

"Bernice, you know what I mean."

"Can you manage that box, too—under your other arm?"

"I'm talking to you, Bernice."

"I hear you but I ain't listenin'."

"You know damn well what I'm saying. Where do you get off —shafting me like this?"

"*I'm* not interested. You asked me where she was and I told you. Period."

"You told me, all right." He picked up the suitcase and large cardboard box with her radio, lamp, and all the junk she hadn't been able to stuff into the luggage. She hoisted the garment bag and typewriter. One fast glance around, making sure she'd not left anything—to become a talisman of bad luck, used by enemies against her. She had to come away clean, entirely.

They marched across campus without saying a word, a strange, sad procession—a shambles of human relationships. He not only sensed her hostility but was throwing it back into her face. He knew she didn't care to hear another word from him and wouldn't mind if she never glimpsed him again, learned nothing more of Kathy's troubles. He sensed the gulf between them and immediately felt himself white—which turned her into even more of a black.

"This the room?" he asked, nudging open the door with the suitcase.

"Put it down anywhere," she said, as if he were the porter.

"You going to sleep on that beat-up sofa?"

"It's all right." How could she rid herself of him?

"I guess everybody's still in the dining hall."

"Guess so."

"Bernice—what happened? What's the matter?"

"I got a headache. Don't mind me."

"What caused it, though?"

"I don't want to talk about it."

He stuck by her side because even though her information hurt, she was the only connection left to Kathy. "Can I ask one more thing?"

"Go ahead."

"If she's not at the Paradise Motel, where *else* could she be?"

"Try the motel."

"I will—okay, I will."

Ever since Billy had asked her the same question, she'd been puzzling over Kathy's disappearance. None of the girls with city apartments would likely offer refuge. Kathy wasn't the sort to run off to a Maine lakeside cabin, all by herself—just to get away. Actually, she wasn't pursued so much by either Billy or James as her own urgent sense of the necessity of resolution. Billy canceled out James, but Billy in turn had to be canceled by something else, until at last Kathy came to the big zero, God himself, with all those roundnesses even in the very name. Kathy had to find God before she'd rest with anybody. "You might try the order of nuns who live on a big Hudson estate near Harmon. She was quite interested in that place, I think. Said she wanted to get away from the world."

"*That's* more like it!" Aglow, smiling.

"I better unpack." She felt let down, bereft.

"I'll go find her."

"She hoped to get away from *you*. That's the point."

"Only because she knows she can't. It's too late. We've got this thing going, Bernice. It's really *some*thing!"

"Sure."

"Kathy thinks she has to choose between this world and the

next, but all she's got to decide is whether she'll live with me or not. There's a difference."

"I should think."

"Nobody should confuse *God* with all this. That's her trouble."

"So *you* know the answers."

"I been to God and back. That's a trip worth taking."

The door opened and Sylvie walked in, wearing a yellow flowered dashiki over black pants. "Well, look who's here."

"Hello, Sylvie," James said, reaching out his hand.

"I mean, here's *Bernice!*"

"Yeah, what d'ya know!"

"You tol' me you just had a little bit."

"I'll pile it all in that corner—till Commencement."

"*I* better be off," he said.

"If you find her, then what?" Bernice asked, not so much in curiosity as to try to puncture him still, wherever there was air to let out.

"I've got this job in New York, see."

"You have?"

"A gallery in SoHo. They wouldn't show my paintings, but they offered me a job."

"That's 'cause you're so *pre*sentable!" Sylvie laughed.

"It doesn't pay much, but—"

"Congratulations," Bernice said.

"Enough for me and Kathy to get along on. If I can find a loft down there that doesn't cost an arm and a leg."

"Whoooooooo-eeeeeeee!" Sylvie clapped her hands. "Kathy's all set, then! One senior who got saved! The rest of us are—just like we always been—right, Bernice?"

"Yeah . . . what's gonna happen to us? Who knows . . . don't ask."

"What's the name of that nunnery near Harmon?"

"There can't be more'n one."

"Think I'll have to rent a car to get there?"

"I don't know. How good're you—hitchhiking?"

"They always pick me up."

"I'll bet," said Sylvie. "You're so *pre*sentable!"

"So . . ." Now that James was leaving, Bernice could offer her hand. Something holy even in such a casual departure as this, when it's forever. Upturned, her palm was pinkish-white like his. They clasped fingers warmly, then broke away.

He seemed very touched by her gesture. "Good-by now."

"Good-by '*now*'? I think it's just plain good-by, isn't it?"

"Yeah, you're right, Bernice. I guess it's the real good-by this time." He left quickly, without a nod, for there was no point in looking back.

"Well, Bernice, you're *here!*" Sylvie threw her arms wide so that the dashiki stood open like a great tropical flower.

"I'm here, Sister, at last."

Sylvie's two suitemates strolled in, flattened their palms for touching, smiled. "Look who's made it?"

"Bernice . . . Bernice . . ."

"Stop it, will ya?" She slumped down on the sofa as tears filled her eyes.

"What's the matter, honey?" Sylvie asked, arm around her quickly.

"Oh, shit! Never mind me. I always get this way. When I'm happy."

Strangely enough, they seemed to believe her. They saw her sitting there like one of themselves, but the unseen—the unseeable—wasn't even surmised, since her dark flesh was joined in their company. They all appeared to be together. They'd never know they had only one half of her. Perhaps the least important half. "And don't let's talk about *soul*," she said.

The bell for matins woke Kathy at 6 A.M., but not wishing to be wedged too securely into their Sunday, she didn't come out for chapel or her ration of oatmeal in the refectory. "You feelin' all right?" Ben asked, through the door.

"I'm very busy—thanks."

Later, Sarah and two companions in overalls jogged down the path in front of the mansion, toward the front gates. Four nuns in white robes, dazzling in the sun (Ben and Cess and two friends) paced up and down the small rose garden and purled black rosaries. Once the dogs barked. In the scriptorium, just below her room, she heard a book slam shut. She was aware of every sound in the house, every sight out the window, sensitive as a sick child in an

upstairs bedroom. Her stomach growled angrily and claustropho-
bia over her imprisonment grew; she paced the room.

The distant diaper-sails on the Hudson suggested freedom, the
aimlessness of destiny when one was driven by the wind alone.
Hers was no longer an unexamined life. But more of life had to be
experienced before further study—or prayer—was possible. How
could she get out of this place? When? No doubt Sarah had a
scheme, would appear outside her door after morning exercise was
over.

She felt helpless behind the locked door, incapable of anything
but a mindless vigil at the window, looking down upon the
pebbled road which led to an entrance not discovered yesterday.
The circle drive in front of the house was like a bishop's orb, and
the road leading toward it resembled the shaft of a cross. People
saw bears and archers in the starry sky, just this way.

She recognized James by his stride, from a long way off, even
with his odd haircut. She felt suddenly, completely alive. He came
slowly down the cross toward the orb, stately in his walk like the
paladin returning from the Crusades, hair in a fringe on his
brow—Von Sydow in *The Seventh Seal*. He moved with careful
steps because Penny and Pam galloped beside him, charmed but
ominously attentive.

She rapped on the window when he neared—waved. He smiled
and lifted his arm in a triumphant Che Guevara salute. While she
struggled to raise the window, he rounded the circle and now
stood below. The dogs, hearing the window open, looked up at
her, mouths wide in tongue-lolling smiles, as if they'd made a romantic connection between James and her. "Kathy! What're you
doing up there?" he called, hand to mouth.

"How'm I going to get out?" She shoved the window as high as
possible, unlatched the screen, and slid it up. The cool, calculating
eyes of Penny and Pam studied her every move, mischievous in
their watchdog transgressions (nobody was around, no barking
alarm had been sounded)—as deliberately contrary as their mis-
tresses when they'd jumped into Levi's and let their hair grow.

"The door's locked here." He pulled hard on the knob.

Looking down upon him, with his new haircut, she saw the
shape of his whole head for the first time. It seemed phrenologi-
cally sound; he looked good to her. Suddenly he collapsed in the

middle. One of the dogs had nuzzled his genitals. Slavered him so much there he looked as if he'd come in his pants. "Penny! Pam!" she called, sotto voce, "leave him alone! Go away! Go away!"

"Maybe I could climb up?" He studied the rough-hewn gray stone, block set upon block in palazzo style, with woodbine wrapping around decorative pillars almost to the roof.

"Oh no, don't try." If he fell and hurt himself—broke a leg— neither of them would stand a chance of ever getting out of this place.

He kicked off his shoes and grabbed hold of a vine. "Tarzan does it all the time."

"James—you'll fall! Watch it!"

The kitchen door slammed. Somebody had spotted the intruder.

He climbed the craggy stones while the dogs swirled below, ready to jump and cover him with kissing tongues should he drop. When he clutched the window sill at last, he was red in the face and breathing heavily. "Made it."

"Not yet . . ." She gripped his upper arm, pulling him in.

"There!" He fell upon the window seat. "I'm a second-story man!"

"Ever done this before?" To reach those other girls he'd been seeing? "How'd you ever find me, James?"

"Don't talk, Kathy." He held her tight and stroked her back in long swoops, reconstituting her bodily shape, sculpting her for the world. "Let's not talk—for once."

He rubbed his bristly cheek so hard against hers she knew the blood would be bright red under her skin there. What a relief, just to feel him! She had dreaded the explanations and excuses. "I haven't anything to say."

"Nothing at all. Not even I-love-you?"

"Well, of course I'm—"

Rapping on the door. "Open up! Hey, unlock the door!" Sarah knocked and repeated her command.

Kathy flipped the bolt. Sarah in overalls, steamy and red-faced; a phalanx of blue-shirts behind her, and a couple of white-robed nuns, Cess and Ben. "Mind if I come in?"

"No . . . surely not."

"Who's *he*? The angel Michael?" Sarah stomped into the

room, good-humor tough, playing out a role before her cohorts: having the last say. "*This* what prayer does for you, Kathy? You've got powers, child!"

Appreciative laughter.

"This is James, my . . . friend."

"What's he doing here, on a Sunday morning?"

"Ma'am, I'm sorry if I—" he began, "if I disturbed your worship, but you see—"

"Let *her* explain."

"This is the end—of my visitation. We're going now."

"Where's the donation?"

Kathy opened her nightcase and drew out a five-dollar bill. "Here—is that enough?"

"Not exactly generous."

"James, have you got anything?"

"Never mind," said Ben, moving closer into the room, her gown bestowing command upon her, head lowered, the bonnet like a carapace. "If she's going, she's going. Isn't that enough?"

"Amen!" Cess echoed.

" 'The Lord shall preserve thy going out and thy coming in from this time forth,' " said Ben, smiling.

Sarah looked James up and down, very slowly. "Tell him before he leaves," she said to Kathy, "to button his fly."

James quickly repaired himself. "We haven't been . . . doing anything in here."

"Don't talk, James."

"Like Kathy says—I just got here," he continued, ignoring her, certain of his usual charm. He even scratched his left foot with the toe of his right, as if to call attention to his pride of natural-self. "I sure haven't been here all night, if *that's* what you're thinking."

"The dogs slopped over him," Kathy said. "It's not his . . . his —you know."

"Everyone—step back—clear out of the room," said Sarah. "This business doesn't concern you."

"I believe it does, Sarah." Ben didn't move, as if now *she* would take over the convent, become the new Mother Superior.

Kathy noted with relief that James kept his composure, half smiled with genial good will, as the girls pressed close—but he was careful not to glance at any one of them too long. She was proud of his classy instincts, his ability to handle himself in any situation. Make it all a kind of game. She took his hands and said: "Close your eyes, James."

He did. "Okay—why?"

"Never mind."

"You've no business being here, that's why," said Ben, nodding to Kathy, amused. Sarah would be undone this way, best of all.

"No business." Boldly, like a naughty child, Cess reached up to stroke his blond head.

He was startled but kept his eyes shut, held on tighter to Kathy's hand. Giggling, others reached out, touched his shoulders and arms, fingers light, as if to establish his reality, or in a blind-man's buff party game, pin the tail on some donkey. "Don't look," Kathy warned. She felt the suppressed gaiety of the crowd —they'd passed out of Sarah's control altogether. If only he continued to play his role—even though they flicked him, nudged him, like bluegills in a lake—tiny busses on his arm, thigh, buttocks. "Close your eyes, James, and keep hold of my hand." It was the only way for them to go from one medium to another, through vales of shadow and mirrored walls, from this world into that. From here, into their own world.

"What the hell's going on?" he asked her.

Shuffling feet, a kind of buzz in the room from whisperers.

"Encounter . . . Don't move, James."

They brushed fingertips across his lips, chest. They were all over him, alive in their sanction to explore. They even touched him in the crotch where the dogs had, and he seemed to retract, or try to —back up into his body, in a semblance of his androgynous state before he was a male. These nuns!

"When can I look?"

"Shhhhh . . . it won't come to anything. Let them—do what they want."

"They are!" he said, flinching. "My God, are they *ever!*"

Ben tilted back her head and lifted her lips to his, ever so lightly, then smiled ecstatically at Kathy, as if she'd made her a sister through him. They all began taking turns kissing him. Someone pushed Sarah forward, though she clearly loathed the whole charade, but just as she stepped close—no one knew for sure what she might do—James opened his eyes. "My God! Let's get the hell outa here!"

He dragged Kathy along, but she pulled loose to pick up her nightcase. "James, not so—"

Down the hall stairs, two at a time. "Hurry . . . come on!" Out the front door.

Penny and Pam took up the flight, barking playfully at their heels, running ahead and then circling back. "This gravel's killing me! I left my shoes back—" He hopped to the grass.

"Let's find them."

They turned and saw the sisters spilling out the front door, dashing toward them. "Oh my God," he said. The sight gave wings to their feet. He guided her to the little gate behind the stone pilasters of the great, ornamented iron grille. He lifted her up and over, then jumped the barrier himself. "Made it!" he laughed. The aroma of crushed new grass arose where they lay. He found her lips near and kissed her once, then they scrambled to their feet, hearing the nuns close by on the other side of the wall.

They marched away from the convent entrance, farther into the world. Route 9 lay just ahead and some traveler would stop, pick them up. "I can't walk far, Kathy. My feet are bleeding."

"Oh, James! I don't want you to waste a drop—don't want you to suffer!"

"I don't feel a thing, yet."

"Look! You're leaving a red trail on the grass. Let me see the cut."

"Forget it."

The nuns were pressed against the bars of the gate and standing silently on the crossarms. "Wave back, James. See, they're waving us good-by."

He saluted them. "What the devil was going on in there?"

"You'll never know."

He glanced at her, pained, as if afraid she were trying to trace the old demarcation line between this world and the next.

"Only because I don't myself, James."

"It worked, then?" He seemed to guess what she was thinking without her having to speak it—the surest sign they were emotionally connected. "You found God?" He stood on one heron leg, wiping blood from the ball of his foot.

She was horrified to see his precious life spilling from him. "Oh, what can we do about all this blood?"

"*Do?*" Smiling, he squeezed his foot so that more blood flowed, cleansing the wound, then he stood upright on both feet and wiped the bleeding member on the blades of grass, making a bright red swath. "Nothing—there's nothing to be done, Kathy."

"But it's—it's your life's blood—"

"I know."

"Seeping away!"

"That's why we can't waste any more time. *Come!*"